The Warrior Code

By M. L. Strong

DEDICATION

To my wife Michele. She is my best friend, my life partner, and my swim buddy. Without her firm support, I could never pursue my dream to write.

Chapter One

The blast sent a massive shock wave in all directions, tossing the lead-armored Mercedes four feet into the air. The car twisted slightly then came down on its side, screeching and groaning as it slid a short distance on the hard, concrete surface of the street.

Despite the car's built-in protection, it was difficult to believe that anyone inside could've possibly survived the effect of the roadside bomb. The well-hidden attackers waited for a count of twenty, hoping the passengers would be foolish enough to exit and make their jobs much easier. A second team, stationed a few yards down the street, focused on the second target.

The second car in the motorcade was also a Mercedes sedan. It was designed with special ballistic glass, effective against most military-grade small-arms fire; but the engineers had never intended for the special glass to stop a rocket-propelled grenade, especially one fired at point-blank range.

The professional driver in the third and last sedan slammed on the brakes to avoid hitting the middle car. His moment of indecision was all the ambushers needed.

The second attack team fired an rocket propelled grenade or RPG round from a distance of twenty feet, scoring a direct hit through the back windshield. The black Mercedes flipped over on its roof, spinning wildly like a child's toy. No one would survive.

The few pedestrians unlucky enough to be close to the attack scattered in every direction. Two bystanders, a mother and her young daughter, lay motionless on the bloodstained sidewalk. Acceptable collateral damage to the attackers.

Chaos reigned on the narrow Colombian street. Suddenly the roar of automatic gunfire erupted from the flat rooftop opposite the smoking motorcade. The Russian-made, belt-fed PK machine gun pumped rounds into the first car then shifted fire to the last car.

In the middle of the security motorcade sat the last untouched Mercedes sedan, wrecks in front and behind, blocked on the narrow street by the remains of the other two cars. One thing was certain: the attackers were experienced in the art of urban ambush.

When it became clear there would be no counterattack from the first and third vehicles, the heavy machine gunner on the roof turned his focus to the middle car.

The machine gunner had been too optimistic. Rifle fire cracked through the early morning air. The two US Army Special Forces (SF) operators firing at the roof were the sole survivors of the RPG attack on the lead sedan.

They made their move as soon as the rooftop machine gun shifted its fire on the third sedan. The bodyguards climbed out of the lead car and crouched down together behind the upturned sedan, using its armored exterior as a shield. Their driver and another special operator lay dead inside the smoking Mercedes.

"That's covering fire. They want us to keep our heads down!" shouted the taller of the two soldiers, a career army man and veteran of six combat tours in Iraq. "Pete, I think they plan to rush the limo and grab the precious cargo."

Any car carrying a VIP in a motorcade was referred to as a limo. It distinguished the vehicle from the others in the mobile security package. The term "precious cargo" was well known among protection teams. It simply referred to the object or person a team was protecting. Special operations professionals were frequently used for this purpose.

"I think you're right, Jimmy!" responded the second soldier, a heavily built man in his early thirties with twice as many combat tours in Iraq and Afghanistan as his partner. "Should we get our ass over to the limo?" He pointed with the

2

barrel of his German-made MP-5 submachine gun toward the middle sedan.

"No, we need to scoot across the street. Get inside their position. If we're lucky, we can capture that big gun on the roof and turn it back on these assholes!"

They both knew their heavy gun team was in the third sedan. Their job was to bring a world of pain down on anybody foolish enough to engage the motorcade. Jimmy knew that was a moot point.

The third sedan was upside down and on fire; the machine gun's rounds had ignited the exposed fuel line under the car. Everyone was dead and there was no way to get to the heavy weapons located inside. Taking the PK machine gun on the roof made sense.

Pete shifted to a position placing more of his muscular frame behind the burning car. He considered his partner's idea for a moment and then nodded in the affirmative. "Yeah, you're right. We'll just get our ass handed to us trying to get to our big guns, and that shithead on the roof has the limo covered." Pete gestured toward the middle car with his chin. He looked Jimmy in the eyes, his face set in grim determination. "Screw it, man! Let's just do this thing."

Special Forces Sergeant Jimmy Ford stretched out his hand. Pete took it and squeezed. He understood deep down inside that the odds of surviving the surprise attack were heavily stacked against them. Both men knew it would be a miracle if they could pull this off.

"Okay, Pete, let's leapfrog as two fire teams. I'll go first, find a good spot to cover you and then wave you over. We'll aim for that alley right over there." Jimmy pointed to a gap between two storefronts on the other side of the street.

3

Pete first looked at the alley then scanned the street for an alternative. He didn't see a better option, so he nodded his head. "Okay, Jimmy, make your move! I'll cover you!"

Jimmy gave his partner a thumbs-up. The two green berets initiated their planned maneuver. Jimmy jumped up and quickly moved around the trunk of the car, sprinting across the street toward the attackers.

For a tall man, he moved deceptively quickly, weaving back and forth to present a more difficult target. Pete watched the tall sergeant make his move then opened up.

He tried to give the sergeant a fighting chance by laying down a withering base of fire with his MP-5 submachine gun. The small nine-millimeter bullet was a good round, but it didn't have the power to punch through the material the attackers were hiding behind.

Pete wished he had his M-4 rifle, but it was too late now. He fired directly at the attacker's rooftop position, spraying bullets all along the edge in an attempt to keep their heads down.

The belt-fed weapon kept up a steady pounding on the middle car; the machine gunner wasn't distracted from his primary mission as the two Americans revealed their presence down on the street. He kept a steady rain of lead on the middle sedan, just enough to deter anyone from attempting an escape.

The sergeant's sprint to the alley did draw the attention of several riflemen staged nearby. They opened fire on the American running across the street, trying to prevent him from reaching the entrance to the alley. Jimmy heard the rifles and saw the bullets hitting the street all around him. The ambush was only two minutes old; but to him, it seemed a lifetime.

Pete pulled out the expended thirty-round magazine and dropped it on the street. He smoothly inserted a new magazine and slapped the charging handle down. It slammed forward loudly as it stripped the first round off the top of the magazine, sliding it into the chamber.

He saw that Jimmy had reached the alley and was ready to provide covering fire. They made eye contact and Jimmy calmly waved Pete across.

Pete marveled at the senior man's poise. Sergeant Ford was definitely a pro. He was the kind of Special Forces or SF soldier they put on army recruiting posters. The kind of leader men wanted to follow.

Pete hoped he could measure up. He waved back. It was painfully obvious that he and his partner were heavily outgunned and probably destined to end their lives in this dirty city. Oh well, he thought, he wasn't getting any younger.

Pete popped out from behind the car and fired at the roof. He sprinted toward the alley, shooting short bursts at the rooftop. It seemed like his partner was a mile away. Jimmy saw Pete start his run, then slid his body out and away from the storefront. He pointed his weapon straight up and drew a bead on the edge of the roof.

The sergeant didn't have an identifiable target, but he could place aimed fire along the edge of the building as a deterrent. Their combined efforts appeared to be working, as shredded stucco drifted down to the street below.

The enemy riflemen ducked down to avoid the steady patter of nine-millimeter rounds. Maybe they stood a chance, after all, Pete thought as he wobbled to the right a little. Nobody was firing back.

Just as Pete made it to the safety of the alley, a group of armed men burst onto the scene near the burning lead car and directly across the street from the two SF soldiers. For half a second Jimmy thought the newcomers were Colombian police officers coming to help; then a burst of gunfire from the new arrivals changed his mind. Pete crossed the alley to stand behind Jimmy along the wall.

"Hey, sarge! What's the next move?" Pete yelled, trying to get his partner's attention over all the racket.

Jimmy didn't answer right away. The alley didn't afford the two operators an easy way to the rooftops. This was taking too long, he realized. They were both running low on ammunition, and the bad guys now were reinforced.

The new arrivals maneuvered around the lead sedan and came to the same side of the street as Jimmy and Pete. Jimmy leaned out a little and aimed, taking the first two men in the chest. He watched the third man drop, exposing the man behind him. Jimmy shot him, too; then his MP-5 bolt slammed back and stopped locked into place. He was out of ammo.

Cursing loudly, Jimmy rolled around Pete and shouted. "Five assholes along the storefront. I got three. Go!"

Pete stepped up to take Jimmy's place and immediately dropped to his knee. He leaned out and nailed two attackers as they were just about to reach the alley. "Only three left! You got any of those Belgian cherry grenades on you?"

Jimmy knew most of the go bag extra shit was still back in the sedan, but he had a habit of carrying a few extras of everything on him just in case.

"Hell, yes! Only four though."

Pete popped out and dropped another armed attacker. The last two ran back across the street and used the burning Mercedes as cover. He ducked back into the narrow alley and pulled his magazine out. He had five rounds left plus one in the chamber.

"Four will have to do. The last two assholes skedaddled back across the street. I have six rounds left. So, as I said, do we have a plan?"

Chapter Two

Jimmy didn't have an answer. There was no way they could get to the limo; and if they did, then what? Expose the precious cargo to all the threat ringing the ambush site? No, they were better off bottled up in the armored car.

Jimmy reached into his leg pocket and pulled out a green plastic strip about an inch-and-a-half wide. The center was perforated and there were four evenly spaced bulges under the plastic. Each was a small fragmentation grenade. The kill radius was only four to five feet, but this fight might get that close before it was over.

He started pushing the bulges against the perforation and continued this until all four mini-grenades were out of their plastic tube. He dropped three of them into his front right pants pocket and held the fourth one in the palm of his hand.

"Jimmy?" Pete was still waiting for an answer.

"Look, Pete, we can't get to the limo and we can't get to the rooftop. We're out of ammo, so we can't take on all these guys. We've done all we can do here. Time to haul ass and bunker up somewhere, high vantage point, like a multistory building. Find a landline and tell someone who gives a shit that we are alive and need extract."

Pete kept scanning every doorway, window, and corner as he thought through his partner's idea. "Well, as much as I'd love to stay and see this thing through, we can't fight without bullets. I'm all in, Jimmy. Let's get the hell out of here."

Jimmy gave his partner a thumbs-up. "Okay. Let's move out!"

Pete returned the gesture then froze. "Jimmy, look out!" His warning was too late. Jimmy's eyes followed the other soldier's gaze upward to the rooftop. The fragmentation grenades seemed to drift down in slow motion. The two men watched frozen in horror as they realized what was going to happen to them. There were at least four grenades in the air now. Dropped by the riflemen who'd found a way to move three buildings over and get to the roof.

Both men attempted to react in some smart tactical way, but it was too late. Two of the grenades exploded with a devastating blast right at head level. The others made it all the way to the ground before bouncing once or twice then exploding. When it was over, the two Americans lay dead, ripped apart from head to toe by the vicious steel casings of the grenades.

The three men sitting inside the limo were trying to assess what was happening outside the car by listening to the sounds of combat outside on the street. The State Department Diplomatic Agent-in-Charge, referred to as the AIC, sat in the front passenger seat. He was a veteran of the post-invasion insurgency in Iraq in 2004 and 2005 and had lost fellow agents to attacks just like this one. He knew the odds of surviving here in Colombia were slim to none.

The AIC frantically worked the car's blue force tracker system, trying to communicate their situation through the use of brevity codes. The attack was five minutes old, but any response would take at least twenty minutes to ramp up and getting to the ambush site required the same amount of time.

He'd tried his cell phone first, but it wasn't getting reception in this area of the city. He took some comfort in the fact that the tactical operations center in the embassy still would be able to track their exact location.

He pictured the watch officer going through the protocols once he or she determined that the motorcade was static and way off schedule. The protocol for an unscheduled motorcade stop was simple.

After two minutes to eliminate the possibility of traffic being the cause for the stop, the tactical operations center would attempt a call via the encrypted radio. If that didn't work, they would switch to the encrypted cell phone to determine the status of the motorcade.

If the AIC still did not respond to the communications attempts, then the tactical operations center would alert local police, directing them to move their assets to the motorcade location with sirens blaring and activate the quick reaction force. He gritted his teeth. There wasn't enough time; they were fucked.

His attention was disrupted by the rapid succession of grenade blasts nearby. He had no idea the sound marked the death of two men in the SF detail. The smoke was thick in the street, billowing from the trail sedan, which had turned into a blazing, white-hot torch.

The smoke blocked the AIC's view of the surrounding environment. It had been impossible to follow the gun battle outside. They could only listen and wait.

"Any chance the boys back at the embassy are rolling in soon?"

In the back seat, Senior Chief Auger was just as confused and disoriented as the AIC. He played the scenario out in his head. The timing of the ambush, the lag before anyone might know they were in trouble, and the additional delay in making hard decisions to launch a heavily armed quick reaction force into the streets without confirmation of the facts on the ground.

"No, we're pretty much on our own for the next ten to fifteen minutes. That's if everybody had their shit together and moved fast, which I doubt."

Auger nodded in agreement, brushing his long brown hair out of his eyes. The hair was supposed to make him look like a State Department guy, but his muscular frame and his demeanor conflicted with that portrayal. Anyone watching him move knew he was a hunter. Diplomatic types move like cattle, not like panthers.

He kept losing focus. Auger had tried and failed to determine how many of the personal protection team members had unassed their vehicles to engage the attackers directly. He heard the sounds of a running gunfight outside on the street, so somebody was engaging the ambushers. But who and for how much longer?

The elite navy commando was the body man for this particular VIP protective mission. His job was to stay in close contact with the precious cargo, no matter what happened. Get him from the embassy to the meeting venue in the city and safely back to the embassy.

He didn't want to put more pressure on the State Department security officer in the front seat. These guys were good, better than most; but they were not trained special operators. Stress was their enemy. SEALs, on the other hand, enjoyed the challenges of combat. Taking risks and winning was what being a SEAL was all about.

He held his questions and listened to echoes of the multiple grenade blasts bouncing off the buildings and then fade, dispersing until there was no sound at all. The machine gun had stopped putting rounds into the limo two minutes earlier. Were the attackers on the run?

The senior chief was frustrated. He needed to know the situation in order to deal with the new reality. The rules stated that you never broke the seal on the armored sedan. The sedan was a rolling sanctuary. Stay put and place your faith in the security protocols; help was always coming.

The heavily-armored windows couldn't be rolled down even a tiny bit to allow him to see outside, but he could open the door a crack to survey the street scene.

He ran over the risks of breaking the State Department's cardinal rule. If the sedan remained locked and sealed, then it could take a considerable pounding from a wide range of small-arms fire. Maybe long enough for help to arrive. But the sedan's protective system wasn't designed to protect against a close-range direct hit from an anti-tank rocket. He sighed in resignation. He knew the right call was to stay put and protect the general.

Everyone on the joint special operations protection team expected the others to be professional and do their duty. Auger was the only SEAL in the group. Although he was relatively new to the bodyguard business, he certainly wasn't new to the business of being a team player. So, he waited. Waited as the Colombian guerillas finished off the two SF soldiers with a few shots to the head and turned their attention to the limo.

Chapter Three

On the street, the Revolutionary Armed Forces of Colombia (FARC) narco-guerillas assembled at one end of the ambush zone and calmly walked online, sweeping the area for any other Americans who might've escaped the two burning cars. Once at the third car, their leader signaled the machine gunner standing overwatch above them on the rooftop to stand down.

The silence was deafening. Inside the limo, Auger thought he heard the scuffling sound of lots of boots moving on either side of the sedan. The smoke hadn't cleared enough to see figures; but they damn sure didn't move like Joint Special Operations Command (JSOC) operators, and that was bad news. Auger sensed that the moment of truth was at hand.

The attackers were forming a defensive circle around the three cars, which finally brought them close enough for Auger to make out through the haze. Auger's thoughts of what to do next were interrupted by the magnetic chunk of a mine or explosive charge being applied to the door of their Mercedes.

Auger turned to the precious cargo, four-star General Mark Alexander, Commander, United States Southern Command.

"Sir, we only have a few seconds before they blow these doors wide open! You have to move to the center of the car, now!"

The tall man in the seat next to Auger had remained poised and quiet throughout the attack. He was used to letting professionals sort things out and execute. He trusted his special operations protective detail and the men of the State Department's Diplomatic Service Division. But he also had ears. He knew things were looking bleak.

He shot a cold look at his navy bodyguard. He wasn't used to taking orders, especially from enlisted sailors. General Alexander was the man in charge of all US military activity in Central and South America. The theater commander-in-chief was in the process of visiting the city of Bogota, Colombia, to show support for the joint American-Colombian counter-narcotics program there.

The general grudgingly shifted his body closer to the center, in compliance with his bodyguard's request. "Well, since you're in charge of this particular tactical situation, Senior Chief Auger, what do you think they'll do once they break in here?" The general's voice revealed just a hint of concern.

Auger thought before answering. They both were wearing civilian clothes. He looked hard at the older man. The general was in his late forties, gray hair, with a solid build. He really didn't look a day over thirty-eight, and that gave the SEAL an idea.

"Look, general, I've got a plan. You and I are about the same size and look nearly the same age. When these guys bust in, just play dumb. Don't let on which one of us is the real VIP. You follow me, sir?"

The general nervously leaned over to look through Auger's window. He could see the guerillas were scrambling to clear the area around the car. "All right, navy man, but your idea better work. They might not want me alive. They could be trying to kill me, you know."

Auger looked directly at the general and grinned. "Sir, in that case, it doesn't matter, we're both toast!"

General Alexander grunted, unconvinced. "Okay, SEAL, we'll go with your plan for now. But what about our ID?"

Auger kicked himself for not thinking of it first. "Good call, sir! Give me your wallet; we'll toss it in here." Auger indicated the secret armrest compartment used to store weapons

13

in the Mercedes. The SEAL took both their wallets and dropped them in, slamming the armrest shut. "Carlos! Did you follow all that?"

The driver twisted around in his seat. "Yeah, boss, I understand the plan. But somehow I don't think they'll want to kidnap the schmuck driving the car."

Auger's response was violently swept away as the car doors blew off with a loud popping sound. The explosion was tremendous in the small confines of the limo. All three men dove to the floor of the car to avoid the flying debris generated by the small breaching charge.

Auger saw Carlos throw up his arms as a man forced himself into the car. On the front passenger side, three rapid shots rang out. The sound caused by the automatic weapon was so loud in the small Mercedes that it momentarily stunned the SEAL.

Carlos's body was blown back into the door on his side, then he slumped forward over the wheel. A second explosion rocked the car, and the door on the general's side of the back seat was violently breached.

The door was hanging by a hinge. The shock wave had momentarily incapacitated the general; he was barely conscious, with blood dripping from his left ear.

Auger watched helplessly as the older man was yanked roughly from the back seat of the car and thrown to the street. This was it. Auger knew he must survive. He began the mental processing that would give him the best chance to make it out in one piece.

The senior chief willed a change of mind-set; he forced himself to go passive. He was a prisoner for as long as they kept him alive. It was best to hope their lie bought them both some time. Stay alive any way you can and sort things out later. He hoped the general would have the sense to follow suit.

On the dirty sidewalk, the general struggled against the two men holding him. He assumed his size would intimidate the smaller Colombian gunmen. He was wrong; it only served to anger the proud young men. They violently kicked him in the mouth, and then all three of the gunmen began kicking him repeatedly as hard as they could.

One guerilla stepped up, struck a vicious blow to the general's temple with the butt of his rifle, and knocked the big American out. A young bearded face pushed itself into Auger's line of sight, blocking his view of the beating. "Venga aquí!" the man shouted angrily in Spanish, emphasizing the command with the barrel of a rifle pointed at Auger's gut.

Auger nodded and tried to look afraid. He tried to comply by sliding across the seat, but apparently wasn't moving fast enough. The end of the rifle barrel was jammed into his forehead with a loud smack. Auger's hands went to his head, and that's when the gunman thrust the rifle tip into his exposed torso.

Auger grunted and fell forward. He was sure the man had cracked a rib with the second blow. The guerilla fighter took advantage and grabbed the American by his long hair, dragging him out and onto the pavement to lie beside the first American.

Once out of the car, the SEAL could see that General Alexander was unconscious and lying in the fetal position, blows from the angry guerillas still being rained down on the unconscious man. A gunman to Auger's right shouted something at him he didn't quite catch. The SEAL turned his head to respond. An explosion of light and pain streaked through the enlisted man's brain as a result of the rifle butt stroke, then there was darkness.

San Diego, California – Coronado Beach

Navy Lieutenant Matthew Barrett cursed as he stared at the glowing green face of his luminescent dive watch for the third time. Damn it! It was thirty minutes past midnight. He was going to be late two nights in a row, and tonight of all nights. Matt knew Tina wouldn't fall asleep. She would wait up for him, probably with her arms crossed, dressed in a sexy nightie. Of course, the nightie would be off-limits. There was always a price to pay with Tina.

Matt hadn't been lucky with women. His first real brush with love, a smart, sexy blonde named Sherry, had tried mightily to cope with the loneliness and fear of being the girlfriend of a navy frogman. Matt's time in Virginia Beach, stationed at SEAL Delivery Vehicle (SDV) Team Two, had been eventful, to put it mildly. A stroke of dumb luck put him in command of a sniper heavy recon task element only a few months out of advanced SDV training.

Against all probability, he'd been ordered to take that unit recon into harm's way. He was a green turd, not even a fully-grown frogman, and he knew very little about his chosen specialty of naval special warfare. He owed the success of his time in leadership to seven exceptional men.

They were the reason he didn't screw up, when after only a few months in command he'd been placed in a combat leadership role. It went well enough to get the job done without losing anybody. He'd learned more in that eighteen hours about being an officer and about being a SEAL than all the training leading up to that mission combined.

The mission was deemed a success by the higher-ups, and a slew of awards were given out to his men for their part in the ordeal. Matt's wounds put him in a six-month-long process of rejuvenation, going in and out of hospitals and enduring painful physical therapy sessions.

Somewhere along the way, Sherry called it quits. She'd had enough of Matt's chosen life. He often wondered if she'd ever gotten married. A great looking woman like that was bound to attract attention. Matt sighed. Tina wasn't Sherry, and Tina was going to be pissed.

Once he'd been cleared operational by the navy doctors, Matt spent one more year at SDV Team Two as the training officer. He then went on to complete two back-to-back combat tours in Iraq as a task unit commander, where the SDV teams mothballed their minisubs and helped win the fight in the sandbox with their brothers in the other teams.

His orders to Basic Underwater Demolition SEAL training, known affectionally as BUD/S, in San Diego, California, was meant to be a rest tour. He took the orders grudgingly. He knew he was getting burned out, they all were. Many of his classmates from BUD/S were on their sixth and seventh combat tours, and quite a few were shot up.

The push was never from the brass. Team guys were designed to fight; it was in their DNA. Once a frogman was able to move, shoot, and communicate, it was go time. That made going to shore duty even more shameful.

He felt he'd been in the zone at SDV Team Two. He fully expected to go to one of the other East Coast SEAL teams and hoped he'd get at least two more combat deployments in before doing his obligatory operations officer tour.

He was getting smarter and more effective, both as a SEAL operator and as a leader; but his feelings on the matter were ignored. His commanding officer had Matt evaluated for post-traumatic stress disorder (PTSD) not long after he returned from Iraq a second time. Everyone concurred: Matt wasn't going to another SEAL team, he needed a break.

Chapter Four

Matt spun around to study the ground between him and the SEAL training facility a quarter of a mile away, straining to spot the truck carrying the oncoming Hell Week shift. It was too dark to see anything. Damn, it was cold!

California nights were always chilly. The temperature didn't tell the real story. Around four in the afternoon, every day in the winter, the wind began to whip up. A Mexican wind.

In the summer, it was a mere inconvenience to bikers heading to Imperial Beach by way of the paved two-lane bike path. But after August, when the sun went down, the temperature dropped and the wind chill steadily increased. A crazy effect, but one every BUD/S student, graduate, and instructor understood.

Matt turned back to address his shift chief, Chief Petty Officer Sanders. "That damn relief crew should've been here half an hour ago. Those boneheads are going to screw up the schedule."

Chief Sanders was always calm and cool. He poured another cup of steaming coffee from his thermos and screwed the cap back on. "Well, LT, Chief Jackson's a good man. I can't believe he'd screw us over on purpose, maybe for the fun of it, but never on purpose." The chief chuckled at his own joke. "There must be a good reason for this delay."

Matt knew the chief was right. He thought of the VHF radio lying on the hood of the gray navy pickup truck. He could always call, but that would broadcast the problem on the command net.

The radio conversation would be monitored, and eventually, the executive officer would learn there had been problems with the shift turnover. Matt decided he wouldn't use the radio. He could send a text, but he had a better idea.

Matt decided to drive to the compound and find out what was happening for himself. He knew the shift leader wasn't supposed to leave the BUD/S class during Hell Week.

He was considered the primary safety officer, responsible on-site for the SEAL students and the ten-man instructor staff. The chief easily could perform the same function; Matt would only be gone for a few minutes.

"You're probably right, chief. I'm just jumpy because I have big plans after this shift's over. Kind of an anniversary thing."

"I didn't realize you were married, sir."

"I'm not. It's our first year dating. Might be our last if I don't get home on time after my shift. This screwup is kind of cramping my style, if you know what I mean."

"Well, sir, we could wait five minutes after you leave and then just mosey on over with the class. Just call me on the radio if you need us to bring the class into the compound any sooner. Nobody will be the wiser. I'll just make them race to the dive tower. Anyone would think you planned it that way."

As Matt considered the plan, the chief put his whistle to his lips and blew once. The straggling mass of Hell Week students froze in place before easing down to the sand. One whistle meant to stop whatever you were doing and hit the ground.

Three whistles meant to continue with whatever you were doing. The chief was going somewhere else with this drill. The students waited, their hands over their ears and their legs crossed in, as if in preparation for the concussive effect of incoming artillery fire.

The BUD/S students were moving like zombies. The chief knew that at this point in Hell Week, pushing them to move quickly was a waste of time. By now, most of the class would

19

have gone on "automatic": zoning out the pain, the cold, and the harassment.

Usually, the last two days of Hell Week were a simple endurance event. The instructors didn't need to create special tortures or games. The weather, the ocean, and the weight of the seven-man two-hundred-pound rubber boats did the work for them.

The chief tweeted his whistle twice, and the blob of sandy wet bodies began to shudder as one-by-one the students began crawling toward the source of the sound. He would direct the pile's direction by moving to one side or the other as he continued tweeting twice. Tweet, tweet. Tweet, tweet. The only other sounds were the ever-present booming of waves crashing offshore and the scraping sound of the sandy bodies slithering forward.

Matt smiled. It was clear the chief could handle things here. "Okay, I like your idea. I'm out of here." Matt grabbed his safety radio off the truck's hood and jumped into the cab. He twisted the key and the truck roared to life.

The chief smiled at the lieutenant and waved as Matt backed the vehicle up. He waved back and rolled onto the sand road leading back to the training complex. Tweet, tweet. Tweet, tweet echoed in the background.

Every SEAL Hell Week shift was composed of an officer and a senior enlisted SEAL. Their primary duty was to ride herd on the younger instructors and make sure the schedule was followed without too much deviation.

Matt realized he was lucky to have Chief Sanders covering his ass. He pulled off his ball cap and ran a hand through his wavy blond hair. He needed a haircut, bad. The truck was set in the four-wheel-drive mode, but it still required skill for Matt to maneuver on the soft sand of the Coronado strand beach.

Within minutes, he neared the back gate to the BUD/S compound. Home sweet home!

Matt had spent the better part of two years assigned to the Navy Special Warfare Training Center in Coronado. He had a great job, as far as instructor billets went. He was the officer-in-charge of the third and final phase of BUD/S training.

The first phase was all about weeding out the weak. This was done in a variety of ways; but ultimately, in a volunteer course, the decision came down to how badly a man wanted to become a SEAL. The students checked out on a regular basis, quitting in pairs, by themselves, and once in a while, an entire boat crew left together.

Hell Week took the half that survived the early weeks and weeded the class out even further. All BUD/S instructors and officers chipped in to help during Hell Week. The groups or shift teams rotated throughout the day. That way the instructors were always fresh and alert.

After Hell Week, what was left of the class licked their wounds and recovered, slowly ramping up physical training over a two-week period before moving on to the second phase of training: dive operations.

The order of dive training and land warfare training had flipped and flopped several times over the history of BUD/S. Currently, land warfare was placed at the end of the course in phase three.

The third phase was the place where the baby SEALs first learned the art of ground warfare. Combat tactics, land navigation, weapons training, and mission planning were a daily staple. Matt loved being the leader of this phase of training.

Demolitions also were taught to the young tadpoles in this last phase. All the SEAL instructors working for Matt loved the schedule. Half of the third phase was conducted on the Coronado strand alongside the other BUD/S classes, and the other half was conducted on San Clemente Island, a part of the Catalina Islands sitting a few miles off the California coast.

Matt's instructor staff knew they were the only BUD/S instructors able to maintain their warfighting edge while still on shore duty. Shore duty was normally two years long. The two years were supposed to be a break between the longer seven-year sea duty tours experienced at the operating teams, but the third phase crew took full advantage of the opportunity to shoot, move, and communicate right alongside the students.

Once on San Clemente Island, the instructors took time to conduct their own weapons proficiency training whenever their schedule permitted. Playing bad guys allowed them time to patrol and practice their fieldcraft. It was a good gig, and the best part was that their professional skills didn't atrophy while away from the wars in Iraq and Afghanistan.

Rotating in to help the first phase guys work Hell Week wasn't so bad. Matt rather enjoyed the five-day-long vetting process. Watching boys become men and men become SEALs. Nothing much had changed in over fifty years. The class attrition rates still hovered around the historical norm of seventy-five percent.

An old saying, burned into a wood plaque hung above the entrance to the facility, bluntly summed up the reality of the BUD/S experience. It simply said, "The cowards never started, and the weak dropped out along the way." The words were harsh, but reflected the reality of the experience.

You volunteered in and you volunteered out. Of the seventy-five percent who didn't finish, approximately sixty percent decided to quit and move on with their lives. The rest were dropped or rolled back for injuries, safety issues, and academic failures. To Matt, the madness he remembered as a student was really a well-orchestrated dance supported by SEALs dedicated to finding the next true warriors.

Chapter Five

Matt couldn't help but flash back to his experience as a BUD/S student, marveling that somehow he'd made it through the grueling process. When you were in the middle of the student experience, time slowed down, unless a bad event was coming; then time accelerated, pushing the student into yet another test of endurance.

Putting one foot in front of the other, living and surviving one training evolution at a time; that was the path to success for him. For the class going through Hell Week right now, it wasn't any different.

Matt slowed to a crawl as he drove through the back gate. The oncoming shift's trucks were parked near the first phase office. They clearly were staged and ready to go, but there were no instructors in sight. Matt cursed under his breath and picked up the radio.

"Blue shift chief - this is blue shift OIC." OIC stood for officer-in-charge, and at BUD/S it held weight. The blue shift's chief responded immediately.

"ROGER - blue OIC - I'm all ears - OVER."

"Chief, continue to bring the kids home. I don't think the group here is leaving anytime soon."

"I'm way ahead of you, blue OIC. I started moving the herd in your direction right after you left. We should be there in less than ten minutes."

Matt again was amazed at how navy chiefs seemed to anticipate and make the right call in almost any situation. But then Matt had always been lucky enough to work with great senior-enlisted SEALs.

"Roger that, chief - I'll wait until I see them entering the compound before I go searching for the oncoming OIC."

"Copy that sir - blue chief out!"

Matt sat in the truck pondering his predicament. The Hell Week shifts rotated in three eight-hour sessions. The first-phase instructors supervised most of the work in each shift and that made sense. These guys knew the drill, understood the evolutions, and were able to extract just the right amount of pain and anguish without stepping over the line.

The other second- and third-phase instructors like Matt assisted by covering logistics and safety. They drove trucks, provided medical support, acted as lifeguards, and arranged chow for the students.

In addition to safety, shift officers were responsible for preparing the formal documentation of any incidents, accidents, or student requests to volunteer out of the program. In the late 1990s, the demanding SEAL course underwent intense scrutiny from liberal congressional delegations.

Some of the visiting staffers felt the training procedures were antiquated and out of touch with modern and more humane techniques.

These political lightweights believed that it was time for a change at BUD/S. In their opinion, a politically correct America could no longer tolerate the harsh reality experienced by the SEAL students. They were able to get the bell removed from BUD/S for a year or so before it was quietly brought back.

Their interference did result in the creation of a complicated assortment of additional legal paperwork. Paperwork designed solely to cover the navy's ass. Quitting was an event that required multiple counseling sessions, logbook entries, and eventually lots of forms and signatures. The shift OIC was the guy responsible to make sure the paperwork was right.

Matt was parked near the student classrooms. He heard the Hell Week class before he saw them. The forty-nine dog-tired students shuffled into the compound. Each boat crew carried a two-hundred-pound rubber boat on top of their heads. They moved to an area just to the right of Matt's truck and waited for the command to lower their black rubber boats.

"Prepare to down boat, DOWN BOAT!" Chief Jackson's voice boomed across the compound.

The class boat crew leaders repeated the command to their six-man crews and lowered the boats to the compound's surface, a rough concrete mix referred to as "the grinder." The IBS, or in official navy jargon, the inflatable boat small, was manned by a seven-man student crew: six paddlers and one coxswain, usually an officer.

The officer, or if one was not available, the senior enlisted man in the crew, sat in the back of the rubber boat, shouting commands to the paddling crewmen and steering with a paddle. It was crude, but it worked, as long as everybody paddled together. If they did not, the little boats spun sideways and rolled over in the rough California surf.

The class leader put the class at parade rest with a barely audible command. The students obeyed, feet slightly apart, hands clasped behind their backs, while the boat crew leaders shuffled up to stand in front of their boats awaiting instructions.

They all wore life jackets, an oversized, bright orange pain in the ass. The nylon straps were routed across the butt and through the crotch, finally attaching to the front of the flotation device.

The straps relentlessly sawed back and forth against their inner thigh muscles. The camouflage fatigues worn by the students provided little protection from the abuse, and the addition of the beach made wearing the combat fatigues an ordeal as sand filled up every one of the oversized pockets.

The crews of young men stood next to their boats three men to a side, their heads dropping to their chests as they fell asleep standing upright. Matt got out of the truck and quietly closed the door. Nodding off in any position or situation was a prudent coping mechanism.

The students were severely sleep-deprived and kept that way. Little catnaps were tolerated and even encouraged by the first-phase instructors on each Hell Week shift. It provided just enough rest to keep the miserable exercise going all week long.

Matt watched as weary heads dropped forward, resting on the padded collar of their life jackets. The sleeping men wobbled a little, but found some way to keep from falling down while taking their short catnap.

A paddle clattered to the concrete and a startled student quickly picked it up, resuming the parade rest position. If the class stayed here any longer, more than paddles would be bouncing off the hard surface of the grinder.

Matt exited the truck and walked briskly toward the first-phase instructor's office. The shift change delay would most likely provide the tired students with a much appreciated unscheduled sleep period, but too much of a break could adversely impact the programmed pace of Hell Week.

Matt sidestepped the shiny brass ship's bell that hung just outside the office and walked inside. He scanned the room but saw it was empty. There were daypacks scattered about on the instructors' desks, indicating that the oncoming shift instructors were somewhere in the compound. On a hunch, Matt left the office, heading straight for the classrooms.

As he got closer, Matt heard men's voices punctuated with laughter. He pulled his jacket sleeve up and checked his watch again. It was twelve forty-nine in the morning. He was truly fucked if he didn't get on the road soon.

He opened the classroom door and found the oncoming shift of instructors engaged in a safety briefing for their first event of the night. Near the back of the classroom, the off-going shift officer was chuckling at something he heard when he spotted Matt coming through the door. His smile faded when he saw Matt's angry, bloodshot eyes.

The delay hadn't been his fault, but there was no way for Matt to know that. The third shift of instructors had been forced by the school's director to wait for the medical team to show up. The doc and his navy corpsman were supposed to conduct a checkup at two o'clock in the morning; but according to the schedule, the students would be too far away for an easy linkup.

To make the original schedule work, the instructors would've had to shuttle the medical team back and forth, messing up the tight Hell Week schedule. Lieutenant Smith didn't want to get into a pissing contest with Lieutenant Barrett; he really admired the man.

Smith knew Matt Barrett was a recipient of the navy's highest award for courage under fire, the Navy Cross. His combat exploits in Egypt a few years back were also well known in the SEAL community.

According to people who were close to the operation, Matt Barrett led a small team of SEALs into Egypt to conduct a reconnaissance of a critical airport in support of a United States rescue operation. His team's original mission was to take a look around and report the target's status to the oncoming raid force comprised of Army Rangers.

The Rangers eventually flew in by helicopter to assault the airport, but that's when things went to shit. The Ranger force got waxed by the Egyptian military. As a result of this disaster, Barrett was ordered to put his SEALs on target and hold the airport until a second raid force could be assembled and launched.

Before it was over, Barrett's eight men had accounted for one hundred and eleven enemy dead, killed directly by the recon team or indirectly by the fire support Matt brought down on the Egyptians. Barrett ended up badly wounded, but all the SEALs were extracted from the airport without loss of life.

Smith decided he would be apologetic and defer to the angry war hero out of respect. "Hi, Matt! Good to see you!"

"Well, Dave, great to finally see you, too!" Matt said sarcastically. "Why don't we go outside and talk about it?" Matt swept his arm toward the door. Lieutenant Smith sighed, stood up, and walked outside. Just outside the door to the classroom was a covered walkway.

There was a pipe running the length of the overhang horizontally for the students to use as a pull-up bar. Smith turned and placed his hands over his head, gripping the pipe.

"Matt, before you get started, hear me out. The old man told me to stay and police up the medical guys and take them with us in the trucks. Our linkup with your shift was too far away to get the med check completed without a lot of shuttling and a big loss of time. You know Doc. He takes forever to get his shit together. As a result, we fell behind schedule for the shift change."

Before Matt could respond, Smith realized the Hell Week class was in the compound. "Looks like my chief called your chief," observed the oncoming shift officer.

Matt shook his head. "Nobody called us. The chief took the initiative to move the kids into the compound until I found out what the fuck was going on."

Chapter Six

Both officers watched as Chief Jackson directed the class leader to have the students ditch their life jackets. The class office saluted and passed the command to his boat crew leaders. There was a flurry of activity and then the class resumed the position of parade rest, all the jackets draped neatly over the tubes of their boats.

The oncoming shift chief strolled out onto the grinder to watch and assess the physical and mental state of the class. Chief Jackson walked over, shook hands, and conferred with the newcomer for a few seconds before shouting out a new command.

"Mr. Gonzales! Have the class move to classroom seven for a safety brief. Move, sir!"

The class leader gave a command for the students to muster in a single-file line and then led them quietly toward the classroom near the first-phase office. Two weeks ago they would've been screaming "Hooyah" as they sprinted to the briefing. In this early hour, they were unwilling to expend any more energy than necessary.

"Come on, Matt. Let's go back inside and listen to the safety brief."

Matt couldn't stay mad. Dave wasn't trying to fuck him over; he was just following orders. "All right, Dave," Matt responded as he turned to follow the long conga line of sandy, tired sailors into the classroom.

The two SEAL shift officers moved to the back of the room as the students found their seats and settled down. An instructor from the oncoming shift stood by the whiteboard. He took a long moment to survey the tired faces, then smiled a big toothy smile.

"Good morning, gents!" The instructor turned to the board and pointed to the upper left corner.

"This morning's evolution I call 'Around the World.' Pay close attention. Any mistake could add miles to your course, and poor leadership will be recognized by the staff with an appropriate punishment . . . for the entire boat crew. So it pays to pay attention!"

For the next ten minutes, he ran his index finger along an elaborate navigation map marked on the whiteboard. To Matt, it looked like the board game Life, except the milestones were places like the Coronado municipal pool, the Hotel Del Coronado, and the base laundry. He knew he'd also suffered this classic Hell Week evolution in his day, but he didn't have a single clear memory of the event.

According to the instructor, the tired students would roam the base and the island of Coronado, looping the course multiple times until the sun came up. The endurance course required them to walk or run with their boats and paddles.

It would be interesting, at least for the instructor staff. The whole thing was a well-designed mindless expenditure of energy that, at this point in Hell Week, would cause many in the class to experience hallucinations brought on by fatigue and sleep deprivation.

The students would never stop moving or stop competing; boat crews vied against each other to earn a few minutes sleep, ten minutes of warmth, or a little extra food. With the closing words of the briefing, the two shift officers moved away from the door.

The lead instructor in charge of the evolution shouted the order for the Hell Week class to man their boats, and the room exploded with the rumble of scrambling students. Student desks toppled over and men fell down. Matt and Dave waited for the herd of students to squeeze through the door.

The two officers walked out onto the grinder and continued to watch the class as they raced to get their life jackets back on. In Hell Week it paid to be a winner. Matt knew this frantic activity was a waste of vital reserves. No one started a fifty-mile endurance race by sprinting the first two miles.

Just then they heard the loud and unmistakable clang of a ship's bell. The sound echoed across the compound and bounced off the walls. Matt and Dave looked at each other before walking over to the first-phase office. There was nothing they could do now, except the paperwork, of course.

The officers arrived just as the third and final ring echoed throughout the school's compound. A forlorn-looking student stood in front of the first-phase office door, his hand still resting on the fancy rope work hanging from the bell's striker.

The young man reached up and pulled off the green helmet liner that signified his status as a first-phase student. The helmet liner was marked in white paint to show his rank and name.

Matt knew what was coming next, so he attempted to beat feet. "Is the turnover complete?" Matt asked.

Lieutenant Junior Grade Smith knew exactly what Matt meant. The officer stuck with this quitter would have a lot of forms to fill out. Smith checked his watch. "Yeah sure, Matt. Get your guys out of here. This bonehead just created half an hour of paperwork for me."

Matt paused. Tina already was pissed at him for being late; a few more minutes wasn't going to matter. "Look, Dave, why don't you get going? I can handle the report on this quitter. He's really my responsibility anyway, since my shift drove him to this decision."

Dave didn't have to think the proposal over for very long. "Are you sure, Matt? I mean, if you are, that would be great!"

"Yeah sure, why not? I'm already in deep shit with Tina. How much more damage can I do if I'm another thirty minutes late?"

Dave tilted his head. "What's going on? I thought you two were getting really serious."

Matt shrugged his shoulders. "Yeah, well she's all into the marriage thing, and I don't know if I want that, at least not yet. Sometimes I think I'd rather have my life simple again. You know? Single and free of attachments."

"Well, if I can help . . ."

"No, I'm just whining, Dave. You'd better get moving." Dave gave up. "Okay thanks, Matt. I owe you one."

"Bullshit! You don't owe me anything. You know the deal. We're in this together–teams and shit!"

Dave reached out his hand. A guy wearing the Navy Cross could get away with being an asshole. But Matt was truly a good guy. "You're right on that point, Matt. But I can still say thanks."

With that, the oncoming shift leader turned to address the nearest instructor. "All right, boys, let's saddle up!"

It took Matt forty-five minutes to interview the young student who quit. The paperwork was tedious and overly redundant. In the old days, if a man rang the bell three times that was it. No psycho evaluation stuff. Just goodbye and there's the door.

Matt was having a hard time keeping the student awake, and the warm office was causing the guy's face and hands to swell. Matt knew that most Hell Week students reacted this way after being cold and wet for so long.

He directed the young man to sign the final document and called in the student duty officer. "Escort this student to the Hell Week tent and help him collect his personal belongings. Then take him to the duty bunkroom. Make sure the roving patrol checks on his status from time to time until eight o'clock when the master-at-arms takes over handling the quitters."

Matt left the phase office and walked over to the instructors' locker room. He stopped before opening the door and checked the time. Boy, was he late! Screw it, he thought. I'll skip the shower and wear my stuff home. That ought to shave a minute or two off my drive to Mission Valley.

Matt could barely stay awake during the long drive back. He pulled his car into the common parking area in front of Tina's townhouse and shuffled his way to the door. Fumbling with his keys, Matt finally entered and quietly climbed the stairs to the bedroom. Tina woke up the second Matt's tired body hit the sheets.

"This isn't working," she said sharply.

Matt sighed. "Come on, honey, not right now! I'm beat. Besides, it wasn't my fault this time."

Tina wasn't buying it. "Matt, it's never your fault! You waltz in here at two thirty in the morning. You never even called to say you'd be late! And to top it all off, you knew I was waiting up for you!"

"Tina, look, I didn't think the shift turnover would take so long. I didn't call because I didn't want to wake you up. I thought we'd wrap things up and I'd still make it home on time. You know how these Hell Week shifts work. We don't call the shots; the students do. I'm sorry you waited so long, but it just couldn't be helped!" Matt rolled over and attempted to end the discussion with body his language.

Tina wasn't going to let up. "Matt, how can we even think about getting married and building a life together if you can't even honor your commitments? For God's sake, this is only shore duty! What will it be like when you get reassigned to the teams again?"

Matt knew Tina was right on that point. She had touched on the only concern he had about their relationship. Married life in the teams was tough. Many active duty SEALs spent over two hundred and fifty days a year away from home.

They often were unable to tell their wives where they were going or when they would be back. Matt realized too late that he hadn't answered Tina's question fast enough.

"Okay, I get it now. I'm just a convenience. You don't really intend to make this work!"

Matt knew he couldn't win this argument. He was pretty sure he loved Tina, but he had his doubts about her ability to deal with his SEAL career. He knew he could always get out of the navy and try to make a go of it on the outside. Tina would love that. But Matt wasn't so sure he'd be happy doing something else.

"Tina, please, can't we talk about this after I get some shut-eye? It's nearly three o'clock in the morning!"

"Sure, Matt," she punched out. "As usual, we'll wait until you're ready to talk about it!" Tina pulled the covers tighter around her shoulders and went silent. Matt smiled. Now he could sleep.

Chapter Seven

When the phone started ringing, the clock radio read five twenty AM. Matt snapped out a hand, snatching the handset from the cradle before the second ring. He listened for a few seconds and then groaned. "I don't believe this!"

The sun poured its rays down on Mission Valley, creating a living landscape of beauty and charm. The Spanish had seen the same quality when they first arrived. It compelled them to place a mission church on the high ridge overlooking the valley. Matt wasn't feeling it; he put on his blinker and took the exit for Balboa.

Ten minutes later, he was crossing the Coronado Bay Bridge. The morning traffic was mercifully light and that allowed Matt to make great time. He pulled up to the security post on the ocean side of the amphibious base, flashed his ID card to the guard, and drove the last hundred yards to the Naval Special Warfare Center's parking lot.

Matt dragged his feet as he went up the two flights of stairs to the second level of the command building. He walked along the outside balcony, which ran the length of the two-story structure that rose up from the BUD/S grinder. He saw that the compound was coming alive, but there was no sign of the Hell Week class.

Matt opened the outer door and entered the reception area placed squarely between the executive officer's office on the left and the Director of BUD/S training's office to the right. It wasn't normal working hours, and the director's secretary wasn't at her desk. The navy commander was standing by the window, looking down the beach toward the Hotel Del Coronado when Matt came into the room.

"Come on in, Matt. Have a seat." The older man pointed to a chair.

"Yes, sir!" Matt answered.

Matt looked around; they were alone. The presence of other senior officers would indicate that he probably was in some kind of trouble or they needed witnesses for some reason. You never knew what might happen in the navy. The institution was famous for axing their leaders for failing to lead.

Tradition stated that officers in charge were responsible for everything that happened on their watch, even if the officer in command himself did nothing wrong. There were all sorts of sad stories about young officers making some mistake and getting nailed. Cutting short their careers before they really got started.

However, they were alone. Apparently, this meeting was for Matt and the director alone. Matt sat down on the chair indicated.

"How're ya feeling?" asked the older man. The director of BUD/S was a prior enlisted SEAL. The rows of ribbons sitting about his left breast pocket reflected a lot of time in the teams. Matt guessed he was nearing an impressive thirty-year career by now.

Matt swallowed hard; his throat was suddenly dry. He couldn't figure out from the tone of the director's voice whether or not in he was in hot water, so he decided to sound curious instead of guilty. "Well, sir, I'm okay, but I am kind of curious why you had me come back into work. I only just left. Did something happen to the Hell Week class?"

"Matt, I received a classified special category (SPECAT) message an hour and a half ago. I was the only one allowed to go into the message center and sign for the document. I know this was an imposition on you, just coming off shift this morning; you probably didn't get much sleep. I had to drive in all the way from Poway. Do you know how far that is from here?" Matt simply nodded. He was sure the director was about to tear his head off.

"What was the message about, sir?"

36

The director leaned back in his ergonomically-designed office chair, a gift from his concerned wife of twenty-two years. "The classified message came from the Joint Chiefs of Staff and the subject of that message was you, lieutenant."

Matt was confused. That and a lack of sleep caused him to do a mental double take. "Me, sir?" Matt murmured. "What could possibly be in a special category message involving me?"

The director continued, "Matt, the message is fairly brief and to the point. You're directed to report to the Pentagon in Washington, DC, within twenty-four hours. The message states that you are going to be placed in charge of a special operations unit being assembled by the national command authority. Nothing more specific." The director paused. "Do you have any idea what this might be about?"

"No, sir," Matt said. The shock caused by the announcement left him numb. "No, sir, I'm attached to BUD/S. You know the deal; this is shore duty. I shouldn't be doing any operational stuff."

The director nodded in agreement. "That's right, Matt. I don't know what clown decided to pull one of my officers out of BUD/S; it doesn't make sense. You and I both know there are plenty of capable officers in the operational SEAL teams on both coasts. Why pick you?"

The director's words were both questioning and accusing. "Your guess is as good as mine, sir. Maybe it's a mistake." Did the director think Matt had something to do with this? Maybe angling for a special project behind his back?

"It might be a mistake, but I'm not going to ask if it is or not. Orders are orders. However, if you get to DC and find out this is a mistake of some sort, I would appreciate it if you would let me know and hightail it back here. I'm short two officers as it is."

"Yes, sir," Matt replied. "I have one more question."

"Yes?"

Matt continued, "Are you sure the message didn't say anything about the reason for all this?"

"No, son, it didn't. The message was clear as mud. Lieutenant Matthew Barrett, United States Navy, is to report within twenty-four hours. This message will act as official orders for all military transportation."

The director stopped reading and looked at Matt. "That basically gives you a blank check to arrange immediate transportation at any military facility in the United States. Do you need to wrap anything up here before you leave?"

"No, sir. I'm good to go. I take it I can't tell anyone I'm leaving?"

"You know the deal, Matt. This baby, whatever it is, is code word access only. You're single, right? Or do you have a special someone who will ask questions if you disappear?"

"Yes, sir, well, sort of. I live with a lady. She's already pissed about the whole SEAL thing. She'll freak out if I play cloak and dagger with her now. If you would, please tell her I had to go to San Clemente Island on an emergency. Say it's a training accident and I was assigned to investigate or something. That will give me a week to sort this Joint Chiefs of Staff or JCS thing out."

The director reached out to Matt and shook his hand. "I'll do my best. You need to get your shit together and roll on out of here. Call me if I can assist in any way."

Matt returned the firm handshake. "Thanks, skipper! I'll let you know when I know." Matt suddenly remembered a problem. "Sir, I guess there is one other thing I am concerned about. I have a heck of a lot of paperwork stacked up on my desk. I saw your request for everyone to get those quarterly budgets in on time."

Matt was a good officer. Instead of whooping it up about his timely escape from the all the administrative bullshit, he retained a sense of duty to his command. "Don't worry, Matt," the older man said calmly. "I'll make sure somebody looks at the stuff on your desk. If you don't get back in time, we'll get input from your phase instructors and get the budget worked out."

Matt left the office holding the SPECAT message folder. He began conducting a mental inventory. He had his basic combat load in the locker room. It would only take a minute or two to grab his gear. As a third-phase instructor, Matt spent quite a bit of time patrolling with the students, so his personal equipment was squared away as a result.

He took a deep breath and let it out slowly. Whatever was going on, it sounded like operating and that was a good thing. He felt the old juices begin to flow. He had a fleeting image of how Tina would react to all this. Well, Matt thought, he had some thinking to do on that subject. Things might not be the same for them when he came back.

The Pentagon - Washington, DC

The Chairman of the Joint Chiefs of Staff glared across the table at the other service chiefs. "Gentlemen, we need a plan I can show the president. How the hell are we going to get our people back?"

The assembled uniformed leaders of the nation's armed forces didn't immediately respond.

"So far, only the navy has put forth a proposal worth looking at seriously. They, of course, believe this is a navy special operations job, and I for one, can see the logic of their argument. Especially since our boys at the CIA think the guerillas will take General Alexander and the senior chief to their main sanctuary on that river . . . what's the name again?

"The Ariari River, Chairman," reminded an intelligence analyst sitting against the wall.

"Right, right. The Ariari River. Seems like a navy job to me. Any thoughts?" The chairman looked at each man around the table, locking his eyes with theirs, challenging them to do something, say something. He knew they were political animals, not really fighters. Always calculating the downside of stepping forward.

A voice to his left piped up. "Yes, sir. As you have already surmised, a river means maritime expertise, and the Special Operations Command in Tampa concurs with my recommendation. We are the force to execute this rescue."

The admiral looked up and down the long table to gauge the reaction of his army and Marine partners to his bold statement before continuing. "As we stated earlier, sir, the best option is to use a select team of SEALs. As you know, these men are uniquely trained to execute operations in this environment.

"A small team of handpicked SEALs will conduct surveillance of the FARC's river encampment, then direct and support the rescue force upon our order. Of course, we'll welcome and require the assistance of the other services in support, as always."

"Admiral, I'm going to reserve my judgment for a moment, even though, as you pointed out, I'm inclined to agree with your logic. It seems to me that patrolling through the dense jungle would be much tougher to accomplish than coming down that river."

The chairman stabbed his finger at the map. "I'm an army infantryman, and I know what I'm talking about here. I'm leaning toward an operational concept consisting of two phases. Phase one: reconnaissance surveillance by the SEALs. Phase two: the rescue of our people. I want to study the rescue options a bit further. All Department of Defense service assets will be dedicated to supporting both phases of this operation. Does anyone disagree or have a better plan?"

No one in the room responded. By their silence, he was comfortable in assuming the navy special operations approach was a decision and no longer an idea. "Okay, then it's settled. What do we want to call this lash-up?"

"How about 'Operation Green Dagger'?" The admiral was in the zone.

Chapter Eight

The chairman looked around the room. Everyone was happy letting the navy put a noose around their own neck. "Okay, Jake. We'll designate it Operation Green Dagger. Any other questions? Comments?" The commandant of the Marine Corps raised his hand. He had decided to contest the assumptions discussed so far in the meeting.

"Yes, sir, I do have a question. I'd like a minute of your time to dispute the navy's logic. I can't believe that it's prudent to allow the SEALs to penetrate so far inland. Sure, it's a riverine environment, but the corps has a long history of successful operations such as this, and, sir, SEALs are still sailors."

The admiral raised an eyebrow and smirked slightly. He was a combat fighter pilot. He'd supported SEALs, and he was absolutely sure they measured up to a Marine rifleman. "Apples and oranges, George, apples and oranges."

"Yeah, I get it. Special operations and all that. In my opinion, the Marines can bring more to the table. While the SEALs are certainly capable warriors, I believe that the Marine Corps force reconnaissance units are the best team we can field for Operation Green Dagger."

"Of course, sir, as you might expect, I respectfully disagree with the commandant's conclusions." The admiral looked sideways at his Marine counterpart and maintained eye contact. "If I may, chairman, I'd like to bring out a few salient points that my esteemed associate may be unaware of or may have overlooked."

"Go ahead, Jake, but make it brief. I thought we'd put this thing in a box three minutes ago." The chairman checked his watch. He was late for a meeting with the national security advisor.

"Yes, sir, thank you. First and foremost, we have predefined levels of expertise in this area. Marine force reconnaissance units are second-tier forces. They are very effective in a conventional sense. Sir, I mean no disrespect to the commandant or the corps, but I do not recommend we send in a second-tier force to conduct a first-tier level mission."

The admiral paused for emphasis. "Sir, in addition, I respectfully suggest you compare the actual credentials, capabilities, and training expertise of a two- to three-man SEAL surveillance team with a force reconnaissance unit. While both are made up of patriotic American men, the SEAL's ability to communicate and send back real-time photography and video stream using state-of-the-art equipment far outclasses any conventional tier-two unit the Marine Corps could put on the ground."

He had everyone's attention now. "The average age of a SEAL is twenty-eight. These are mature men, and the team I have in mind are all highly-decorated combat veterans." The admiral ended his statement with a little smile on his face. He knew the discussion was over.

"Any other thoughts?" the chairman asked, looking around the room. He focused his eyes on the Marine four-star across the table. None of the other joint chiefs felt like jumping in. "All right then. George, I concur with the logic of using tier-one SEAL elements. This is a strategic challenge, and I might add, a politically charged one at that. The SEALs are better for this type of thing."

The chairman turned to address the admiral. "Quite frankly, Jake, if you guys pick the right men you should be able to pull this off."

"I'm way ahead of you, sir. I took the liberty of recalling a potential mission commander, Lieutenant Matt Barrett. He led the SEAL platoon that pulled off that miracle in Egypt a few years ago. He's steady as a rock."

"All right, admiral, I'll leave phase one of Operation Green Dagger in your capable hands." The chairman took one last look around. "Unless any of you have any more objections in this matter, I will adjourn this meeting." He looked around. "No? Good! Jake, I expect the draft operations order on my desk within twenty-four hours."

With that said, the chairman stood up. The chiefs all rose to their feet and remained standing until he departed the room. "Good job, Jake!" the commandant said without looking at the admiral.

The admiral looked at his Marine counterpart. "Sorry, George." The admiral knew his peer was fully aware of the advantages of using a tier-one asset, but it was his job to support the objectives of the Marine Corps. One of those objectives was to capture funding. US Special Operations Command had a huge operating budget as well as its own line of funding in the defense budget, similar to full-fledged military service.

The commandant nodded. "No issues, Pete. Congratulations." He'd lost this round. The budget game was straightforward.

The threats drove the mission and they drove the spending. After the attacks in 2001, amphibious infantry wasn't as sexy or as vital as counterterrorist capabilities. The Marine Corps had fought the rising emphasis on terrorism in the late nineties, and after 9/11 they found themselves stuck as a conventional force in an unconventional war.

To achieve the required transformation, the corps established a special project in 2004 to create a new force patterned after the famous WWII Marine Raiders. That new unit had grown from an idea to operational status since then and was an evolving component of the Special Operations Command (SOCOM) fighting force.

Marine Special Operations Command (MARSOC) stood up in 2006 and since that time had grown and developed into a uniquely capable contribution to the arsenal. However, despite the success to date, the SEALs still were getting most of the maritime special operations missions.

The commandant needed to get his men into the Special Operations Coomand or SOCOM order of battle. He wanted to finally convince the Joint Chiefs of Staff and the SOCOM commander that his MARSOC guys were ready for full equality on the battlefield.

"You should get out of here, Jake. You have an operations order to write. Do you need any help?"

Jake smiled. "You bet, George. I appreciate any help you can give me. The mobility piece is a bear. We need to define the parameters, establish the potential assets to support Operation Green Dagger, and transmit warning orders. If you can do that for me, I'll focus on the OPORD to Tampa." Both men left the room and got to work. Despite their passions, they were Americans first.

Medellin, Colombia

Hernando Chavez stood on a pure white balcony overlooking the city, quietly smoking a fine cigar from his private collection. He was tall for a Latino and still in good shape from twice weekly racquetball sessions. He had a handsome face, with the high fine facial bones of his Spanish ancestors.

Even though he was one of the richest men in the world, he knew something was missing in his life. Gone was the thrill of the early days, when running coca leaf and protecting his jungle processing plants filled his hours with danger and the promise of personal combat.

Chavez wasn't the smartest businessman ever to ply the coca trade, but he'd evolved to become the most ruthless. Those days were gone. His businesses continued to grow as if on autopilot; he wasn't involved anymore. He lived a life of luxury, a pampered aristocrat without a true challenge to stimulate him.

As a young man, Chavez would roam the deep green jungle of Colombia like a conquering conquistador. Marking territory for himself, boldly calling out his competitors, and shrewdly identifying locations for future processing facilities.

If anyone got in his way, he eliminated them. It took years and a lot of luck, but his efforts paid off. Flying under the RADAR just enough to avoid federal intervention until one day he was too powerful for them to even try.

In a moment of insight, Chavez realized the value of cultivating an alliance with the country's disenfranchised, the poor, the downtrodden, many of whom had gravitated to the rebel movement, the Fuerzas Armadas Revolucionarias de Colombia, better known as the FARC.

This insight and his diplomatic skills led to a symbiotic relationship with the FARC guerillas. They protected his property from rivals and the Colombian military, and he funded their growing paramilitary operations. It worked beautifully.

In time this unholy alliance allowed Chavez to bind the FARC to him, allowing him to roam freely throughout Colombia, safe from both his enemies and from the government. Any official who asked too many questions about Chavez's activities soon wound up dead. Then there were the Americans.

The Americans were trying to help the Colombian government in their fight against both the drug trade and the FARC. They knew about Chavez, his drug kingdom, and his funding of FARC operations.

They'd charged him in absentia and were vigorously seeking to extradite Chavez from Colombia to face American justice. However, no matter how hard they tried, they found that serving those warrants in a country Chavez owned was an exercise in futility.

Few knew that Chavez's main purpose in traveling abroad so frequently was his need to organize his financing and distribution channels in Europe and Asia. The American CIA was probably aware of some of his global reach, but he doubted they knew everything about his intentions. Chavez owned vast estates in at least five countries.

His record keeping was meticulous, and he trusted no one to do this mundane task, preferring to do the work himself as he always had. He conducted himself as a legitimate businessman in each of these countries and had greased the palms of all the important players in each to provide a deterrent to the Americans.

The proceeds from the Chavez coca trade were laundered several times through various banks in the Cayman Islands, Cuba, and the Dominican Republic. He owned these banks, which made the laundering simple and neat. Chavez used a sophisticated encrypted software program that made it virtually impossible to trace any of the laundered dollars back to him.

Once clean, he took the laundered money and gave most of it to selected money management people and investment advisors in the US, Great Britain, Germany, and Dubai. They invested in the world's fastest growing companies, hedged currencies, bought natural resources, and multiplied his wealth.

It took money to make money and Chavez made a lot of money. The last step involved the use of dividends, interest, and sale proceeds. This flow of funds went to more than thirty countries, to brokers who handpicked choice real estate properties and built an impressive portfolio worth hundreds of millions of dollars.

It was safe to say that only the income generated from his legitimate investments had grown to rival all the money he was making on the front end of his operation, the coca trade itself, and that was the problem. The efficiency and legitimacy were making him richer every day, while he sat on his ass feeling useless, his mind going to mush. His semi-retirement had become a form of a death sentence. Then, just when he was as depressed as he could be, the Americans gave him something to live for.

Chapter Nine

The primary architect of the American campaign to kill or capture Chavez was the general in command of US Southern Command stationed in Panama. General Alexander had proven to be highly effective in working with the Colombian military and police. He helped them plan and coordinate their efforts; and with the help of the FBI and CIA, he'd helped them to find the moles within their own organizations.

The general also had brokered a joint Colombian-Venezuelan effort to defeat the FARC along their shared border, interacting hand-in-hand with United States special operations units to deftly cut off the flow of young recruits joining the FARC from Venezuela.

The disaffected students were easy marks for the communist revolutionary propagandists. They fed their fears and confirmed their phobias while filling their empty heads with the vision of a communist utopian paradise. All they had to do was join the worldwide revolution. The message was simple, deceptive, and it worked.

At first, the clumsy attempts of the Americans were nothing more than an inconvenience. A nuisance intended to capture a few headlines in the war against drugs for the politicians back home in their campaigns to get reelected. But things were different now.

The drug problem rose until it approached epidemic proportions. The problem was debated: supply side or demand side? Which was to blame and which was the right place to deter the trade?

The Americans decided to focus on the supply side; it was easier to execute drug interdiction missions than to face the more complicated challenge of jailing or rehabilitating millions of users in the United States. A few public messaging ideas were implemented and pursued halfheartedly, but the new war on drugs was going to be a real war and it would happen outside America.

Never before had the Americans used their special operations and intelligence capabilities to such great effect. The change in the environment was sudden and violent. The Americans were everywhere at once, hitting the crops, the production labs, the distribution points, and the transport system that moved the bulk product into the United States.

Chavez took losses. He immediately realized that the Americans were deadly serious. He sprang into action. He called his leadership together in Havana and outlined a counter to the American attack on their livelihood.

It worked. It took time and they had more losses, but eventually the tide turned. Chavez and his top management developed new ways to hide the crops and the other facilities.

They moved raw coca offshore to ships and then to neutral locations in South America and the Caribbean, where the Americans were restricted or denied arrest authority. They also devised new ways to smuggle the end product into the United States, using air and sea transports flagged under countries friendly to the United States and originating from anywhere but Central America.

The war slowed down to a grind. Then the Americans changed their strategy. Instead of attacking and eliminating production infrastructure, they began to target the heads of the various cartels.

Chavez himself was now a target. The Yankees were out to get him, to ruin him and to destroy the empire he'd built so meticulously. It was clear to him then that waiting passively, without taking action, was a losing proposition. He wouldn't be a victim.

First Chavez needed better information: more details about the military and government units tasked with bringing him down. He went even further; he wanted to know where they lived, the names of their wives and children. In this effort, the Cubans proved invaluable.

Cuban intelligence was arrogant, but they could be bribed. Besides, the Americans were a common enemy. They sent a massive amount of data based on years of deep cover intelligence operations. Now Chavez was ready to respond to the American's aggression.

Unlike the Colombian military, the American professionals in the military and intelligence agencies were difficult to bribe. They were well paid, patriotic, and well-educated. He might be able to bribe a few low-level players-- TSA lackeys at the border or ports--but no one significant. This left him with one path: retribution against soft targets.

His planners provided him with several scenarios, and eventually, Chavez settled on using terror. Terror was the tool of last resort, a tool for the weak, those unable to change the world through force of arms or revolutionary upheaval.

He considered and then rejected the direct approach of simply assassinating American leaders. Taking out one or two key people might work in a third-world country, but America had lots of generals and politicians. They would simply replace and move on as if nothing happened.

After much deliberation and analysis, Chavez and his top lieutenants decided the best way to make America stop their attacks was to make it more painful for them to continue them. Americans were sentimental and had always been open to being manipulated when hostage-taking was involved.

He would begin a reign of terror and use hostage-taking as both the offensive and the defensive strategy. The Americans would yell and stomp, but they would never bomb a potential hostage location. This gave Chavez the leverage he needed. This gave him an actionable plan.

The American people were easy to manipulate and influence. Their media would keep a hostage crisis in the news every day, magnifying its effect tenfold, and strangely insinuate that their own government was at fault, the root cause of the crisis.

Their media would insist that the Americans themselves created the conditions that led to the kidnapping, all the while demanding that their government do everything possible to secure the release of the hostage or hostages.

All Chavez had to do to start the chain of emotional self-flagellation was grab an American. Any American would do, he supposed, but then it occurred to him he could kill two birds with one stone.

What better target than the architect of his problems, General Alexander of the United States Southern Command? The mastermind of the attacks against Chavez's coca operations and his family was not only a good target, but he also was responsible for the loss of Chavez's only son, Rodrigo. From a hidden location somewhere in Panama, the general and his murderous staff had plotted the demise of Chavez and his guerillas.

The general didn't personally murder his son, and he likely didn't intend to kill the boy; but he did plan the air strike and gave the orders that resulted in Rodrigo's death. In Colombia, there was only one way to right this wrong: a blood feud now existed between himself and the American general. The general just didn't know it yet.

After careful planning, Chavez himself handpicked the operatives to conduct the attack and kidnapping. The intelligence was easy to gather. The Americans had patterns. A few weeks after choosing the target, Chavez got a break. The Cubans contacted him with the general's schedule; he was coming to Colombia.

The Americans traditionally moved with pomp and a sense of haughtiness that irritated Central Americans, but this time the habit benefited Chavez. The special armored sedans used by the US embassy in Bogotá were accessible, and with a few bribes, easily tagged with GPS tracking devices several days before the general arrived in-country.

Chavez's leaders had informants everywhere, but the GPS trackers were the ace up his sleeve. The day before the general's arrival, Chavez guaranteed there would be no interference from the local police or military units by distributing a few well-placed bribes.

The general finally arrived, and the three armored sedans were moved to the airport two hours before the American plane landed. Plenty of time to rally the strike team and get them into position on the main street leading from the airport to the US embassy in the capital.

Everything fell into place as Chavez watched the plane's arrival via a direct video feed. A camera on top of a nearby commercial building had a perfect view of the landing, and he watched as the entourage exited the plane, entered the cars, and headed for the airport entrance.

The ambush site wasn't covered by surveillance cameras, so he waited by the phone to hear the report. The plan was executed flawlessly, but the firefight was more prolonged than Chavez had expected.

The target's bodyguards had turned out to be US special operators, and they were unwilling to die easily. Twelve out of the twenty-man team he sent in were now dead. Two or three of the survivors were severely wounded and struggling to stay alive.

His elite fighters were hard to find. Intelligent men who were loyal to a fault and capable of professional discretion were valuable. He made a mental note to recruit replacements as soon as possible. Chavez left the balcony and walked into his sitting room. Now the Americans would understand. He was going to extract a heavy price for their interference in his affairs.

Chapter Ten

The Colombian Jungle

Auger was thrown violently to the ground and repeatedly stomped on by a guerilla. The air whooshed out of his lungs and he struggled to breathe. Other men stood nearby, laughing and goading their friend while they screamed obscenities in Spanish.

How much pain could this gringo handle? Auger didn't understand much of what they were saying, but he did know he had to get to his feet or they'd break his ribs.

With his hands tied behind his back, Auger struggled to roll over until he was face down on the ground. He scooted back until he was at last resting on his knees, forehead pressed into the hard dirt. The attack did not abate. One of the Colombian guerillas began whacking him across his back using his rifle barrel. If this didn't stop, they'd cripple him. He needed to end this somehow.

Stand up! Auger's mind screamed the command. The senior chief ignored a particularly brutal blow and pressed himself into an upright kneeling position. He ducked a wild stroke aimed at his head and got to his feet. Standing, his full height intimidated the smaller men. The Colombians backed off a few steps, assessing the situation.

He was an impressive physical specimen, but it was the look in his eyes that gave them cause for concern. They had the guns and the numbers, but all of the young men moved back a bit, giving him some room. One of the guerillas indicated by pointing with his rifle that he should walk around to the front of the truck.

Auger could barely see around the rusty vehicle. He made an effort to survey his opponents, their strengths and hopefully their weaknesses. There was a group of fighters, four or five at most, gathered near the front of the truck. Auger took muster. Counting the two or three goons having fun with him, there were a total of six to seven armed men guarding him and the general.

He quickly assessed the situation. He was now somewhere deep in the jungle, possibly hundreds of miles from any town or city. Even in his battered condition, a dash through the jungle might work, but then what? He took stock of his captors. The guerillas were relaxed, even comfortable. That usually meant that they were on home turf--no immediate threat from the Colombian military and plenty of friends operating in the area.

No, he would bide his time. Running would end badly. Besides, his mission was to protect the general. He had no idea what the older man's condition might be or even if he was alive. He needed a plan that took this into consideration. If his principal was dead, Auger was free to act on his own. If alive, Auger had to figure out a way to get them both out of this mess. He'd wait until there was a clear opening, an opportunity to escape.

He knew help would be on the way soon enough. When he closed his eyes, he could see the preparations in his mind. Communications, coordination, detailed planning, and the forward staging of support units. Of course, the ever-present need for logistics management, and somewhere out there, a special ops team gearing up to execute a rescue.

Whoever they are they would be cocky, self-assured combat veterans. Bragging and joking with each other as they prepared for what they might see as an easy bread and butter operation: get in, get out, don't fuck around. All in a day's work. He said a silent prayer that whoever was selected was good, really good.

He could be patient because he had faith in the process. This faith gave him a sense of purpose, too. He must stay alive and he must keep the general alive; time was not on their side. His brain drifted back to the rescue fantasy. The strike assets would be requesting detailed satellite coverage right about now. They would conduct a time-lapse walk back to the moment of the attack then watch the flow of events as captured by the eyes in the sky, from the beginning to the end of the attack.

Tracking movement in the dense, triple canopy jungle might be too difficult for even America's spy satellites. He guessed the intelligence agencies had most of the big FARC camps identified already.

They could detect thermal signatures emitted by fires and even humans. They likely would target all the camps, using their technology to look for the sign a unit was tracking to a camp and then using Intelligence-Surveillance-Reconnaissance (ISR) drones to get a closer look at the camp with a high degree of increased activity.

The drones were a great asset in the desert and mountains; but in the jungle, they were limited. Any attempt to fly directly overhead might be detected and cause the guerillas to scatter. The best the drones could do was monitor thermals from an oblique standoff distance.

Auger realized this caused an issue for pre-attack intelligence collection. The good guys would need to put boots on the ground--a recon team to find, observe, and report the camp activities, capabilities, and vulnerabilities.

It would take more time that way, maybe four or five days before insertion. Snipers made sense, too. They could assist the assault force once the rescue began.

He could've planned the entire thing from soup to nuts with ease, but he decided to stop thinking about the possibilities. He knew it was only a matter of time. As long as Auger kept his head, he had a fighting chance to make it out of this scrape alive.

The SEAL scanned the immediate area again for a sign that the general was traveling with him. He seemed to remember there had been another crate in the back of the truck, but nothing had moved inside during the long ride. A sharp jab to the ribs returned his attention to his immediate problem: teenagers with rifles.

The little smiling man in front of him was having loads of fun, prodding the bigger American with his rifle barrel. Auger was rudely pushed onto a narrow jungle trail where his concerns about the general were put to rest. A few steps to the right lay the principal.

The general was lying on a makeshift stretcher surrounded by a bunch of new faces, reinforcements. Great, Auger thought, a new group of guerillas. He seemed okay. At the very least he was alive. The new group of guerillas was older and appeared more seasoned than the ones handling Auger.

The two escort teams met on the trail and, after a brief exchange, Auger's buddies left and he was handed over to the new boys. Hopefully, they were more professional than the first group, who were filled with teen angst, he thought to himself. May as well find out.

"So, you must be the country folk!" The senior chief's quip was answered with a sharp rap to the head. I'd better cool it, Auger thought. A few more hits like that and I won't be able to balance my checkbook anymore.

On cue, two men lifted the stretcher holding the general. The old man moaned. Maybe he's been sedated, guessed Auger. The senior chief remembered that just before the goons knocked him out, the general had received one hell of a beating.

"Venga! Venga!" The insistent voice belonged to a grizzled old coot he hadn't noticed before. He urged Auger to start walking while pointing an old bolt-action rifle at his back.

The old man's coal black eyes spoke volumes, reflecting the harsh life he'd led. Auger nodded ever so slightly in deference to the old man and did as he was told. He may be old and skinny but he's probably capped a few people in his time. Best to be polite and respectful, for now.

The group moved out, and Auger noted they didn't seem to be in a hurry. The patrol moved at a casual pace, conserving their strength in the oppressive heat. Auger recognized the indications immediately. This was going to be a long trek.

The guerillas weaved back and forth, dodging tree branches and avoiding washouts in the trail. Auger followed at a leisurely pace and appreciated the low level of effort required. The path was well-worn, and it meandered through the dense vegetation without giving Auger a clear sense of direction.

From time to time, they'd all stop to switch out stretcher bearers, drink some water, and take a piss break. The jungle was so thick it reached out and touched you on all sides. As the morning grew longer, the heavy air became stifling, making it difficult for Auger to breathe.

He was in excellent physical shape, but he hadn't been in Colombia long enough to acclimate before the protection mission. He was just going to have to suck it up and adjust to the heat and the moist air in real time.

Auger looked up. Maybe his hope that the satellites could find them was misplaced. The triple canopy of vivid green blocked any possible view of the sky. Was the technology good enough to penetrate this shit?

Hopefully, the heat signature of the truck that took him from the city to the jungle had been tracked. Maybe they could look at that point of departure and draw a line to the nearest FARC camp and determine where the guerillas were taking them, that is if there weren't a shit ton of FARC camps.

Auger knew the spooks back at the national security agency were experts at recognizing routine activity, so they probably could watch the likely camp candidates and identify anything out of pattern, like the arrival of a large patrol with prisoners. They could then pinpoint the anomalies, analyze them, and identify Auger and the general's location. At least that was the theory. He hoped they were as good as advertised.

The senior chief's stomach growled loud enough for a guerilla to pay attention. Man, I'm hungry, he thought. I wonder if these guys are planning on ever feeding me. Then again, maybe they don't want to waste food on a man marked for death. The initial confusion over who was the actual VIP would, most likely, be resolved when they reached their destination. They didn't go to all the trouble of ambushing a VIP and not have a picture at least.

Auger walked all day without a break. Twice the guerillas gave him water. He pondered the probabilities associated with escaping. Based on the size of the canvas backpacks, his new best friends were expecting to be in the field for two or three days. He knew he could go longer than that without food, as long as they kept him hydrated. He really wished he could speak to the general, assess his condition. So far, the big guy had been silent.

Auger knew he might be able to slip away at night, find help somehow. Or at least make a statement before dying, get hold of one of those weapons and take a few of them with him. Auger knew either fantasy was silly. His mission was the safety of the general. So, unless he died, Auger was on the hook to stay. Auger absentmindedly wondered for the hundredth time if anyone back home was on top of this problem.

Chapter Eleven

The Pentagon, Washington, DC

Matt stood in the waiting room shuffling his feet nervously. This was his first visit to the Pentagon. The feeling of intimidation was overwhelming at first, but the longer he stood there the more relaxed he became. The Pentagon was nothing more than a huge office building, and he was a warrior surrounded by clerks and politicians. Easy day.

It was interesting to watch so many senior officers from the various services moving about the hallways, scurrying up and down the passageways. He noted that most were not in good physical condition, a fact that confirmed Matt's assessment that he was in the world's largest nest of staff pukes. Top-heavy paper pushers trying to rule their military kingdoms from a desk, never getting their hands dirty, at least anymore.

He still wasn't sure why he was there. His orders had been clear as mud, and the sense of urgency he'd felt in Coronado didn't seem justified considering the long wait once he'd arrived. After three hours, a civilian security guard waved him over to an information desk near the main entry turn styles.

The staff personnel at the information desk confessed they were impressed with the origin of his written orders, but were as confused as Matt as to their meaning. They decided to make a call rather than allow him access. The young lady hung up the phone and smiled. He was given visitor credentials and directed to go back to the waiting area; someone would be arrive shortly to escort him to his destination. Ten minutes later, Matt was greeted by a tall army colonel.

"Lieutenant Barrett?" he asked.

"Yes sir," Matt replied. "I was told to . . ."

The colonel interrupted Matt, extending his hand. "My name is Colonel Rushworth. Please be patient, you'll soon know more than you really want to know." Colonel Rushworth reinforced his mysterious comment with a wink. Matt followed the colonel up the escalator, adding to the stream of people coming in to work in the famous building. It was a long walk, and Matt felt silly about his anger at being made to wait so long. The facility was so large that getting anywhere was a test of endurance. At last, they arrived at a large door.

Matt was directed to drop his cell phone off outside. He placed it in a rack of twenty or so phones already being held hostage and walked through the door. Matt was ushered into what appeared to be a small briefing room. Three men sat around an oval conference table. None of the men stood up to shake Matt's hand. One of the men, a navy admiral, pointed to a chair.

"Please take a seat, lieutenant." Matt couldn't stop staring at all the fruit salad on the man's chest. Each colored ribbon represented a different military award, and the four stars on the admiral's collar were certainly impressive. Matt spotted an elaborate badge positioned just under the man's breast pocket. It suddenly dawned on him that he was sitting across from the Chief of Naval Operations (CNO).

The man to the CNO's right was wearing a suit. He was in his early fifties, with a touch of gray at the temples. He had that air of authority that comes with access to the top; he was one of the untouchables. The man oozed arrogance from every pore. Matt was sure this schmuck was CIA or maybe NSA. He decided then and there that he disliked him. At the end of the table sat a gentleman Matt recognized immediately. The Chairman of the Joint Chiefs of Staff. His mouth opened a little involuntarily in surprise. What the hell was this all about?

"Welcome, Lieutenant Barrett. I trust your trip from San Diego was pleasant?"

Matt betrayed himself by swallowing hard before answering. "Yes, sir, thank you, sir."

The chairman began with introductions. "Mr. Barrett, this is Mr. Collins, the assistant to the director of operations for the CIA." The suit stared back at Matt before offering his hand. Great, Matt thought. Some insecure idiot that wants to play head games. Matt returned the handshake and then promptly ignored him. The chairman took all this in before introducing the admiral.

"This is the Chief of Naval Operations, Admiral Jackson." Matt smiled and shook the offered hand.

"It's nice to see the navy here, sir." Matt wanted the admiral to know he might need an ally. Matt turned his attention back to the chairman. "Please excuse me, sir, if I appear a little confused."

"That's understandable, Mr. Barrett."

The chairman slid a plain, yellow eight-by-ten envelope across the table toward Matt. "Lieutenant, the contents of that folder will explain some of the issues we are going to be dealing with during the pre-mission planning phase for Operation Green Dagger. We have two Americans in jeopardy, lieutenant. They've been taken hostage, and we presume they are being moved as we speak to a large base camp south of Bogotá, Colombia. You will find the details and background information in the envelope. All our intelligence resources are at your disposal."

Matt wasn't getting it. "Sir, what does this have to do with me? I'm assigned as an instructor at our special warfare training center. I'm not in command of a SEAL troop or platoon."

"Son, you have been selected by the navy, with SOCOM's blessing, to lead a very special team. Initially, the team will be responsible for conducting reconnaissance and surveillance of the guerilla base camp in question. The camp is located on a river in the Colombian jungle. You and your fellow

SEALs have been tasked with helping find and rescue General Alexander, Commander, US Southern Command, and one of his SEAL bodyguards." That got Matt's attention.

"Who's the SEAL, sir?"

"Actually, I believe you know him. His name is Senior Chief Auger. I understand you two worked together at one time."

Matt's heart sank; he couldn't believe it. "Auger? Are you sure, sir?"

The chairman didn't change his expression. "That's right, son. All we know right now is Colombian guerillas, affiliated with or actual members of the FARC, ambushed a vehicle convoy in Bogotá and took General Alexander and your friend." He paused to allow the information to soak in. Matt overcame his initial reaction and stopped staring at the table in front of him. He turned his head and focused on the chairman's words.

"Please go on, sir."

"We tracked the bastards by satellite. They drove into the jungle then we lost contact with them. Lieutenant, we don't have much time. You need to choose who you want on your three-man team and assemble them in Panama. We have people coming in to brief you on the events that led up to the hostage taking, the capabilities of the FARC guerillas, and their tactics. They'll also make sure you have all the information you need to plan and execute your mission."

The chairman looked at the bank of digital clocks on the wall showing times from all around the globe. "You have less than seventy–two hours to assemble and brief your team. Spend a few minutes after this meeting and sketch out your immediate logistics needs so we can get that ball rolling. Remember, lieutenant, if you are able to locate the hostages, you will not attempt a rescue. Your team's job will transition to rescue support. Do you understand?"

Matt nodded. "Not a rescue, standoff surveillance only. Yes, sir, I understand."

Admiral Jackson cleared his throat. "Good. We don't expect three men, even three SEALs, to go up against the FARC on their home turf. There's a SEAL platoon in isolation right now preparing for the rescue phase of the operation. They'll be staged close enough to the camp to be able to react to your reporting. They will insert and conduct the rescue once you've found the general and your friend. Do you have any questions about the objectives of this operation?"

Matt shook his head. "No, admiral, I think I've got it down. You want me to go in and find these bastards and see if our people are still alive. If they are, you want me to report that fact and then roll over to fire support for the raid. Pretty straightforward."

The chairman got Matt's attention. "That's exactly right, lieutenant. You were chosen to lead the way on this operation because of your combat experience and because you have proven you can think under pressure. Your actions in Egypt are proof of that. Good officers, the ones who know how to lead men, are rare, even in special operations. Pick your team wisely. You need to pull this off right, the first time." The chairman stood up to leave.

Matt jumped to his feet along with the rest of the people in the room. "Yes, sir. You can count on that. I know just the men for this job, and it won't take long to put the team together."

"Good, that's no less than I expected," the chairman said. "Admiral, I concur with your decision regarding Barrett. He'll do a great job! I wish we had more like him!" The chairman left the room, followed by the suit and Admiral Jackson. Colonel Rushworth waited until they left, then spoke up.

"Matt, take a few minutes to review the material in the envelope. You won't be able to leave here with the envelope, but there will be a lot more intelligence material waiting for you in Panama at our isolation area. It's enough to get you started thinking for now. If you already know who you want on this mission, give me the names. I'll chase them down and send them to Panama ASAP!"

Matt barely heard the colonel. He knew who his top picks were, but he had no idea where they were or if they were still in the teams. He wrote the names down and slid the piece of paper across the desk to the colonel. Then he sat down and opened the envelope. Colombia wasn't Egypt or Iraq. He had little to no experience in jungle operations, but he didn't give a shit about that. He was going to get Auger out of that camp.

Chapter Twelve

Fort Pickett, Virginia

The gloved hand gently pushed the branch aside. The SEAL sniper shifted his weight ever so slowly, adjusting his field of vision. He now had a clear shot. The target area was a simulated urban compound. A training site referred to as a mobile operations in urban terrain (MOUT) facility.

The instructor cadre set up various scenarios to help train students how to deal with the difficult task of fighting in a city environment. American military forces historically learned, forgot, and then relearned the bloody lessons of street fighting because of apathy between wars and an arrogant perspective that the last war would never happen again.

Well, it did happen again. Operation Iraqi Freedom put Marines and soldiers in the urban environment once again. Ill-trained for house-to-house fighting, tactics their World War Two counterparts would have recognized immediately.

The SEAL sniper lay in wait, assisted by a second SEAL who acted as security. They comprised one of four sniper pairs positioned around the MOUT facility, and they were focused on their slice of the MOUT in front of them.

A SEAL assault team was about to attack. The primary mission of the four sniper pairs was to identify which of the MOUT buildings was holding two American pilots, prisoners taken after their imaginary plane crashed.

Once that location was determined, the assault force would swoop in and rescue the two men. The snipers then would transition from surveillance and reporting to direct action mode, eliminating any threats to the assault team outside the walls of the building in the MOUT.

But for now, the SEAL snipers remained hidden around the training town and continued to provide up-to-date intelligence information. Their customer was the ground force commander, who was located with his command and control element on a hill near the MOUT.

They were conducting this raid in broad daylight so the SEAL Team Four training department could videotape their actions on the objective. Video cameras were positioned throughout the MOUT area and inside the rooms occupied by the opposition force role players and the prisoners.

The opposition force consisted of reserve army personnel. As infantrymen, they were competent ground fighters, but they knew their task today was to die. They would follow those orders, but they planned to make it as difficult as possible for the SEAL rescue team.

The SEAL snipers also were being observed and graded by the training department on their ability to coordinate their marksmanship skills. Upon hearing the execution code word over the secure radio net, the four sniper pairs would execute their shots simultaneously, taking out their assigned sentries before picking up squirters, enemy soldiers running out of the buildings or trying to escape the MOUT.

The sniper fire was also the signal for the rescue team to leave their concealed position on the edge of town and move rapidly to the target building. Once there, the breachers would separate from the assault team and place high explosives on two ground floor windows as well as the main door to the building where the prisoners were held.

Once the explosives opened the way into the building, the assault team would rapidly enter through all three breached access points.

From his vantage point, the SEAL ground force commander could observe the evolving attack and orchestrate solutions to problems as they arose. The mission commander was assisted in his efforts by two SEALs, a radioman and a rifleman responsible for the element's security. Code words and critical information flowed back and forth via scrambled SATCOM radios.

From time to time, the radioman passed the information updates along in the form of intelligence reports to the SEAL task unit commander, who was in orbit five miles away in a supporting air force AC-130-gunship.

During the mission-planning phase, the SEALs were provided with critical information from SEAL Team Four's training cell. The key to the tactical puzzle was the location of the two American hostages. The training cell's initial intelligence was wrong, something the seasoned operators expected.

That's why having eyes on the target always trumped pre-mission information. The snipers confirmed to the ground force commander that the hostages were being held on the second story of the hotel near the center of town.

The SEAL snipers also verified the location of all enemy targets operating outside the buildings. There were men on two or three of the rooftops in the immediate vicinity of the hotel, armed with Romanian-produced AK-47 assault rifles.

Petty Officer First Class Sam Oberman watched one of the men on the nearest rooftop scanning the trees intently with his binoculars. Oby had the wind and knew the range using his laser range finder. This guy was toast.

The man on the roof seemed to be focusing most of his attention toward Oby's position, but his demeanor indicated that he was completely unaware of the danger. "What time is it?" Oby didn't want to take his eyes from the scope.

Petty Officer Third Class George Donaldson was scanning their side of the MOUT facility with a pair of high-powered German binoculars. He glanced at his watch. "Two minutes to eight. I can't see the assault team, Oby. They should've been in position by now."

"The assault team's coming through the sewer. They'll enter the MOUT, then use a side street to approach the target building. My guess is they are coming up through the manhole covers right around now."

Donaldson knew the plan. The rescue team was going to stage next to the target building sixty seconds prior to the assault. The side street chosen was unobservable from the roof of the target. A natural blind spot in an otherwise open urban plan of streets and common areas.

If everything went according to the rehearsal, at exactly eight o'clock the demolitions breaching team would lead the SEALs as they rushed across the open space from their hiding place and execute the takedown.

Upon their arrival, the demolitions team would place a special light breaching package on the two windows on the side of the target building. Then they would creep up and place a larger charge on the main entrance. Small, hand-held shields were carried to protect the breachers from the blast.

The explosions would stun the occupants of the building for a moment or two, just long enough for the assault team to enter through the smoking entry point created by the breachers and take down the first floor. The breachers would stay out of the way until the assault team entered, then join the tail end of the flow of special operators.

"Yeah, Oby, I know how it's supposed to go down," the young scout said. "I just wish I could see that they were in position."

Oby snorted. "Did you ever stop to think that if we could see them, the bad guys could see them? Don't worry about the assault team. They know what to do. Just focus on helping me identify secondary targets once the shooting starts. What time is it now?"

"Forty-five seconds to execute." Donaldson's voice was all business now. Oby was right. Each SEAL was responsible for his own piece of the action. BUD/S taught you that. The team was well-briefed, well-rehearsed, and well-led.

He knew the assault would be successful unless Murphy got involved. Murphy's Law stated that if anything can go wrong, it will go wrong. In special operations, it was wise to say a small prayer to Murphy to hedge your bets.

Of course, mistakes were bound to happen. The two SEALs had witnessed quite a few during complex exercises like this one, and Oby was a combat veteran who could attest it happened in real combat, too.

That's why they practiced all the time. There is no such thing as a perfect mission when you pushed the performance envelope every training day. Most SEALs believed a perfectly executed exercise was a waste of training time, since nobody learned anything when nothing went wrong.

Donaldson swept his binoculars back toward the target building. "Thirty seconds, Oby."

"Roger that," acknowledged the sniper. "Watch for the assault team moving from their first breach position to the door."

"There they are!" The scout could see a line of men snaking around the corner of the MOUT hotel. He shifted his view to the rooftop sentries. "Everything's still cool topside! Ten seconds to execute."

Oby pushed the selector switch to the FIRE position. "Heads up," he whispered. The scout didn't respond. Oby inhaled fully, then slowly let air escape from his lungs. He stopped halfway through the exhalation and held his breath. Oby began squeezing the trigger.

Chapter Thirteen

BOOM! BOOM! BOOM! The three breaching charges detonated two seconds late. The explosions were amplified by the proximity of so many empty cinder block buildings in the MOUT, and the sound echoed off every building.

Oby didn't wait to confirm he'd nailed the first of four mannequin targets representing the enemy on the rooftop. He smoothly shifted his crosshairs to rest on the head of a second sentry dummy. The weapon jumped in his hands. This time he saw the plastic head explode.

"Topside targets waxed!" Donaldson scanned the windows and then looked at the base of the building. "No secondary targets in sight."

Oby didn't answer. He shifted his scope to each window on the target building, methodically moving from window to window. Donaldson was correct. He couldn't find any new targets to shoot.

He kept his eyes on the windows anyway. The dumb shits always wanted to come out and take a look. Sure enough, a mannequin's head slid slowly into view, just high enough for Oby to take a shot.

These training guys are great! It was tough to set up a training evolution where all the players participated fully. Oby took the shot. The mannequin flipped back out of sight.

He could faintly hear shattering glass and the sounds of struggle emanating from the hotel. So far, so good. Everything was going according to plan. After the assault team entered the building, they quickly secured the ground floor.

Meanwhile, the other sniper pairs were executing their tasks. Dropping all the exterior targets in their field of view. The assault team "killed" two more enemy combatants as they ran up the stairway toward the second floor. In the first fifteen seconds of the assault, the SEALs eliminated eleven bad guys, a very respectable body count, considering none of the SEALs were yet killed or wounded.

Oby heard the assault team firing a rapid series of shots as they cleared the second floor. "How does it look?" he asked.

"Still clear everywhere I can see," responded the scout. "Our kill zone is empty. There are no visible targets."

The firing suddenly increased dramatically. "Sounds like they found the hostages," observed Donaldson.

"Yep," remarked Oby. "Unless those crafty training guys set a trap for our boys over there."

Donaldson lowered the binoculars. "You really think so? What a bunch of bullshit if they did."

Oby continued to sweep the crosshairs of his high-powered scope back and forth, looking for fresh targets. "I was on an assault last year. We went charging in there and started clearing the rooms one by one until we hit the fifth floor. The training department had a wall of desks and chairs piled up in the hallway. Every time we tried to take it down, they opened up on us."

"So, what did you guys do?" Donaldson said, placing the binoculars back in front of his eyes.

"We sent a six-man team up the stairs to the sixth floor. They cleared that deck and used ropes to lower themselves down to the fifth-floor windows behind the barricade. They tossed in a few flash crash grenades and came in through the windows shooting. We had the floor, but no hostages."

"They weren't on the fifth floor?" Donaldson was having a hard time keeping up.

"No, they weren't," Oby continued. "The training guys moved them just before the attack. They moved them through a sewer access door in the basement of the target building. It took a while, but we found them alone, tied up in the building next door."

"Man, that's bullshit!" Donaldson had less experience than his sniper partner, but he'd been a SEAL long enough to know how the game was supposed to be played. The hostages were always in a bad position when a team came in hard, fast, and in broad daylight.

During such a dynamic entry and assault, there was nothing to stop the hostage takers from putting a bullet into their hostages out of spite or a desire for vengeance. The SEALs counted on hard-hitting action and speed to overcome even a prepared enemy, hoping they would be more concerned about dying than killing hostages.

"Violence of action" was a tactical concept crucial to the success of small unconventional units. It meant never letting the other guy have the drop on you. Hit him first and hit him hard. Never give your adversary a chance to fight back.

The bottom line was simple. It was far better for a small team of SEALs to go in and eliminate the bad guys in their sleep rather than call them out onto the street like an old western movie to determine who had the fastest gun.

Any biker who's survived a bar fight knows that violence of action works. In a bar fight, if you start to shove and poke while talking trash to a seasoned street fighter, then they'll just hit you over the head with a stool or a beer bottle mid-sentence. Fight over.

Immediate escalation of violence is so shocking and so unexpected that virtually every opponent falls victim to the tactic. Applying violence of action to hostage rescue scenarios entailed using the rude impact of shock, combined with precision firepower, in a coordinated and deliberate fashion.

Ideally, that put shooters everywhere at once. The element of surprise wasn't always enough. You had to get the other guy to stop and wonder what was going on. Make him blink. Then it was much easier to take that guy out of the equation.

The assault team brought the rescued hostages downstairs to the main entrance. The team leader was on the radio net, methodically sending out a detailed status report to the command and control element. They, in turn, passed the report to higher authority circling above.

The earpiece crackled to life in Oby's ear. "Stand down; the exercise is over. All players muster at the target building's main entrance."

"Roger that," Oby said out loud. "It's quitting time, buddy!" Oby started packing up the equipment staged all around him.

"That's cool," Donaldson commented. "Because I desperately need to get a big ass, ten-legged bug outta my shorts!" Oby laughed.

If this exercise had played out to the end, the assault team would've gathered all the sniper and breaching teams together at a control point identified in the mission brief. The ground force commander's element would join them and get a final headcount before patrolling to an off-target helicopter extraction site.

The preferred formation shape for tactical travel on this mission configuration was an oval. The hostages would move in the middle, protected on all sides by members of the assault team.

The ground force command element also would occupy the center, communicating with the extraction helicopters and coordinating ground markers, such as colored smoke during the day and pop flares at night.

The extraction birds would be called in, and the SEALs and hostages would load up and depart to a safe zone. Today's exercise, however, was different. It focused only on actions in the objective area. The training staff only intended to debrief the attack and rescue sequence in and around the target building.

Oby and Donaldson slid backward out of their sniper hide and threw their heavy packs over their backs. The two SEALs casually walked down the steep hill toward the MOUT facility, carrying their rifles and watching the ground to avoid getting tripped up on the way to the base of the hill.

SEALs were flowing into the center of town from all around. A good many were exercise graders, safety personnel, or role players.

There were a few third-party observers, too. The SEALs were an important national asset. It wasn't out of the norm for a congressman or a senior executive from one of the three-letter intelligence agencies to want to watch SEAL training.

The general collapse of formality in the MOUT was referred to by SEALs as "going admin." The term also was used to taunt a fellow SEAL who cheated, slacked off, or tried to cut corners during training exercises.

"Oby!"

Oby recognized the voice of SEAL Team Four's assistant training officer, Lieutenant White, coming through his earphone. This couldn't be part of the exercise. The training officer wouldn't be using Oby's real name over on the radio. "Yes, sir, this is Oby," Oby replied.

"You and Donaldson get down here ASAP. I need to talk to you, Oby. I have a priority message from the commanding officer for you. I already told the team leader and ground force commander that you aren't going to be with them for the final headcount and debrief."

Oby was puzzled by all the cloak and dagger stuff. "Whatever you say, boss," he replied, pressing the talk button on his small radio.

"What's up?" Donaldson could see Oby was troubled.

"Don't know. They said the old man sent me a message. Lieutenant White says it's important. We need to find him down there. He told me to ignore the post-mission muster."

"That's weird!' Donaldson observed. "Are you in some kind of trouble?"

"Not that I know of," said Oby. "I guess we'll find out when we get into town." The two SEALs picked their way through the thick underbrush. At times both men cursed the tangle of vines and dead plant life. Eventually, they broke into the open, clearing the tree line forty yards from the edge of the MOUT facility.

Chapter Fourteen

Oby spotted Lieutenant White standing, hands on hips, next to the concrete building directly across from the target. He also observed the rest of the troops gathering for initial feedback from the graders. This would only last ten minutes. A full detailed review would be held the next day and those often lasted for several hours.

The assistant training officer saw them and waved. Oby gave a little wave back. He was starting to worry. Did something happen to one of his parents? His sister? He'd been around long enough to suspect the odd request wasn't anything good.

The training department was diligently moving about, cleaning up grenade canisters and spent brass. Some of the instructors headed upstairs to dismantle the barricade in front of the hostage room on the second floor. Still others were picking up the pieces of shattered cinder block where the breaching team blew the wall.

The gooey grease used to stick the charge against the door had splattered all over the wall. The SEALs were responsible for cleaning up any mess made in the army's training facility. Soon, an army range control sergeant would arrive to clear the MOUT and certify it clean and ready for use by the next unit. There was a lot of work to do.

Oby and Donaldson walked over to where Lieutenant White was waiting. "So, what's up, boss?" Oby asked, closing the distance. "Well, Oby," the lieutenant started, "It seems you've received special orders back at Little Creek." Oby stopped dead in his tracks.

"Special orders?" he asked. "I thought I was in trouble!"

"No, you're not in trouble. The orders were SPECAT. Nobody but the old man and you can look at them. I've told the troop you'll be heading head right back to the creek. When you get there, go straight to the CO's office, he's waiting for you."

"If it's SPECAT, its real-world shit!" Donaldson blurted out. Oby thought for a moment.

"I need to take my long gun, sir. Especially if it's the real deal." All snipers are issued five different specialized weapons. Oby's other weapons were in the team armory in Little Creek.

"Fine, Oby, you do that. But promise me you'll get your butt on the road right away. My ass will be in a sling if you don't show up soon."

Oby stuck out his hand. "Sure thing, sir. I'm moving as we speak." Oby shook hands with Donaldson and said a quick goodbye. A pickup truck, the driver at the ready, was idling nearby. Oby jogged to the truck, threw his gear in the back, and jumped in the front seat.

He hid his rifle by covering it on the back seat with a poncho somebody left in the cab. His heart was pounding as the truck pulled away from the MOUT area. Real-world missions were the reason all SEALs trained with such intensity. He was pumped!

Stuttgart, Germany

Petty Officer First class, Boone Kilpatrick shook his head, his overly long blond curls reflecting the bright sunlight. These idiots can't even draw a straight line, he thought. Boone was temporarily assigned to the naval special warfare unit in Stuttgart as a reconnaissance instructor.

His home command, SEAL Team Two in Little Creek, Virginia, had been asked to provide a man with experience in reconnaissance and surveillance to give a class to the bored SEALs, who had been drinking and skiing too much in their winter wonderland. Someone, he didn't know who, thought it made sense to send him. Lucky him.

Boone's job, for the time being anyway, was to refresh the SEALs in the fine art of target sketching. An old-school skill that the SEAL teams realized they needed to recover after several years in the sandbox using nothing but advanced technology. Most of the men in the room hadn't drawn a recon sketch since BUD/S, and it showed.

Boone wasn't the greatest artist himself. But he could draw a straight line. He also could write neatly and legibly. A critical skill if you're making maps and charts for someone else to use. The five SEALs in the classroom seemed incapable of executing either requirement.

"This exercise is simple, gentlemen," he began the lecture for a second time. "All you have to do is duplicate the drawing I've placed on the whiteboard. By duplicating the drawing neatly enough for someone else to read, you're halfway to becoming real recon artists."

Boone didn't believe a word of it. As if to punctuate the end of his sentence, one of the SEALs in the back dropped his number two pencil, snapping off the sharpened end. His head bobbed and his body jerked around as he struggled to escape the confines of the small student desk in pursuit of the writing implement. He began to use the pencil, then sheepishly rose out of his chair, walked to the wall mounted sharpener, and began to make noise.

This is a waste of time, Boone thought. None of these guys want to be a point man, let alone part of a surveillance team. What I have here is two M-240B machine gunners, two SAW gunners, and a demolition guy. The sixth student, a skinny ensign, left to go to the bathroom two hours ago.

Why are they even in this class? Why did they send me over here? Boone walked to the front of the classroom and checked his watch for the hundredth time. The digital watch face mocked him; he still had two hours to go.

Boone made a decision. "All right, guys, we only have five more minutes left before we're through for the day. All that I ask is that you finish this drawing so we can move on to the rest of the curriculum tomorrow."

The five-minute warning seemed to perk the class up. The SEALs frantically worked to finish the drawing assignment now that they knew the end was so close at hand. Boone was sure he'd take some shit for ending the session almost two hours ahead of schedule, but he was through wasting his time.

The door to the classroom opened a crack, the rusty hinges complaining loudly. Boone heard the odd sound and looked at the source. Did the ensign finally finish his business?

One of the administrative naval personnel for the unit was standing in the doorway holding a note. He beckoned to Boone to come over to the door. Boone glanced at the class. They were all scribbling away, ignoring him and the man at the door.

He walked over and grabbed the piece of paper handed to him. It was a memo from the unit's operations officer. Boone raised his eyebrows. The note said he was being ordered to Panama. Panama? SEAL Team Two was responsible for Europe and the western Mediterranean. Panama was SEAL Team Four's area of operations.

"Hey, Boone!" one of the denser SAW gunners shouted out. "Can we get out of here now?" Boone nodded without looking up from the note. He stepped aside absentmindedly as his students bolted for the door. Why Panama?

Boone walked back to the desk and collected his things. He left the classroom and walked rapidly down the passageway toward the operations office. This has to be a mistake, but it gave him an excuse for ending early. Boone smiled.

FARC Base Camp – Colombia

Auger was suffocating. The knotted T-shirt used to gag him was pulled so tightly up against his nose he could barely draw a breath. To make things worse, one of the guerillas was sitting on his chest. After two days of slogging it through the jungle, the guerillas had linked up with yet a third group.

The newcomers numbered around nine shooters, and they looked different somehow, maybe younger. Men in their prime, younger than his current escorts, but older than the first group to lead him and the general into the jungle. Maybe these were the frontline fighters, he mused.

It was near sunset, and the combined guerilla force was assembled on the trail, huddled up and listening to instructions growled out by a man with a pockmarked face and a dark scar across his neck. The man on Auger's chest stood up, and he was able to breathe at last. He was yanked to his feet, and once off the ground, he could see the terrain stretched out ahead of him.

A low ridge ran perpendicular to the trail about twenty to thirty yards away on his right. For now, he was content to catch his breath and focus on the scarred man. From what little he could tell, he was watching a mission brief of some sort. There was a sense of urgency in the man's tone. Were they about to engage with someone? If so, was it the home team? His heart beat a little faster. Would these assholes kill their captives if overwhelmed, or would they let them go?

He took another look around. The ridge was high ground. Anyone following this trail would be exposed and at a disadvantage should a team hit them from above. The man with the scar looked at Auger and barked an order in a mix of Spanish and a local dialect.

The two guerillas closest to him responded by grabbing him by the shoulders and, part dragging and part shoving, moved him forward and upward to the ridgeline. Once there, the guard shoved him violently to the ground again. He heard the others moving into position all along the ridge.

Chapter Fifteen

Auger didn't have to wait long before his new best friend came over to sit on his chest again. The men were whispering instructions now. Auger assumed this meant the intended victims were close, real close. It only took three minutes before everything calmed down and only the sounds of the jungle reached Auger's ears; the ambush was set.

The minutes crawled by. His legs and hands went numb, and the hard points of his shoulder blades were on fire from being pressed into the small stones and rocks on the jungle floor. The ground under and around him seemed to crawl and move with a life of its own.

Auger's shirt and pants were now home to a wide array of insects that burned, bit, or just wiggled. It was enough to drive him insane if he focused on the sensations.

Eventually, he fell asleep, for how long he couldn't determine. When he did wake up, he didn't feel refreshed. Waking up only allowed his mind to register the pain. Auger knew something was up when he felt the man sitting on him nervously shift his weight and slide to one side, going prone.

Auger heard the classic sounds of warriors getting ready for a fight. Bolts sliding forward slowly, whispering, slight adjustments in body position. Up and down the firing line, the guerillas were getting ready for a fight.

What a bunch of amateurs, he thought. Who sits for almost an hour quietly waiting to spring an ambush, then when the moment arrives, puts a round in their chamber? He decided that based on his professional observation, two or three SEALs could kick all their asses.

Auger spent the next few minutes detailing in his mind's eye how he would've set up the ambush. Claymore antipersonnel mines on the flanks and one back behind the team for rear security. Add in machine guns, forty-millimeter grenade launchers, and the world's best riflemen, and all you needed was a target.

A SEAL ambush was a real thing of beauty. These idiots, on the other hand, were in a rough skirmish line, no more organized than students on a firing line at the training range. Pathetic.

His fantasy was interrupted by the sound of crunching boots coming down the trail. Heavy feet, men tired and at the end of a long walk. They couldn't be US troops. Conventional American infantry would never patrol in such a sloppy manner, especially in a combat environment.

He could see the outcome as clear as if the fight was already over. Whoever they were, the FARC guerillas saw them as a threat, Colombian soldiers most likely. The tired men slogging their way up the trail were as good as dead.

The narrow jungle trail made a tight hairpin turn to the left, angling away from their position on the ridge like a check mark. The ambush position on the ridge was contoured the same way, placing the victims below them in a well-defined kill zone, with shooters on both flanks of the soldiers. The guerillas waited until the soldiers were bent around the trail, and then they opened fire.

A shattering blast of light and rapid firing signaled the initiation of the ambush. The guerilla's fire was sporadic. They couldn't see well, and their training didn't include learning the principle of sustained firepower.

Each man picked his target and fired in his own manner at that target. A few targets were being hit repeatedly, and others were, for the time being, untouched. Everybody was firing on full automatic, without discipline. Auger knew they were burning up ammo at an incredible rate.

He knew what came next. The firing began to die down, not by command, but gradually, determined by each rifleman. Then there were lulls in the shooting, ten seconds of quiet before more shots were fired, then silence again. Auger guessed the dummies executing the ambush were probably reloading at the same time.

The man next to Auger was spraying bullets in earnest, expending his magazine in less than ten seconds, then taking over a minute to reload. The man's hot brass casings sprinkled down on Auger. A few made their way down the collar of his shirt.

Everybody was firing and people were shouting in Spanish, but nothing seemed to change one way or the other for several minutes. Auger couldn't distinguish the fire of the soldiers from that of the guerillas.

He just assumed that as long as the guerillas kept firing there must be somebody firing back down below on the trail. He was happy to be on the reverse slope of the ridge where he was relatively safe.

Auger suddenly felt a pang of guilt. For the last half a day, his only thoughts were about himself. Except for a fleeting glimpse during the first turnover between groups, Auger didn't have a clue if General Alexander was dead or alive. Was he still with the group fighting on this ridge? He strained but couldn't see anything while on his back. There were only fighters on either side.

Auger was considering his options. He was gagged, so shouting the general's name was out of the question. His handler wasn't mounted on his chest for the time being, but sitting up was an invitation to a bullet in the head, fired by the good guys down below.

He realized in frustration that he would have to wait. If the guerillas truly believed he was the general, the ruse may have backfired. They could have dumped his body off on the side of the trail long ago.

Just then the pace of firing abruptly stopped. He heard a few grenades detonate, but he was sure the guerillas had won the day. Now it was time to clean up the kill zone and count bodies.

The ambush had taken forever, a full ten minutes by Auger's calculation. A sloppy mess executed by a bunch of third-rate amateurs. BUD/S students could do a better job. A few more shots rang out and then silence.

A flurry of excited commands was shouted out in Spanish, generating frantic movement all along the ridge. It looked to Auger like the fighters were being sent to sweep down and through the kill zone in a haphazard manner, every man running down and into the trail on his own.

Almost immediately, a short flurry of automatic weapons fire exploded from a few yards on the other side of the trail. The guerillas were the winners. They were sloppy and ill-trained. They'd chosen what looked at first glance to be an excellent site, but there was more to selecting a good ambush location.

Auger wasn't sure, but the firing seemed to indicate that there were survivors on the far side of the trail. He guessed there was some sort of terrain feature, camouflaged by the jungle, that provided shelter from the bullets rained down onto the trail by the FARC guerrillas.

He rolled onto his belly and eased forward until he could see the trail and the cluster of confused fighters. They'd just discovered that the opposite side of the trail slanted away steeply from the path. This feature had apparently provided an escape for many of the soldiers.

With the lower ridge formed by the trail protecting them, the soldiers were free to roll down the steep decline, and once on flat ground, either run or wait for the attackers to cease fire and sweep the trail. By exposing themselves, the ambushers became the ambushees. "Boy, these guys are all FARC'd up," he mumbled. Then he laughed at his little joke. It had been a long time since he'd found anything to laugh about; it felt good.

It looked like one guerilla found this out the hard way. He was lying dead on the trail. The veteran fighters in the guerilla group yelled for everyone to hit the ground. Then the wiser men among the prone bodies casually rolled six or seven grenades over the ridge and waited. A few more grenades and a few shots later, it was all over; this time for real.

A few minutes later, two men half crawled and half walked up to the ridge and closed the distance to where Auger lay. He had a fleeting thought that he'd probably blown the best chance he'd ever get to escape, but he still didn't know where the general was. The two men reached down and jerked Auger to his feet.

His legs were half asleep, so he promptly collapsed under his own weight. He was heavier than his handlers, so the three of them came crashing down. Auger pitched over as he fell and hit the ground with his face. The guerilla who fell on top of him cursed and struggled to stand up. Once on his feet, he began kicking Auger viciously.

The SEAL knew the drill. He curled up in the fetal position as tight as he could, hoping the beating would tire the small Colombian before he did any real damage. He covered his head and waited. The brutal attack ended, and the young fighter shouted for Auger to stand up.

When Auger failed to react, the man struck him in the shoulder with the butt end of his rifle. Auger inched closer to the man's feet, making it hard for the guerilla to use his gun as a club again. It worked. The second man said something and the attacks stopped.

Auger's legs were screaming in pain as the blood rushed back into the tissue. He was lifted to his feet a second time and was greeted by a new face. This new handler was much stronger than the first two men. He had little problem guiding and controlling Auger through the dense jungle, over the ridge and down to the trail below, all with one hand gripping his shoulder. Once they reached the trail, Auger was allowed to sit down Indian style.

There were bodies all over the place, and the stench of death and gunpowder mixed with the jungle humidity to create a terrible cocktail. He tried to breathe through his nose in short intakes and exhalations. Then he noticed a large man with gray hair lying behind him.

General Alexander! The general was breathing, so he was alive. The general sneaked a quick look at the navy SEAL. His face was covered with dried blood and dirt, but his smile spoke volumes. Auger nodded. They were both still in the game!

SEAL Team Three–Coronado, California

Lieutenant Jared Stone, platoon commander of FOXTROT Platoon, SEAL Team Three, reported to his commanding officer as ordered. He'd been pushing paperwork for hours, having just finished a training trip at the SEAL's Niland desert training facility. His platoon was the team's designated hostage rescue platoon, and he loved every minute of it.

Jared's guys were the unit responsible for short notice emergencies associated with maritime platforms in distress. Their geographic area of responsibility was the Pacific theater of operations. FOXTROT consisted of two troops of eight men each.

Stone's men were adept at taking down ships and oilrigs and rarely trained for anything else other than weapons proficiency, the very purpose of their recent trip to Niland.

Jared wasn't sure why he'd been called to the captain's office. First, he assumed that one of his men had gotten into trouble. He thought that theory through and realized if that was the case, he'd be in front of the operations officer or the XO, not the skipper.

That meant he was in some kind of trouble personally, and it must be serious. The CO didn't waste time on trivial issues. He knocked on the door frame and waited. Captain O'Connor looked up absentmindedly then gestured for Stone to enter.

"Morning, captain." Jared decided to act cool and calm.

"Morning, Jared. Have a seat." Captain O'Connor indicated a plush couch against the wall. As the lieutenant sat down, he couldn't help but see the old man's professional history splashed on every wall in the room: plaques, flags, paddles, strange carvings, and other mementos of all kinds.

Chapter Sixteen

Afghanistan, Iraq, memories of the teams, and personal experiences Captain O'Connor cherished. Someday, Jared thought, I'll have all this, a history worth putting on display. Someday I might even be captain of my own SEAL team.

The captain was ignoring Jared. A minute or two passed until O'Connor finished up a short stack of paperwork. Next to him on the large desk was another stack twice as high.

On second thought, Jared observed, maybe he didn't want this job. Jared hated paperwork of any kind. The captain finally stroked a final signature, leaned back in his chair, and looked over at Jared.

"Son, your platoon is being placed on a high state of alert. This is a real world, national command authority directive. You will be going to San Clemente Island where you will be placed in isolation. I don't know much about this whole thing, but I do know your platoon has been designated as a support asset for a highly classified rescue operation. This should be right up your alley."

Jared realized he was tense, bracing for the bad news. He let the air out of his lungs and sat up a little straighter. "Sir, will I receive a tasking order or intelligence package to work from?" Jared's heart was beginning to race.

"As I said, lieutenant, I don't know much yet; but I will push to get you everything you need."

"Yes, sir, I understand." Jared really didn't understand, but that was okay. He was going to lead his platoon into combat. It's what they'd trained for and why they sacrificed a normal life for a life in the teams.

"I expect that some aspects of the general mission scenario will be fed to you while you're in isolation out at the island. Remember, isolation is just what it sounds like. No contact between your platoon and the rest of the world. Take all your standard hostage rescue equipment and basic loadout, but don't neglect to take your heavier weapons. This could turn out to be something other than a platform takedown. If that's the case, you don't want to get stuck with only submachine guns and pistols."

"I see," Jared said. "Sir, my platoon's still in the compound. We returned from the desert two hours ago. Can I pull them together really quick? I'm afraid the chief might start cutting them loose to go home."

"Sure, that makes sense. Go ahead. By the way Jared, I think this is a good deal for you. Keep your guys straight, practice, and work on your skills out there so when the time comes you are sharp; but don't push too hard. The adrenaline can jack you up to the point that no amount of training seems to be enough. I know; I've been there."

The older man stood up. For a man in his early forties, he looked great. Years of physical training kept him lean and hard. Any civilian would guess the skipper was thirty, not forty-two.

"The security classification for this project is top secret, SPECAT. No one else in the SEAL Team Three is to know the nature of your mission or even where you're going for isolation."

Jared was ready. "Yes, sir!" he said, jumping to his feet. "Excuse me, but is that all, captain?" The captain smiled. He was jealous of the young lieutenant. He wished he were still young enough to lead a SEAL platoon.

His time in the saddle had been challenging and, in some cases, humbling. His greatest claim to fame was that he'd led or participated in over forty combat missions without losing a single man. Stone was a good man. He'd get the job done and bring his SEAL platoon back in one piece.

"Get out of here, son, and good luck!" The SEAL captain extended his hand. Jared shook the offered hand, pumping it a little too vigorously.

"Thanks, sir. We won't let you down!" Jared turned and left the office. Man, oh man, he thought. The boys are going to shit!

Tocumen International Airport – Panama

Matt shifted his weight to his left foot, hoping to provide relief for his right one. He'd been waiting in this spot for an hour and a half. His contact said the other two members of his party were due any minute. "This is total bullshit," Matt mumbled out loud.

Matt was firm about his picks for the mission. Everyone tried to talk him out of pulling Boone out of Stuttgart. He wasn't stupid. He had his pick of over two hundred combat-proven SEALs from either coast. He chose Boone for a reason; he was the best. The mission planners were tied in a knot trying to accommodate the timeline. Matt knew time was critical, but he still insisted on Boone and he got his way.

It had been five years since the mission in Egypt, five years since he'd last seen Boone. After the fight at the airport, Matt was transported to emergency medical facilities in Germany along with his chief and machine gunner, who also was wounded. It took three months for him to be released, and when he returned to SDV Team Two, he found the troop he'd commanded had been rebuilt and was under new leadership.

It made sense; his reconnaissance and surveillance troop were beaten up by the ordeal in Egypt. Time marches on. More experienced guys like Boone moved on to another troop or, in some cases, they were up for rotation to another SEAL team. The natural military cycle of replenishment, rebirth, and training began with new guys filling the empty positions in this old troop.

93

"Hey, bullet trap!" The voice originated from Matt's left. He turned and saw the infectious smile of his former point man.

"Hey, butt munch, you're late!" Matt laughed and Boone jogged the last few yards and embraced Matt in the standard team guy bro hug.

"What the fuck, sir? One minute I'm teaching finger painting in Germany, and the next minute I'm told zip shit, nada, and thrown on a plane for sunny Panama. They won't tell me what this is all about. But who gives a shit? It's the job, right?"

Matt surveyed his first pick for the mission. Boone was tall, a natural athlete, and a blast to be around. If he ever had bad moods, nobody would know by watching him. He was sniper-trained and had served in that role in Matt's SDV Team Two Troop. He looked good, a few signs of aging here and there in his face, but that was to be expected.

Boone married a few years after the experience in Egypt. He was happy and thought seriously of leaving the navy to stabilize his home life. He was dedicated to both ideals, and one had to go. But before he executed his plan to leave the teams, a tragic car accident took his wife and two-year-old son away from Boone.

Matt had heard the story form other team guys who served with Boone during this terrible time in his life. To make it worse, it happened while he was deployed; he never had a chance to say goodbye.

Something like that had to take a chunk out of the man's heart. According to the details he read in Boone's file on the flight to Panama, the cherry SEAL became resolved to become a sword, a warrior dedicated to the teams, his brothers in arms, and to America. Boone was a good choice.

As if reading Matt's mind, Boone decided to strike first. "I know you heard about Nancy and Adam. It was a shit deal. I was told they died instantly, so that's some consolation. I don't think about it much, just try to stay busy. By the way, you still with that hottie? What was her name, Cherry?"

Matt wanted to say something about Boone's loss, but the point man's face said drop it, so he rolled with the change in tempo. "No, dumbass, and her name was Sherry."

Boone tilted his head slightly. "Team guy curse?"

Matt nodded "Big time. She couldn't handle my being shot. She tried, she really did; but the healthier I became, the more depressed she became. All she could focus on was time getter shorter and shorter before I was fully operational again. When that day arrived, she gave me the speech."

"Sorry to hear that, boss. You're a good officer. The teams need guys like you, a modern Templar knight living large for god and country. I'd like to think I'm living that way, too."

Matt laughed. "You make failure sound like a promotion. Templars, eh? I guess so, maybe. Not sure I like the celibacy part, though."

"Fuck that, sir! We're frogmen. We are duty bound to procreate and spread our loving arms around the planet, even as we decimate the heathen enemies of America."

Matt was getting warmed up. It felt like the two of them were together only yesterday. He started to respond in kind, when his attention was drawn to a figure fifty yards away walking purposefully in their direction. He pointed with his chin. "The great long gunner arrives!"

Chapter Seventeen

Sam Oberman, a graduate of Boston College with a degree in biology, couldn't hear the compliment; but he could see his fellow SEALs' lips moving, so he assumed bullshit was flying at his expense.

Team guys always fucked with team guys. That is unless you were a fucking new guy, normally referred to as simply an FNG, then nobody talked to you. Being made fun of was the way warriors kept things loose in an uptight profession.

"You're late! I was about to go find a Marine sniper to take your place!" Oby took two long final steps and offered his hand to the navy lieutenant.

"Now LT, you know you'd only end up carrying the guy! No Marine can outshoot a SEAL, and there is only one great SEAL shootist, and that's yours truly."

Matt laughed, returning the handshake. Boone stepped forward and delivered a bro hug to his SEAL brother. Oby stepped back and lifted one eyebrow. "Shit, Boone, was that a hard-on I felt?"

Boone smiled. "Fuck you!" he shot back, laughing. "I'm not that happy to see you again."

The three men stood for a moment sheepishly looking at each other. Strong emotions swirled around under the surface. Emotions that could only truly be shared by men who had fought and bled in combat together.

"It's good to see you again, big guy; it's been a while," said Matt. Oby looked fit and trim. The past couple of years spent at SEAL Team Four clearly had matured him. He seemed poised and confident. Not the young pup Matt remembered.

Oby lowered his voice; this was no place for a conference. "Good to see you guys, too! So, what the hell is going on? They wouldn't tell me shit back at the team area."

Matt glanced at Boone, then back to Oby. "We'll fill you in later, Oby. This isn't a good time or place to bring you up to speed." Matt looked around to emphasize their lack of privacy.

Boone nodded in agreement. "That's right, old buddy. One thing is for sure, though, we're going to be butt deep in spent brass on this one. Oby, my man, it's time to get down and dirty again."

"Like Egypt?" Oby asked, referring to their shared combat experience two years earlier. "That was a goat rope."

"I hope not," quipped Matt. "We're waiting for our support crew to arrive by plane, and there was supposed to be a contact meeting us here to get us into that hangar." Matt tilted his head in the direction of the large commercial building thirty yards away.

"Not spooks again I hope." Boone, Matt, and Oby remembered the agency guy who gave the orders before their troop went into a shit storm in Egypt.

Matt checked his watch. "No, Boone, not this time. JSOC's sending a command cell, and one of the Naval Special Warfare (NSW) groups is sending a standard support team." Matt shielded his eyes and scanned the horizon. "We're where we're supposed to be. Where the hell is everybody else?"

"Probably still back in Bragg or Tampa polishing their boots." Boone wasn't fond of rear echelon types. However, he had great respect for the support folks embedded in the teams. NSW techs were vetted and selected to mesh with the culture of the brotherhood. The SEALs couldn't execute most of their complex missions without their help.

"JSOC?" Oby asked, confused. "Why not send a command element from one of the teams?"

Matt decided not to tell them about the SF men KIA in the ambush. The green side of JSOC had a vested interest in getting the two hostages back and delivering some payback at the same time.

"Once we get to a secure location, I'll fill you in; but I can tell you there is a good reason JSOC is involved and that the job is a combat recon. Something thirty other snipers from any SEAL team are qualified to do."

"So why pick us? And why jerk us out of our jobs to create a non-standard mission unit? No offense." Oby smiled looking at Boone.

"It's this simple. They chose me to lead and allowed me to pick my team. And poof! Here you are!"

Boone shook his head. "That's got to be some kind of bullshit, boss. We, I mean the teams, don't do shit that way."

Matt nodded in agreement. "Tell me about it. I was running a Hell Week shift when I received orders to the Pentagon. I should be their last resort, not their first choice."

Oby cleared his throat. "Well, you are the hero of Alexandria, the slayer of demons, and the man who wears the Navy Cross. Who else could they pick?"

Matt took a slow swing at Oby's head, and the sandy-haired sniper easily avoided the blow, laughing. Boone joined in the running joke. The guys in the teams were all heroic. The job demanded heroism.

It was a given. The big awards tended to go to leaders or key players in bigger operations. Such high visibility virtually assured that the men and officers involved would be recognized.

The men of Matt's SDV Troop all contributed to making the mission in Egypt a success. They all received valor awards and deservedly so, but somehow Matt didn't feel right about the award he'd received. The Navy Cross was the second highest medal for heroism next to the Congressional Medal of Honor.

He'd only done his job, the job the navy and the teams prepared him to do. Nothing more, nothing less. The old troop knew the topic was sensitive, so it was exploited for fun as often as possible.

The three of them had a good laugh and then began to exchange stories as they waited. The sun was hot and they were not acclimated to equatorial conditions. The nearest hangar was locked up tight, and here in the forgotten corner of the commercial logistics area of the airport, there wasn't a person in sight.

An hour passed after the reunion with Oby, and the burning cement toasted their feet without mercy. Matt messed around with the buttons on his navy issue dive watch. He mumbled a curse as he tried unsuccessfully to set the watch to show the correct time in Panama. Boone watched amused as his boss fumbled around.

"I just do the math in my head LT. Those watches are too tough for me to figure out, and besides, I liked it better when you only had to pull the stem out and presto the time changed!"

Boone was a computer fanatic. Back in the states, he spent hours every night surfing the Internet and playing games. He considered himself fairly well-versed in the complexity of high technology, but those dive watches were something else altogether.

"You're right, I suppose," said Matt, shielding his eyes with his hand. He looked up and stared into the sun. "I think I know how to do it, but my fingers are too fucking big for the buttons!" Matt continued to scan the sky. Boone spotted the plane first. A tiny speck visible just above the horizon.

"Look right over there, LT." Boone pointed at the small object looming larger and larger as it approached.

Matt and Oby looked in the direction indicated by Boone. The navy C-9 passenger plane landed and began the long slow taxi to the private aviation side of the airport. The C-9 was a small passenger airframe that looked like a commercial airliner, not a military aircraft, and that was the point.

The sound of a vehicle approaching caused the three SEALs to spin around. A small grey sedan pulled up in front of the nearby hangar. Matt watched as a man and a woman stepped out of the car.

The man went straight to the hangar and unlocked a small side access door, walking into the building. The tall dark-haired woman walked to where Matt and his two friends waited. All three men watched without saying a word.

The young JSOC analyst was drop-dead gorgeous. In mid-thigh length shorts and a sleeveless top, there was no way of identifying her branch of service or rank. Her dark brown hair was worn loose, flowing over her shoulders. She had the body of a swimsuit model, and aside from the oversized sunglasses obscuring much of it, she had a pretty face to go along with the body.

"This is going to be interesting," Boone mumbled under his breath.

"Steady, boys. This could be a trap. JSOC sent this lady to disarm us, knock down our defenses, and . . ."

"Have our way with us," Oby finished Matt's sentence.

Major Lane Sanchez smiled a knowing smile as she closed the last few yards to stand in front of the recon unit. "Matthew Barrett, I presume." She held out her hand.

Matt took it and shook it mildly. Her grip was impressive. Up close, she looked less swimwear model and more cross fit fanatic. Matt got the feeling she wouldn't be a cartoon personality. This woman had depth.

"Yes, I'm Matt, and these two guys are my teammates, Boone Kilpatrick and Sam Oberman."

The analyst shook both men's hands. "My name is Major Brooks. JSOC sent me to assist with the mission planning and intelligence piece. You can call me Lane around here and for the duration of the mission."

The last part of her speech was nearly drowned out by the sound of the C-9 taxiing off the access runway and onto the large concrete pad in front of the hangar. Matt noticed the small navy emblem was painted over.

From the point of view of casual or focused observers, the airplane could be a mail carrier. So far Matt was impressed with the way things had been organized, but now he needed to get inside the building and get his hands on the target package.

They followed Lane into the hangar. There were three rectangular cargo containers standing empty to one side of the large structure. Matt led the way over to the first of the three containers. "All right, guys, we'll be storing the mission equipment in these ready boxes. Use the one on the left for your personal stuff." Matt pointed to emphasize which box he meant. "The other two are for weapons, ammo, and comms gear."

"You're still not going to tell us what's going on, huh boss?" Oby asked.

"All in due time, Oby," Matt replied. "All in due time. I'd rather give you the pitch at one sitting rather than bits and pieces."

Boone couldn't help himself. "I've already got this whole gig figured out."

"Oh yeah?" Matt replied sarcastically.

"Yeah!" Boone fired back. "This is how I figure it. The president of the United States has decided that some asshole down south needs to learn some new manners. Of course, when he turned to his experts and asked for the very best the country had to offer, they said, 'Navy SEALs, sir!'"

"The president, no less!" Matt was only partly listening. He'd opened the first container and stowed his personal gear in the back. Oby and Boone did likewise.

"Yeah, the big guy!" said Boone, continuing the silly theory without skipping a beat. "Of course, once we've completed the mission, we'll all be given the Congressional Medal of Honor, free homes, and never have to pay taxes again!"

"Hey, Boone, you got an agent? You're a natural if you ever start writing screenplays!"

Matt chimed in, "The kicker is you don't get the medals and the perks unless you never speak of your glorious heroism to anybody. No book deal, no movie deal, no video games. Nothing."

Oby and Boone laughed. They all knew the deal, and they had experience in the waiting game. It was clear nobody was going to learn anything until the LT was good and ready to tell them, but Boone wasn't ready to quit just yet.

"No, I don't have an agent; but come to think of it, that wouldn't be a bad idea. So, what do ya think, LT? Will this mission make a good book? Maybe a movie?"

Matt and Oby both laughed. "Yeah, in your dreams, man!" Oby taunted.

"I don't think you'll be seeing a movie deal anytime soon!" Matt said, piling on. It felt good to be back together again. The three SEALs finished the task of storing their personal bags in the container.

The support crew was piling into the hangar, and the large doors were sliding open to accommodate the pallets of communications equipment, food, water, desks, chairs, everything needed to convert the empty space into a working combat operations center.

Chapter Eighteen

Lane Sanchez turned away from her JSOC colleague and walked to where the SEALs stood near the containers. She checked her watch and gauged the time against the mission planning parameters. She was satisfied they were doing well so far. "Matt?" She stopped a few yards away and gestured for the LT to join her.

Matt glanced at his partners. "You guys stay here. I'll see what she wants."

Lane smiled in a stiff, professional way as Matt walked up and she extended her hand. "I want to bring you up to speed on the timetable."

He shook her hand and tried to avoid looking down at her impressive body. "When can I tell my team what this is all about?"

Lane thought for a moment. "I understand your sense of urgency; I share it. We have techs sweeping this space, and once they're done, we'll convert the third cargo container into a secure space for the more sensitive aspects of planning and briefing. It's already kitted out with insulated walls and a white noise generator."

Matt needed to tell Boone and Oby so they could begin working the mission plan. This logistics crap wasn't his concern.

"When?"

Lane saw that Matt was moving from irritated to pissed. "I know you're anxious to get started, but give the process another hour and then you can brief your men. In the meantime, you can grab cots off the pallets and set your team up over there." Lane pointed to a far corner of the hangar.

Matt looked where she pointed and grunted. "All the comforts of home. That is if you have twenty people running around your house back home." Matt turned back and smiled at the attractive intelligence analyst. Lane saw something in the look and decided it was time to give Matt the snake eater speech.

"Lieutenant, I'm sure you're convinced your charms are irresistible. From the way your men's eyes keep scanning up and down my body, I'm sure they think they're in the game, too. Let me assure you that, aside from special briefings and countless warnings from friends and my superiors, I have no intention of fucking anyone on the mission team."

Matt's jaw dropped. "Wow! You must be under assault all the time from the boys back in Tampa to feel the need to give that speech to a total stranger. I'll tell my dogs to put their tongues back in their mouths and leave you alone, and I can assure you I'll do the same for the duration of our stay."

He turned and rejoined Oby and Boone. The three of them went to the sailor who looked like he was in charge of the cargo offload process and was steered by him to a specific pallet where they went to work looking for the cots.

Lane watched with just a twinge of guilt. Her speech was a defense mechanism, and it was unfortunate she was required to use it so often. The SEALs were very cute and each had their own special twinkle in their eyes, especially their leader. This time the speech was as much about her inclinations as that of the special operatives she'd just offended.

The Colombian Jungle

Auger's feet were swollen. The heat, walking on broken ground without boots, and the general stress on his body were conspiring to weaken him. His arms were covered in lacerations from the angry plant life found everywhere in this jungle. In short, this sucked. The only positive was that he was able to keep eyes on the general now.

The guerillas had decided to put them together, another sign that things may be going against the home team. The little tells were all Auger had to go on. His intuition told him that the deeper they moved into the Colombian jungle, the safer they should feel. But all signs pointed to a general expression of anxiety in the men near him. Maybe the closer they moved toward a known FARC site, the more likely the Colombian military was to pounce.

Like all SEALs, Senior Chief Auger was a graduate of the escape and evasion school known as SERE training. SEALs and navy pilots were mandated to attend the course. For SEALs, SERE was attended not long after SEAL Qualifications Training or SQT ended.

The course presented facts about being captured and details of a life spent imprisoned by an enemy nation or terrorist group, as seen through the eyes of former captives.

These course developers and sometime lecturers were once hostages in some cases, but more often they were former military prisoners of war.

After the lectures and case studies, the men were ushered into a changing room, discarding their uniforms, their rank, and the presumption of authority, power, and privilege that went with those ranks.

They donned plain clothing. Shapeless, unmarked, and unremarkable, except for the sameness. Each man was brought down first by stripping away the vanity of their position. That's when the prison camp phase began.

Auger remembered the mock torture, the blaring music, and sensory deprivation. He vaguely remembered his attempt to escape and the retaliation suffered by his cellmates when he was caught. They were all punished because of his actions. His crime affected the others, and his macho view of the world changed immediately. Heroes didn't cause pain. He'd survived the course and grew as a professional and as a man.

He needed to bring those lessons learned to bear now. He wasn't a senior chief and he was no longer a SEAL. He was a survivor, and he needed to reframe his worldview. He must learn everything about the jungle, memorize the names of his captors, and note every weakness of every guerilla fighter.

He also must remember what happened when he escaped in SERE school. Any attempt to leave would cause blowback on his principal. Nobody escaped if they couldn't escape together.

He'd lost track of time. How long since the ambush? He noticed the general was animated, moving more and more as time went on. That was a good sign. He'd taken a dreadful beating immediately after the hit; and based on what he'd seen, Auger hadn't expected the older man to survive.

He suddenly realized nobody had inquired as to his name or status. His best guess was that these were soldiers of the cause. No deep thinkers here. Pick up the packages and get them to, to where? Where the hell were they going, and was anybody tracking their progress?

His hope was the intelligence types were locked on all the main FARC bases and would pick up on the delivery of two prisoners. The satellite capabilities were such that the boys in naval intelligence should be able to count his teeth if he smiled towards the sky.

If they weren't watching the bases, Auger was pretty sure he and the general were fucked. The record for American prisoners in Colombia was something like seven years. SERE school was a cake walk compared to that possible future.

Isolation Hangar - Panama

Matt, Boone, and Oby sat in uncomfortable, gray, metal folding chairs inside the secure commercial container. A short, balding colonel stood in front of them. He began his general intelligence briefing by covering the weather in the operational area. Matt, Boone, and Oby stared at the detailed topographic map of central Colombia.

"Gentlemen, you will be operating in the nation of Colombia. The topographic map depicted here . . ."

This was a standard briefing. The guys in green uniforms always started with the big picture and the soft information like weather. The afternoon wore on as the experts trooped into the container one by one.

Each briefer provided the SEALs with general and specific information, directly or indirectly related to their mission tasking. At long last, they began to discuss the meat of the mission. The final briefing pair, both wearing glasses, entered the room. These were the target analysis guys.

Throughout the proceedings, the three SEALs sat quietly. Matt, of course, knew the target and the mission. Oby and Boone played the game, sitting quietly, not asking questions, but letting the process draw them into an understanding of the whole picture. They sat and absorbed the fire hose blast of data. Every so often they took the time to jot down critical details or a question for later.

Any details they wouldn't commit to memory, such as assigned call signs, frequencies, and vital ground coordinates, were written down or issued to them by the briefers. They would attempt to memorize as much as possible, but they'd still bring a fair amount of command and control data with them on the operation.

The focus of their activity would be in the triple canopy jungle well south of Bogotá, Colombia, near the Ariari river. The three SEALs felt comfortable operating in the environment as described and were comfortable with the depth and breadth of support involved. After four hours, a raw-boned Special Forces major arrived. It was time to get down to brass tacks. This is it, Matt thought.

"Gentlemen," the major began. "Your mission, by order of the president of the United States and the national command authority, is to conduct a surveillance and reconnaissance operation along the Ariari River basin south of Candilojas, Colombia. This area is controlled by the communist Colombian guerillas known as the Fuerzas Armadas Revolucionaries de Colombia or FARC and the Colombian cocaine cartel. As you may remember from earlier briefings today, the symbiotic relationship gives these two groups plenty of reason to work together against any outside intruder."

The major reached out to pull a sheet of paper up and over the back of the easel. "Gentlemen, the purpose of your surveillance and reconnaissance is to determine the location of General Alexander, Commander, US Southern Command, and Senior Chief Auger, a navy SEAL who was assigned to protect the general. Both were kidnapped during a premeditated ambush in Bogotá one week ago."

Matt watched the expressions on his teammate's faces. It'd been two years since the mission in Egypt and the breakup of their reconnaissance platoon. Oby and Boone barely registered an emotion upon hearing the news.

Matt knew they were tight with their former troop chief. He guessed they didn't want to show anything in front of non-family members. At a minimum, it increased the level of commitment to succeed.

Matt hadn't been aware SEALs were being used for VIP personal security detachment work. Ever since the twin trade tower attacks, SEALs and their green SF counterparts had dropped all missions and duties to focus on Afghanistan and then

Iraq. Things were winding down from the peak of combat deployments in 2011, so it was logical that SEALs were being freed up for special duties again.

Apparently, his former troop chief had found what, on the face of it, looked like easy duty. No tedious workups on the road, no long combat deployments in some godforsaken country. Moving with a VIP was living the high life. Five-star hotels, limos, Gulfstream Five jets. Matt didn't blame Auger for taking the job. The man had earned it many times over.

Chapter Nineteen

Matt forced himself to turn off the mental images of his former mentor and friend and tried to focus on the major's words. As he spoke, the army officer pointed to the wall map, his finger touching an area colored blue.

This area, according to the major, was completely controlled by Colombian guerillas and had been for over ten years. He strongly emphasized the danger of operating in this zone of guerilla control.

"Men, despite our best efforts and those of the Colombian government, the guerillas remain in control of this area and have survived all efforts to eradicate them. Assume every civilian is sympathetic and that half is on the FARC's payroll or working for the cartel. These folks act as a natural security alarm system; it's why the Colombian military has failed so many times to operate here."

Matt knew that the cocaine cartel pumped money and weapons to the guerillas, so the Colombian army was probably outgunned and even more likely bribed into indifference. The guerillas would know every inch of every jungle trail, every ridge, and every ravine. They'd have the distinct advantage of preparing to fight invaders wandering around in their backyard.

Matt assumed all the locals would be sympathetic to the guerilla cause, if for no other reason than that their sons, husbands, and fathers likely were pressed into the guerrilla forces. Matt realized that the element of surprise, so critical to special operation missions, wasn't likely to be available to him and his recon team.

The major finished the last portion of his mission-tasking brief and relinquished the podium to a tall, gray-haired gentleman wearing a five-hundred-dollar suit.

"Here it comes," Matt whispered to Boone. "You can never trust these guys!" Boone nodded without answering.

The newcomer introduced himself as Mr. Simmons. He appeared very confident, sure of himself in what must've been an environment unlike the ones in Washington, DC, where the suits made policy and sent men to their fate while sipping tea and coffee. The stranger had an upright bearing and a way of standing that gave Matt the impression the guy might have military experience.

The older man cleared his throat, not out of nervousness, but as a way to get everyone's undivided attention. "Gentlemen, we have received fresh reports of ambush activity ten kilometers from the river here."

He stretched out his arm and pointed to the map. "This activity is very close to where a guerilla-operating base is located, one we think holds, or will soon hold, our hostages. In addition, our national intelligence assets, utilizing state-of-the-art thermal imaging capabilities, show a rather large area of human activity on the Ariari River right here."

The smooth-talking agency man pointed to the river on the map again. "We believe the hostages were en route to this location when the ambush occurred. By now they should be near or on the base and secured against a rescue attempt."

Matt saw Boone raise his hand. "Sir, why don't we just grab them now if we know so much about where they're being held?"

Simmons smiled. Matt thought the smile was condescending, like a schoolmaster hearing a foolish thought from a student of questionable intelligence.

"Son, we believe there's a very high probability the guerillas would execute them if we go in there with guns blazing."

Matt agreed. His recon team needed to find the exact location and condition of the two Americans. The US couldn't resolve this crisis in this case with a demonstration of power. They needed to be patient. The major returned to the podium.

"The security council is convinced the guerillas will use the stronghold to keep the prisoners secure until negotiations can be entered into with the United States. You three men are to infiltrate the area of the primary base camp. Once there, you will observe and report on any and all camp activity. We need to know the number of enemy troops. Is there any anti-air capability in the camp? And, if possible, ascertain whether or not the hostages are at that location."

Oby raised his hand. "Yes?" replied Simmons.

"Well, sir," Oby began. "I understand what you want us to do, but maybe I'm missing something. Are you saying this is only a look-see operation? I mean, sir, if they're there, shouldn't we try to grab them?"

Oby's question floated out there in the open for a second or two. Matt had been thinking the same thing. Why jeopardize the lives of any more Americans? Why find the hostages and not do anything about it? So far none of the briefers had mentioned anything about Matt's team attempting a rescue.

Simmons looked at the major and the major nodded. He paused before answering Oby's question. "Actually, you and your team are restricted in this matter. Your job is only to report what you observe, nothing more. Under no circumstances are you to attempt a rescue."

Simmons pused for emphasis and made eye contact, one SEAL at a time before continuing. "I'm sure you'd agree that three SEALs, while they may be a match for most small units they may bump into, would be stretched pretty thin attempting to rescue from a camp with upwards of sixty heavily armed and experienced fighters. Consider your limited firepower and the very real possibility the hostages may be wounded and unable to travel. It's out of the question."

Oby didn't buy the pitch, but he was too smart to show it. "I understand, sir. I just wanted to make sure there was a rescue being planned."

Oby's stare communicated what everyone there in uniform already knew. Nobody trusted the spooks from the CIA or NSA. Simmons glanced at the major, avoiding eye contact with the SEAL sniper.

The major caught the look and decided to tell more than he'd intended to tell the recon team. "If you must know, there is a rescue team in isolation. They'll execute the mission if, and only if, you three are successful in finding the hostages."

Matt knew his teammates wouldn't voice their true feelings about the spooks' answer to Oby's question, but to see Senior Chief Auger, their friend, and comrade, sitting as a hostage within reach, and not do anything about it?

That wouldn't sit right with any frogman. Professionally, they may agree with the major's clinical observations and prohibitions, but if the hostages were capable of moving . . .

Matt wanted to close the loop. "Let me get this straight, just so everybody's on the same sheet of music. You want the three of us to go in, find this base camp, and report on all the activity in the base camp. I'm assuming you want real-time information flow instead of sitreps."

"That's correct," said the major.

Matt continued, "Then you want us to feed answers to a pre-selected rescue team so they can come in and save the hostages."

Simmons and the major both nodded in agreement. Good, the SEALs weren't going to cause a problem. He was more at ease now. The major smiled. "Yes, lieutenant, that's exactly what we want you to do. Whether or not you remain to act as a point position for the rescue force will be decided based on the needs of the rescue team commander. Do any of you have more questions on your mission tasking or the immediate area of the target?"

Boone, Oby, and Matt looked at each other. Matt answered for the SEALs, "No, sir, I think we have a handle on it. Is there another secure area available where we can start planning this mission or is this box the best we can do?"

The major looked at the agency representative to see if there was anything else on the agenda. Simmons shook his head without speaking. The major then made eye contact with Matt.

"Lieutenant Barrett, you and your men can use this entire area for planning and rehearsals. I understand that will cramp your style, but the FARC has a sophisticated network here in Panama and we'd rather not telegraph our intention by moving you around the city."

Matt took a deep breath and thought through the challenge. "We will need boats and the ability to test the gear in the water. Can you make that happen?"

The major nodded. "We'll figure out a way to provide you with all of that. We also have all the materials you'll need-- photos, maps, etc.--set up in here for you to use as you see fit. Information about the logistics of your infiltration also is available in a workbook marked "mobility." Most of the normal SEAL options for infiltration have been listed, and all unconventional mobility assets in the theater also are listed in the book in case you want to try something new."

Matt smiled. "Yes, sir, I think that does it for now." Matt could look forward to getting to work at last. He knew Boone and Oby also were eager to start working the problem sets.

The major finished. "Once you determine how you want to insert, we'll set up the logistics timeline. We'd like your team to insert into the op area, infiltrate to the target, and begin sending out reports within seventy-two hours from right now."

Seventy-two hours until they had to be in position, observing the FARC camp? Matt considered the time crunch for a moment. Forty-eight hours to plan, twenty-four hours to get in and find the target. They were a little rusty working together, but most of the process would be straight recon standard operating procedures or SOPs from the old days.

Matt looked up at the major. "That's no problem, sir. We'll go ahead and start working on this ASAP. If you don't mind, can you arrange to have some pizza or something sent to us? We've pretty much been on the go for the last forty-eight hours, and some chow would be great."

The major chuckled. "I got it, lieutenant. Do you men have a preference?"

Boone chimed right in, "As long as it doesn't have anchovies, I don't give a shit, sir!" The tension was at last broken as everybody joined in the laughter. Matt had the last word.

"Great, then it is done. Oby, Boone, let's get rolling!"

Chapter Twenty

Chavez's private residence–Mexico City

Chavez paced back and forth in the small foyer. He was residing temporarily in one of his many homes, an exquisite high-rise penthouse, kept for convenience to conduct business in Mexico City. He peeked at his watch in nervous anticipation that at any second the doorbell would ring, announcing the arrival of his visitor.

Chavez walked briskly back into the main greeting area adjacent to the parlor, ignoring the well-appointed surroundings. An interior decorator had worked hard to give the space a sense of regal splendor, and it worked. The penthouse was opulent, properly befitting a man of Chavez's wealth and social stature.

He halted his pacing to study the row of photographs sitting on a low ornate table. The family pictures were beautifully appointed in ornate silver frames. His pretty wife Reza, who never complained about the traveling and lack of privacy in his life, and his wonderful daughter.

His daughter was safely away from his world, excelling as a second-year student at Harvard University in the United States, under an assumed name for her safety.

Finally, there was his firstborn child, his son Rodrigo. Chavez found it very hard to look at his son's image without succumbing to a rush of painful emotions. Two years, two long years since his son's death. Two years since the light of Chavez's life was extinguished from the face of the earth by the Colombian military under the leadership of the Americans.

Chavez had sought revenge against the various pilots involved in the air strike, discretely distributing convincing amounts of cash for information. He used his contacts within the Colombian military to do his dirty work for him. But he didn't

117

stop there. He'd also made sure the families of the pilots paid the ultimate price for his son's death. It was a bloody way to get payback, but Rodrigo's life was worth so much more. He had no regrets.

Once the small players were taken care of, Chavez turned his attention to the people who targeted his son and ordered the murder: the American leadership, both political and military.

He spent vast amounts of money looking for leads, and eventually, he hit pay dirt. His sources informed him which senior members of the United States military had orchestrated the entire strike.

Chavez also was able to learn that American Special Forces, operating in coordination with the Colombian military, were guiding the strike. Their objective had been simple: stamp out the guerillas and the source of their funding, the cocaine cartel, Chavez's own coca operation.

Chavez's master plan was in motion. First, grab the Commander of the US Southern Command, General Alexander, the man responsible for approving the attack that killed his son. He wanted to make the Americans initially believe that the kidnapping was a random act perpetrated upon them by the guerillas.

He'd issued a false ransom request; his enemies would work that problem for a few weeks, all from the wrong angle. He had no intention of releasing the general.

While this drama was maintained, Chavez's agents were positioning themselves in the United States to kill the general's family--not only his wife and his two grown sons, but also the grandchildren and the general's mother, his last living parent.

If all went well, the final act of revenge would be his to perform. Chavez wanted to be there, telling the general about the tragic loss of his family, showing him baby pictures, pictures of his son growing up, and finally the picture he had only looked at once: his son's mutilated corpse lying in the rubble of a building bombed by the Americans.

He would make certain the murderer knew what he did. He would tell him, in graphic detail, the fate of his own family. He wanted to see the general's face react in agony as he contemplated his evil life and the pain it brought to so many innocents. Then, after a sufficient amount of time to allow the man to fully understand his failure to protect the ones closest to him, Chavez planned to fire a bullet into the man's brain.

A loud rapping emanating from the front of the penthouse interrupted his thoughts. The large brass knocker hammered two more times on the front door; his visitor had at last arrived. Chavez went to the door, opening it to reveal a man waiting in the hallway. Chavez waved him into his home. A brief exchange took place.

Chavez offered his thanks and handed him a small business card. Encoded in the address and phone number of the business card was an account number for a Swiss bank. Funds had been deposited in the visitor's name. Payment for a job well done. He escorted the visitor to the door and closed it softly behind him. Now is the time to act, Chavez thought. It's time to set the rest of my plan in motion.

Guerilla River Base Camp–Colombia

Senior Chief Auger tripped over a root and fell down, flat on his face. These falls were worse with his hands tied behind his back. His chin was raw from making contact with the jungle floor far too many times. His legs throbbed and twitched uncontrollably from the sheer stress of nonstop movement.

He wasn't getting fed, but that wasn't the biggest problem; he needed water. The guerillas were giving him just enough to keep him moving, but his muscles were cramping up

119

more and more. He realized that if the lack of water and the beatings didn't kill him, the lack of sleep surely would.

The patrol stopped near a small clearing in the jungle. All around him Colombians chattered excitedly. Auger rolled over on his right side to see what all the fuss was about. In the distance he saw a group of men chatting and working, building a thatched hut.

They were well-organized and focused on their task. There were other huts and people going about their business. The SEAL realized with relief that their journey was over at last, he'd arrived at the guerillas' main base camp.

The river camp was impressive. The cleared area in the center sloped gently down toward the riverbank in several broad steps or manmade plateaus. The plan of the camp was less fortress and more about safety, a place to rest and train.

The edges of the jungle hid most of the camp from where Auger lay. His visual survey was rudely interrupted when he was jerked to his feet and ushered forward with a whack from a rifle butt across his shoulder blades. The blow staggered him, almost driving him to the ground again.

As he entered the bustling camp, he concentrated on memorizing the layout of the place. The vegetation on the camp's perimeter had been cleared back from the river about seventy yards, but only the undergrowth. They had left the first two levels of the overhead jungle canopy--a smart move, he thought. Leaving the tallest trees intact provided overhead protection from aerial observation.

Down by the river, two felled trees stretched out into the water. It was obvious to Auger that the guerillas were using the trees as a makeshift pier. Ten or so dugout canoes were tied up and trailing together with the river current. A cluster of five to six men was unloading weapons and supplies from one rather large canoe. There were no guards posted, at least not in plain sight. That confirmed his earlier insight; they felt secure in this place.

Auger's handler stopped him, then pushed him to the ground indicating with a grunt that he was to sit down and sit still. Auger was fine with this order. The perspective was better from his new location. He now had time to understand the camp and its population a little better. One thing he noted immediately: everything was being managed efficiently.

He saw armed men pitching in to assist with menial tasks with little or no direct supervision. These people have a strong sense of purpose, he thought. They're not a bunch of bums trying to escape the responsibilities of life in the cities. They feel a bond that goes beyond obedience. Senior Chief Auger felt his first sting of despair. It would be very difficult to manipulate anyone in this crowd of true believers to help him.

Auger's thoughts were interrupted by a loud thud. A muttered complaint in English confirmed the identity of the man lying on the ground next to Auger.

"I'm happy to find you safe and sound, my friend!" the senior chief spoke in a whisper.

"Ah, yes, my young traveling partner, how are you holding up?" The general's voice was firm.

"So far, so good. I've checked out the camp, and I think we'll have a tough time breaking out of here."

General Alexander noted the pessimism in Auger's tone. "More bodies mean more activity. More heat. Finding this place will be a piece of cake for the NSA boys. I think it's best we just sit tight and try to survive this place until the cavalry rides in to save us."

Auger never had an opportunity to continue the discussion. A fierce kick struck him square in the back of the head. Sparks shot out in Auger's brain as he struggled to maintain consciousness. Next to him, the general was receiving his share of physical abuse, too.

Two young men were making a point, or bored, it didn't matter why; the beatings continued until Auger's mind went to a happy place. He found himself doing this more and more as he lost strength and became numb to the attacks.

When they were too tired to continue the punishment, one of them yelled at the Americans to stop talking. Ah, thought Auger, talking was a capital crime in this camp. He faded out of consciousness.

When he came around again, his head and face throbbed with pain. Ants and small insects crawled in and around his ears and eyes, feasting on the warm blood smeared all over his scalp and cheek. He attempted to blow them off his face, then rub them off against his shoulder, but that just made the little beasts more angry.

Chapter Twenty-One

Auger wasn't religious or trained in meditation, but he'd been in enough dismal situations that he'd learned how to mentally escape for a while. He started by compartmenting the pain and focusing on pleasant thoughts; conjuring up memories of his time in the teams always worked.

This time he decided to think about his fellow BUD/S classmates, the determined young men who went through the world's toughest commando training with him. He remembered the names of his Hell Week boat crew, the guys who helped him get through that crucible of pain by offering a strong hand here or an encouraging word there.

He remembered eating the candy stashed, before Hell Week began, by his boat crew in the wall of sand bags packed along the barracks wall to protect against flooding. The little victories were important in Hell Week.

His mind drifted away from BUD/S and onto another subject. He'd met his wife, Susan, toward the end of the four-month-long SEAL Qualification Training or SQT. A wonderful woman, she'd sacrificed a good career as an executive pilot to marry Auger.

She'd endured his tours of duty and no notice alerts, adoring and supporting her navy husband. Their marriage had been unique in the teams. Unique because it survived much longer than any SEAL operator had a right to expect a marriage to last.

Auger subconsciously recognized this path was leading to a bad place. It was a threat to his morale to dwell on his failed marriage. He knew this, but still, he couldn't stop the flow of feelings and pictures. Yeah, he thought, it'd been a perfect marriage, a true love match. But, in time, the days away from his wife took their toll. Susan became bitter and resentful of the navy, and especially of the teams. She missed her old life and her husband was never home.

Their emotional separation grew until she started to seek the company of others. Sure, she put on a good show whenever they were together, so Auger never realized what was going on behind his back whenever he left on a trip.

After two years of lying and intrigue, Susan confessed to him she wanted out. His reaction had been passive, very professional. Fine, he'd said. You're not happy being married to a SEAL, and I don't know how to do anything else. Let's end this thing.

Ironically, they parted friends. And from what he understood, she never married the other guy in her life. He didn't stay in direct contact with her as the years added up after the divorce. However, he did hear from a third party that Susan went back to her career, and according to his source, she was now finally happy and successful.

Senior Chief Auger's thoughts were interrupted by the distant sound of crunching boots. He forced his mind to pull away from his memories and reestablish focus in the here and now. In a second or two, his attention was back on the present, unpleasant situation. A harsh voice barked a command in Spanish, demanding that Auger do something.

The SEAL didn't have a clue what the man wanted. He stared up at the young man from his spot on the ground using his right eye. The left eye was sealed shut with dried blood. The fighter standing over him was in his early twenties, smooth-faced, trying hard to make a macho impression, but failing to quite pull it off.

Not a hardened jungle warrior, Auger thought, probably a recent recruit from the city. He guessed the kid had been in the jungle five, maybe six months at most.

The young guerilla turned to look at the big American, pointed his rifle at General Alexander's head, then looked right at Auger. He yelled at Auger for the third time. The message was clear, even if the man's Spanish wasn't. Fail to obey and the general was going to eat a bullet.

Auger nodded his head in the affirmative, but maintained a stupid look on his face. He hoped he was conveying that he still didn't understand but wasn't resisting the order.

Playing stupid only pissed the man off even more. Auger winced in pain as he was kicked violently in the ribs. The SEAL rolled back and forth, trying to avoid the full impact of the blows and show by his body language that he was incapable of following any command.

The Colombian appeared to suddenly figure out why Auger wasn't complying. He reached down and grabbed Auger by the ropes wrapped around his wrists and pulled him to his feet.

Auger stood up painfully then went right back down to his knees. His legs were rubbery and unable to hold his full weight. His right shoulder began to throb. There was a good possibility he'd dislocated it somewhere during the long trek in the jungle, and being jerked around by his wrists wasn't helping.

The young man had a change of heart or a change of tactics; Auger wasn't sure which reason moved the young man to gently help him to his feet. He held Auger in place for a moment until the SEAL became steady. Auger acknowledged by nodding his head that he was ready to stand on his own.

The Colombian's eyes expressed compassion as he released Auger and stepped back, resuming the role of the guard, his eyes squinted and his lips snarled. This kid wasn't a killer, he recognized, at least not yet. Auger heard grunts and hard slaps coming from behind him.

The general was receiving his share of misfortune. The senior chief took a measured step, then turned ever so slightly to steal a peek at the general. His brother captive looked a lot worse than Auger felt.

The right side of the older American's face was swollen and discolored. His right eye was completely closed, and there was blood crusting over a wound on his forehead. The kid in front of Auger stepped up and jabbed his rifle barrel into his gut.

The strike wasn't violent enough to drop the SEAL, but it showed that it was time for everybody to resume their roles. He stood straighter and moved in the direction indicated by the guard, deeper into the camp.

Auger concentrated on putting one foot in front of the other. He had a flash of memory. In the teams, the incremental training process they used was called "baby steps." You learned to shoot in twenty small movements, to jump, dive, and plan the same way.

He smiled through cracked lips; this walk through the camp was a different kind of baby steps. Auger half stepped and half shuffled ahead and was somehow able to move fast enough to please his handler.

The escorts pushed and prodded Auger and the general slightly to the left for a few minutes and then back again to the right. Auger stopped and took a look around. This pause generated a growl from the guard, who was all business now that everyone was watching. In front of them was a hill rising up from the camp to dominate the FARC position on the river.

They were eased forward, and Auger took advantage of the elevation to look back at the camp from this vantage point. The horseshoe clearing had twenty or thirty huts of various sizes and shapes. His quick mental math put the population somewhere between forty and sixty people; most were men, but there were a fair number of women, too.

He turned his head back around and concentrated on the climb. He and the general were shoved up against the moderate incline until they stood on top of the hill. Auger stood there next to his protectee, looking at the two small cages constructed of crate parts and tree branches, their new home.

"Well, general, I guess we should feel lucky it's not a firing squad!" Auger's voice was hoarse from lack of water. His attempt at humor rang hollow, not even eliciting a grunt from the other American. General Alexander stood with Auger, watching the guerillas discuss the guard routine. It was apparently a very difficult thing to organize.

"What do you think they have planned for us, senior chief?" As bad as the general looked, he sounded a hell of a lot better than Auger. Auger realized that somewhere on the jungle trail, he'd started to feel sorry for himself. He silently vowed to follow the old man's example and suck it up.

"Well, sir, they aren't going to kill us. I'm pretty sure about that. They went to a lot of trouble to snatch us and bring to this place." Auger's logic was self-evident. The guerillas had only recently built the two cages. From the very beginning of their long jungle trek, the objective had been to keep the Americans alive for this, their new home away from home.

"Hostages then? Are we to be pawns in a great game or simply a cash flow asset, bodies for bucks?"

"Yes, sir, I think you might be right on both counts, but I think they want more than just money. Maybe concessions of some sort from the United States, changes in our foreign policy down here in Colombia, or something similar? They don't kidnap a general as important as you for just money."

The general nodded. "Are we still keeping the secret? I mean who's the general and who's the SEAL?"

Auger looked at the general. "Yes, sir, we are. The story is simple, and you have to commit to it one hundred percent. I'm the general. Whatever they have in store for you, that's all on me. Understand?"

Before the general could respond, one of the guards pivoted sharply and instructed the two Americans to stop talking. The order was made clearer when he pointed his rifle at Auger. They both got the message. Auger took advantage of the silence by checking out his immediate environment.

He could see just about everything from the hilltop. That also meant everybody in camp could see the prisoners. No dead space, no cover or concealment to assist them if by chance the general and Auger escaped the cages. The closest place to hide was the tree line, fifteen yards away from the cages.

The door of the first cage was opened, and Auger was directed to walk over and crawl inside. He got down on his hands and knees and worked his way into the tiny space. The enclosure was no more than four-by-four feet in size.

He curled up in the fetal position, pulling his knees up to his chest in order to fit and watched through the slats as the guerillas jammed the general into the other cage.

The general was a much bigger man than Auger, and the cage wasn't nearly big enough. The guards stepped back and then looked at each other. Auger was sure they'd realized the same thing, but would they do anything about it?

Chapter Twenty-Two

The senior chief decided it was time to take inventory. He was alive, he wasn't severely injured, he knew where he was, and he knew a lot about his adversaries. He must take advantage of staying in one place for a while.

Catch up on sleep and recharge. This was similar, but again so different from his prior POW training. During the navy's escape and evasion school, he thought the whole fake prisoner drill was pretty much a joke.

All SEALs and navy pilots attended the rugged SERE course fresh from their BUD/S and SQT experience. As a result, most SEAL students in SERE school were able to slide right through. The rough handling and verbal abuse were silly after what they had experienced at BUD/S.

Not so for the navy pilots. For them, SERE school was a traumatic and often life-changing experience. SERE school was a reality check. A harsh demonstration, but only a demonstration, of what a prisoner of war goes through trying to survive.

Cold, heat, sleep deprivation, and lack of food all conspire to break a man down. Even the simple act of standing perfectly still can eventually cause pain and anxiety. All of these were experiences students endured in SERE school.

The difference between SERE school and the real thing, Auger was beginning to realize, was that in SERE school you knew they weren't going to kill you. The school played games, but then eventually the games ended and you went home. This, the senior chief understood all too clearly, was no game.

Naval Special Warfare Command–Coronado, California

Admiral Fitzpatrick pounded his desk. "Why the hell didn't we send the ready platoon? Who came up the stupid idea to pick a couple of guys out of a hat?"

The tall SEAL commander absorbed the tirade without flinching. He'd worked with the admiral for two years. He knew that once the emotional blast ran its course, the admiral would become calm and reasonable. It was a process the younger naval officer had no choice but to endure.

"I don't understand how someone in the Pentagon got involved in the first place. They pick the job; I pick the mission team! Whatever happened to standing operating procedures? Whatever happened to recalling standby units? Do you have a fucking clue?"

Commander White quietly stood his ground in the face of the admiral's tirade. "Look, admiral, I know I'm the plans officer, but this came down as a SPECAT tasking straight from the tank. Both JSOC and Tampa signed off on this. You know that I, of all people, understand your frustration. I'm the planning officer for the whole SEAL community. I've spent an incredible amount of time and resources preparing SEAL troops and task units, on both the east and west coast, for war or contingencies short of war. Testing them. Rating and ranking the various platoons."

Commander White wasn't arguing, he was stating facts. The tank was the planning and briefing center in the Pentagon. This mission tasking wasn't frivolous, and the joint chiefs weren't jerking the admiral's chain.

They probably had a legitimate reason for bypassing normal channels; and once his boss calmed down, he knew the old man would salute and do his best to support the mission as directed. He continued to walk the admiral through his own frustration, while at the same time giving him time to calm down.

"You know how it works, admiral. We put our best units on alert status. Those men sacrifice their personal lives by being a cell call away from going to war. But, sir, I have no idea why the national command authority decided to circumvent that process. I do know, regardless of how we were tasked, that every team captain, every officer, chief, and enlisted SEAL will want this mission to be a success, and that includes me, sir."

The commander saw the admiral raise his hand, signaling the commander to be quiet. "Steve, please sit down." The admiral had regained his composure while listening to Steve's speech.

"Look, Steve, you don't have to lecture me about what should've happened. I know what should have happened. And I don't have to remind you that the national command authority has the right to do whatever they damn well please. But three guys?"

"Hear me out, sir. Three SEALs actually make sense," the commander interrupted.

The admiral wasn't in the mood to listen. "The teams are going to get one hell of a black eye if this ad hoc group goes down to Colombia and screws up! Of course, if and when that occurs, nobody will care if I whine that I had no control over the selection of these men. This is still the United States navy, and I will be held accountable! Now, Steve, I want you to focus on figuring out how can we regain control of the operation. If that isn't a possibility, then I need a plan on my desk to handle the aftermath if this operation goes sideways."

Commander White studied the floor for a moment. "Well, admiral, one thing we could do is look into the records of these men. If we can find any problems or flaws, then we can be prepared to prove they were poor choices. In essence, sir, you could tell the national command authority we should run the operation and select the players because it failed to vet the talent properly. Ask them to shift operational control to you so we can fix this before it's too late."

The admiral pondered the comment for a moment. "Commander, I don't think you'll find anything derogatory in the records of these men. I've taken the liberty of checking up on them myself. The officer they've chosen, Matthew Barrett, is a holder of the Navy Cross. The other two gentlemen are eminently qualified and are both holders of the Silver Star medal for valor under fire. All three have served multiple combat tours; I don't think attacking the choice of these men is the answer."

"Well, admiral, if I could inject one or two points. I've looked into their records. At least in the case of the officer, Lieutenant Barrett, he was a very poor student in BUD/S, sir. His record shows he barely met the minimum standards to graduate. He also nearly flunked out of SDV minisub school. As a matter of fact, he was placed on probation at SDV Team Two because they believed he was a substandard officer."

The admiral straightened up. "Drop it, commander! That young officer has the equivalent of a graduate degree in combat leadership, and you're sitting here rambling about his grades in elementary school. No, we've missed the opportunity to take the operation back under our management. That leaves damage control.

"I want another SEAL recon team in isolation by midnight tonight. I want them training around the clock as a backup team, in case they have to go in and take over this mission. I want to have this option in my back pocket, Steve. Meanwhile, I'll try to pull some strings and get the navy guys in Tampa to push for a SEAL rescue force. I think it'll fly, considering the navy is leading the charge so far."

The commander knew when to quit and go with the flow. You didn't rise to higher rank in the navy by arguing with admirals.

"Alright, sir, I'll get a four-man recon team into isolation ASAP. I'll also take the liberty to select a platoon for the rescue phase and get them into isolation, too. San Clemente ought to work nicely. The third-phase BUD/S students left the island last week, so we'll have good operational security, and the airstrip next to the camp will work nicely as a pickup point for the rescue platoon when it deploys south."

The admiral moved to the window. From his office, he could see down the Coronado beach. He also could see the West Coast team compounds and the BUD/S facility. "Make it happen, Steve. Do it quickly! The pace of this mission timeline could pick up without warning, and I don't want to lag behind events. Be ready to act!"

"I'm on my way, admiral!" Commander White picked up the top-secret folders and walked briskly out of the admiral's office. As he worked his way down the corridor to his office, he reflected on the admiral, the man responsible for every navy SEAL on the planet. What's happened to him? He mused. Why is he so concerned about how he looks, about his career?

Admiral Fitzpatrick had once been known as an operator's operator. He first saw combat in Desert Storm and continued to earn a solid reputation for leadership and judgment over the years in Yemen and Iraq. Now, the commander realized, the admiral was only concerned about getting his third star.

Republic of Panama

Boone scratched his head. "I'll tell you what, boss, these maps don't help us for shit! I mean, take a look at the overhead photography. All the paths, rivers, or streams we might want to use for navigation are invisible on the photos. They're all covered up by triple-canopy jungle! I don't know how the hell we're going to find any legitimate landmarks."

Oby slid over to see what Boone was talking about. He studied the overhead photography and then checked the map against the images. "Yep, sure as shit, this is going to be a ball buster. We won't know where we are, and movement through this crap will be nearly impossible."

"Every time it rains the waterways all change anyway," Boone added. "Intel says the small waterways overfill and merge with each other or larger waterways, and that shakes up whatever picture you were relying on for navigation.

Oby leaned back and put his hands behind his head. "If they put a time restriction on us, we won't be able to guarantee we can keep pace, not in this terrain. LT, you know as well as I do that it takes about two hours to quietly patrol a thousand yards over broken ground, so it will take twice that time to move the same distance through the jungle like this, and that's in the daytime."

"Moving at night would double that again--that is if you could keep a steady compass bearing in the dark while avoiding mangrove swamps, streams, and the bush," Boone added.

The problem set wasn't overwhelming; they'd all three been involved in hairy missions before, and in comparison this was pretty straightforward. It was the stakes that made this one feel different. The emotion associated with saving one of their own, a man they knew.

Chapter Twenty-Three

Matt listened to their running commentary with interest. This was the process. Weigh each idea, attack it from all sides, and either reject it or absorb it into the plan. "So, what do you guys suggest then, tell them we can't do this?" Matt asked, stepping up to the dry erase board where he'd begun scribbling a list of unanswered questions related to the mission.

"Now you know better than that, LT." Oby ignored Matt's jab. "I know Boone's the scout guy and all that, but the way I see it, this base camp is supposed to be on the river, correct?"

"Go on. You have my attention," said Matt.

The SEAL sniper continued. "Well, what if we say to hell with all this jungle patrol bullshit and go straight down the river? You know, like navy guys. SEALs and shit!"

Boone moved to the map table again to take another look. The point man looked at the map for a second, then locked eyes with Matt. "You know what, boss? Oby's right! If we can get inserted upriver from this base camp, just stick to the river and move downstream under cover of night, then we'll eliminate a whole lot of problems. Make it easier to find the camp, too!"

"That's the ticket, LT!" Oby chimed in. "We could use a rubber boat! Hell, we could even swim or use a scuba re-breather like our LAR Fives if we were dropped close enough."

Boone doubled down. "Hell, sir, they wouldn't even see us coming if we did that."

Matt stood there soaking it all in. He loved watching the wheels turning. This is what being in the teams was all about. All SEALs cared about mission success. They were constantly studying, trying to improve their knowledge of the art of war.

135

Whenever a SEAL troop sat down to discuss a new mission tasking, each man in that group knew he had a vested interest in the success of the mission. Every SEAL, therefore, invested a lot of time, energy, and emotion into pitching ideas and debating possible solutions. The best ideas eventually ended up in the rehearsal cycle.

During the rehearsal cycle, everyone had a chance to give real-time feedback as well as review video imagery of the rehearsals. Most team guys were cutthroat when it came to criticizing each other, but they had to be. This was the best way to bring out solutions that worked. Matt knew he was lucky to have the operating experience of Oby and Boone on this mission.

"So how do we get a rubber boat in there?" Matt asked. "Parachute drop? It looks dense in there and wouldn't an insert that was close enough for swimming to the camp be close enough to be heard in the camp?"

"I don't know, boss," Boone answered, realizing Matt had just approved the river infiltration idea. "I see your point. A helo insert would have to be farther upriver, far enough away to avoid being heard, but too far away for us to swim to the target."

Boone paused then had an idea. "Look, we could have a larger boat drag or carry a rubber boat down the river to within reasonable launch distance and then release us. Or maybe we could steal a boat from a village upriver, use that to make a longer navigation run to the camp."

Oby disagreed. "That just ain't going to work. Everybody up and down that river's going to be wearing farmer duds, not uniforms, and they hate the Colombian army. If they see anybody coming down that river in a military boat like our rubber F-470s, the word will be out, sure as shit. By the time we get close to the camp, the guerillas will be sitting there eating popcorn, waiting for the light show to begin!"

"What about dropping a boat upriver from the back end of a helicopter?" Boone thought out loud.

Matt looked at his point man. "You know what Boone, I think you have an idea there. Instead of soft ducking a zodiac from the back of a helo, we can drop an indigenous boat instead. Let's figure out how far upstream we have to be for the helicopter not to be heard by those in the immediate vicinity of the camp." Matt looked again at the map.

"We need that information so we can plot the insert point and then determine the viability of this idea. If the distance is workable, then we have what we need to set these preparations into motion right now."

Matt looked for flaws in the plan. "So, if we aren't going to use one of our rubber boats, we need to procure a craft, something the locals would not pay much attention to as it floats by in the night. We still should consider bringing along the re-breathers just as a method of getting from the boats to the shoreline if needed."

"What kind of boats do the Colombian locals use on this river?" Boone asked out loud.

"I'll bet that hot intel chick could find out for us!" Oby said, grinning.

Matt nodded in agreement. "She's an asset, so we should use her."

"I'll take care of it, boss," Boone spoke up. "I'll be back in an hour or so."

Oby laughed. "She's trapped in this hangar with the rest of us. Why would it take you an hour?" Boone didn't answer; he just smiled and left the container.

"Oby, while Boone's attempting to lay the cover model, why don't you get a hold of our air force friends here and see what kind of aircraft we can use to deploy the indigenous boat and how we can configure the aircraft to accommodate the boat once we find one."

"You got it, boss. I'm on the move."

"Great." Matt, responded. He watched Oby leave the container. They didn't have much time left, but this was always the hardest part of the mission. Figuring out how they were going to gain access to the target itself without getting caught.

Once on target, their standard operating procedures for reconnaissance and surveillance would kick in. Matt turned back to the dry erase board and continued writing a draft mission timeline.

San Clemente Island–California

The platoon officer, Lieutenant Jared Stone, heard his SEALs grumbling as they jumped off the large navy truck and onto the hard ground. "Hey chief!" one of the men yelled. "What the hell are we doing out here?" He watched as Chief Sampson stopped dead in his tracks and scowled at the questioner.

"What the hell do you care, Jones? Your job is to go where the big boss in Washington tells you to go! Now start tossing that gear out of the truck and move it into the weapons cleaning building. Let's go, people! We're burning daylight!"

The SEAL chief turned and walked to where Jared was standing. LT Stone was one of the few African-Americans in the teams and one of half a dozen officers in the elite organization. The chief ignored the mumbling and moaning going on behind him. "Hey LT!" he called out. "When are we going to sit down and work on this training schedule?"

Jared looked at his watch then looked at the chief. The man moved like a mountain cat. Tall, lean, and covered in rippling muscles. More of a climber than a weight lifter. His senior enlisted advisor was an intimidating personality, even among SEALs. Jared felt very lucky to have him in the platoon.

"Well, chief, I was going start to work on that but it turns out Ensign Barton here has quite a few ideas to share."

Jared saw Chief Sampson's face contort in a show of mock pain. "Ensign Barton, I'd really appreciate it if you'd just sit on the sidelines for this one. No offense, sir, but this isn't exactly a practice mission. How about the LT and I work out the schedule and we'll brief you on it when we're done?"

The young ensign's face fell. "But, chief, I'm an officer! I'm supposed to be the one who calls the shots, not sit back and watch, and I'm a good planner!"

Jared knew Chief Sampson didn't want to put the young officer down, especially within earshot of the enlisted guys. One of his key tasks as a platoon chief was to help the young man learn from his mistakes and grow into a confident leader. If he did his job well, Ensign Barton would command his own SEAL platoon someday.

SEAL officers were all operators, all graduates of the same basic and intermediate training as the enlisted SEALs. In the navy, warfare pins signifying an officer's specialty were worn over the ribbons on the top left breast. Navy officers' pins were gold and enlisted men with the same specialty areas had pins that were a dull silver.

Only the SEAL community allowed the enlisted men to wear a gold, naval special warfare specialty pin on their uniform. This was a nod to the tradition and the reality that all SEALs went through the same shit together; every SEAL, officer, or enlisted man went through BUD/S, SQT, and pre-deployment training together.

Every man in a SEAL unit knew he could count on the men around him, because they were all cut from the same cloth and had survived the same crucible of the rigorous selection process. The SEAL pin, referred to as the trident, was twice the size of any other navy warfare specialty insignia, a symbolic distinction not appreciated by the navy's jet fighter community.

Jared and the others in his platoon knew that his second-in-command had very little time to get his shit together, even with Jared and the chief mentoring. SEAL officers routinely were placed in command of missions with significant consequences. They were assigned incredible amounts of fire support, intelligence support, and mobility options.

In the other services, these same high-level or high-value missions would be entrusted to more senior leaders, such as majors or lieutenant colonels. It wasn't out of the question to see a SEAL lieutenant junior grade or lieutenant briefing and leading high-impact operations. Young Ensign Barton was on the fast track to either glory or disaster. The choice was all his.

The chief let up a bit. "Look, sir, we don't have much time. Let us brief you on the training plan and you critique our decisions. That way we have to explain our logic and maybe you can find areas where we can do better."

Jared watched the ensign's expression change. "Sounds like a plan to me, chief."

The chief nodded. "Good. We could also use your help in tracking the range setup and ammo staging. What do you think?"

"I think the chief here is smart as a cat," the ensign noted. "He has a way of keeping me busy without hurting my feelings. Roger that, chief, I'll take care of the logistics. Jared, let me know when you are ready for the training schedule critique."

Chapter Twenty-Four

Jared noticed the ensign's tone was dry, making it clear he was not very happy. But he was impressed with the young man's insight. He'd seen right through the chief's manipulation, which showed he was a quick study. He watched his second-in-command turn on his heel and leave, heading for the operations office.

"He's a good man, chief. We need to start giving him a bigger piece of the pie."

"I know, sir," Chief Sampson said, watching the departing officer. "At least he has a spine. Did you see his eyes? I thought for a second he was going to take a swing at me!"

Jared laughed. "Well, I'm counting on you to make sure that doesn't happen! So, where were we?"

"Sir, do you know anything more about this mission we're preparing for? It would sure be easier to tailor the training to the task if I was a bit more dialed in."

Jared shook his head. "I wouldn't hold anything back from you, chief. You know everything I know. This smells like a readiness drill, and I doubt we'll finish whatever we're doing here before they call an end to the exercise and bring us back to San Diego. However, to paraphrase my favorite chief, you should always train like the next call is the one that sends you into harm's way. Let's play this that way."

"LT, I'm with you on this one. In my opinion, the rescue scenario contains several critical steps that we need to break down further and address. We're talking about getting everybody in the platoon up to speed on open-terrain contact drills for use in a jungle environment. Shit, we haven't touched any other type of training since we were designated an urban operations platoon. Fast rope inserts, breaching, room-entry choreography, precision shooting skills, yeah, we're hot shit when it comes to that stuff. The jungle is different; we both know that."

"I see what you mean, chief." Jared was running down a mental checklist of critical skills. "Here's an idea: what if we put the training schedule together in phases, representing the natural evolution or progression of the mission scenario as we understand it right now?"

"So, we'll train through the phases, but evaluate the strengths and weaknesses as we go. I like it! We can then focus on a particular phase or performance element in a phase to maximize on time correcting what needs to be corrected, right?" The chief was already plotting the phases in his head.

"Exactly!" Jared responded. "We run the whole mission, soup to nuts. Then we isolate the steps of performance that require the most training emphasis and use our remaining time to fix what we need to fix."

"Okay, sir, so let's get started!" The chief pulled out his notebook. "Phase one, we assume this hypothetical recon team does a bang-up job and finds the hostages. They succeed in pinpointing the site with a global positioning system. We receive the uplink and X marks the spot."

Lieutenant Stone knew his chief was on a roll. "That's right, chief. We start planning our mission based on the assumption we have an accurate target location and know the position of the hostages. That way we can hit the camp fast. Our platoon comes in; then we roll right over into a direct assault, take down the target, and rescue the hostages."

"Check, LT! Then we can work on moving the hostages out of the immediate target area and extracting the team from the environment. You string that all together, and you've got all the mission phases."

"And, therefore, the training and rehearsal sequence," Jared added. "Have we missed anything, chief?"

"No, sir, but . . ."

"What's the matter?"

"Two things. We don't know how many hostages to rescue so we don't have a clue about how many we'll be marshalling and protecting until a larger force relieves us and takes them off our hands."

"And the second concern?"

"LT, this feels like the Philippines. We're West Coast frogs, and that's the jungle area of combat operations right now in the Pacific. The teams already have guys staged in Guam that can do this job just as well as we can, and they've already been acclimated to the heat. Why pull us out of Coronado and stick us on this rock? Why send us?"

Jared didn't know the answer. "Good observations, chief. As I said earlier, it all points to an exercise and not a contingency mission. I'd add a third concern to yours. If this is a real operation, who is the recon team that's feeding us the target location and verifying the status of the hostages? What are their capabilities?

If this was an exercise, we would've been provided all that information and likely planned to link up with that team so they can take us straight into the camp."

The chief saw where this was going. "So, it's an exercise that feels like something else. It appears to be in the Pacific, so the Philippines or another jungle island in the Pacific. That's our team's regional orientation, but you have a point, boss. The exercise target folder would have been packed with stuff for us to sink our teeth into if this was all based on role-play and not true operational security concerns. Maybe it's the duck rule in play."

"The duck rule?" Jared wasn't following.

"Yes sir, the duck rule. If it walks like a duck and quacks like a duck, it's probably a fucking duck!"

143

They both had a good laugh and when that subsided, they looked at each other in a strange way, coming to the same conclusion. "Fuck, sir, this is the real thing."

"I think you're right, chief," Jared said grinning. "So, let's get hot with your plan. Get your initial planning cell together and have the rest work on setting up the training areas and logistics. We don't have a lot of time, so let's try to get things rolling early this afternoon and aim for completion sometime in the early evening. Then we'll spend the evening going over everything. If it looks good, we'll hit the ground running tomorrow."

The chief was nodding in agreement. "Then the results of the rehearsal tomorrow will determine the training schedule focus from that point on. Got it, boss!" The chief was satisfied they had arrived at a sound approach. He slapped the SEAL officer on the shoulder. "This will be a piece of cake, sir. It's not like we've never done this before."

Jared nodded. "Yeah, chief, I'm not too worried about the training side of this. I'm more worried about my men getting shot at."

The chief's smile faded a little. "Yeah, I know what you mean. But shit happens, sir. You can't sit around and worry about it, does no good. Well, sir, I'm heading out!" The senior enlisted man left Jared standing alone and headed for the operations office to find the ensign.

Bordentown, New Jersey

Alice smiled warmly. She couldn't stop laughing because her daughter had a bad case of the giggles. Alice had played that stupid Barney tape a hundred times, but her little Jackie never failed to enjoy it anyway. She walked over to the kitchen counter and picked up the business card lying there.

The Pentagon officer had been polite but firm when he stopped by the day before. He gave Alice the card with instructions to call if anything strange happened, anything out of the ordinary. He'd been reluctant to elaborate about the army's cause for concern.

She knew her father was in trouble and that threats had been made against her family and against her brother's family in California. After breakfast she'd call the nice young man and tell him about the sounds outside the house the night before. Alice looked back again at her daughter. It was time to start the day in earnest and that meant saying goodbye to Barney.

Alice gathered up loose toys and put them away in a cedar chest made by her father. The general, as the family referred to him, was an amateur woodworker, that is when he wasn't spending most of his life outside the United States. The box wasn't perfect, but it meant a lot to her and she knew that when her daughter became older, she would cherish it, too.

As she finished picking things up and went to the kitchen to unload the dishwasher, she suddenly got a weird feeling in her stomach. Alice couldn't put her finger on what was bothering her, but it felt strong, an intuition. She glanced at her daughter to make sure she was safe. The child smiled back and waved. Alice smiled back. The feeling was forgotten as swiftly as it had come to her.

The bomb blast rocked the sleepy little neighborhood. The shock wave was so intense that it damaged homes over a hundred yards away and broke windows up to half a mile further. Car alarms wailed in every direction, reacting instinctively to the violent explosion.

At ground zero, what was left of Alice's small three-bedroom house stood engulfed in flames. Throughout the neighborhood, people sheepishly crept out of their homes to see what possibly could have happened. Did a gas main explode? Once out on the street, Alice's neighbors saw the truth; there was nothing left of their neighbors' beautiful home.

"Oh my God! Somebody do something!" yelled a woman dressed in sweat pants and an over-sized white T-shirt from across the street. As more and more people gathered to stare in shock at the devastating scene, the question they all shared was "Why?"

"I've called 9-1-1!" shouted a well-dressed man nearby.

"They're in the house! The family is still in the house!" This observation came from a woman, who was running down the street and only just arriving in front of the inferno.

Her comment was correct, but it was now a moot point. There wasn't anything left of the structure. Alice and her daughter had been vaporized by the intense wave of fire that initially swept through the home. The fire was simply finishing the destruction.

Chapter Twenty-Five

Within minutes, sirens screamed in the distance. The assembled neighbors soon came to the collective conclusion that no one could have survived such a blast. "This is so terrible," one lady remarked. "So terrible. They had been through so much lately!"

"What do you mean?" a man asked.

"Didn't you know?" she asked. "That poor woman's father was kidnapped just in the last few weeks; the Colombians took him, killed some Army soldiers, too."

"Oh yeah, that's right," he remembered. "The general, the guy down in Colombia. Sure, I remember the story now. He's a general stationed in Panama. Wow, so much tragedy in one family and in such a short time!" The flames licked higher and higher. The fire trucks arrived far too late. General Alexander's daughter and granddaughter were gone forever.

San Diego, California

Army Captain Chuck Alexander stared straight ahead. He didn't dare to look at the scenery; the road was tight in places and it wandered back and forth across the narrow area on the mountainside where a road could exist. He glanced at the digital clock embedded in the dashboard; they were making good time.

The young family was on its annual pilgrimage to a special little spot they knew: a garden untouched by human development. As usual Chuck made sure they arrived just before sundown, with enough time to set up camp before it became too dark. Maybe if he was quick enough, there would be time for a short hike before dinner.

The long drive gave the career officer time to think about his father. He knew the old man was a tough son of a bitch, but Colombians didn't play by the queen's rules of war.

He knew there was a very good chance his dad wasn't going to make it out of this mess alive. His old man had been a tough father, a rigid disciplinarian with an unwavering expectation that his son would follow in his footsteps and join the army.

Chuck struggled all through high school against the idea of following his father into the army, but halfway through college he found himself adrift with no purpose or meaning in his life.

The entire country was angry about the attacks in New York and the Pentagon, and war fever was still in the air. America wanted payback, and he was ready to serve, serve the way his father and his grandfather before him had served, in uniform.

Chuck's thoughts were interrupted by a sharp bang near the rear of the vehicle. A second later, another sharp bang occurred, this time under the hood. The small explosion had buckled the hood, and Chuck stared at the sight of the bent metal in confusion. What could have possibly caused that? A split second later, he realized he'd lost steering control.

Chuck frantically and fruitlessly tried to turn the car to the right to contour with the looming bend to the right in the narrow mountain road ahead. It was pointless.

The car was unresponsive. His last memories were of his wife's face next to him, her hand grabbing his arm, and the screaming of his frightened children in the back seat as the car hit and then jumped the low concrete retaining wall at seventy miles per hour.

It took four hours for the first rescue teams to arrive. The smoke from the shattered car was at first thought to be a rancher burning off scrub brush, so no one investigated. Then a private pilot flying over the crash site on his way to a refueling stop radioed that he spotted a car flipped on its top, on fire and smoking furiously at the bottom of a cliff.

With the pilot's report in hand, the rescue team made their way to the place where the car had busted through the low retaining wall. They were specially trained to conduct difficult mountain rescue operations such as this.

A small crowd of police and firemen stood at the roadside containment wall, staring down at the now smoldering wreckage. It took twenty minutes for the first member of the rescue team to safely maneuver down to the car.

"Hey, guys, my first assessment as to the cause of this accident is inconclusive. The vehicle is too damaged to determine whether they were pushed off the road by impact with a second vehicle or just lost control."

One of the on-site investigating officers quickly wrote down the rescue worker's initial assessment. The tags had been traced to a Charles Alexander, an active duty army officer. Something was vaguely familiar about the name. He asked the rescue leader next to him about survivors.

"Hey, Bob! What's the situation regarding casualties?"

There was a long pause before Bob answered, his voice choking with emotion. "It appears to be a family. One adult male aged thirty-five to forty, one adult female same age range, and two children. One is a boy and the other is a girl. Best guess is elementary school age. All four are deceased."

The group on the road stopped talking when they heard the last sentence of the report. This was now a body recovery mission. After what seemed like ten minutes, one of the police officers cleared his throat.

"You know what, Phil? This guy's last name sounds familiar," he said, turning to the police officer next to him.

"Hmm, Alexander . . ." the other policeman responded. "Let me see. Yeah, I've heard that name recently, too. Isn't there some army big wig in the news with the same last name?"

Both police officers shrugged their shoulders. It would take a week or so before forensics determined the cause of the crash was two small, radio-fired explosive devices attached to the car.

The Pentagon–Washington, DC

The air force intelligence officer stepped into the room and placed a blue folder on the chairman's desk. The nation's senior military officer nodded. "Thank you, Johnson," he said without looking up. He waved his hand, dismissing the junior officer.

The chairman opened the folder and began speed-reading the incident reports. They didn't add much to what he'd already learned watching CNN. The report was full of facts and timelines summarizing eyewitness accounts and providing an analysis of previous day's events.

Domestic terrorist acts? For what purpose? Why kill two innocent families on either side of the country? He scanned the FBI white paper outlining their assessment. The FBI determined the deaths were part of a vendetta, a sophisticated pair of professional assassinations.

Somebody had marked General Alexander's family for death. The FBI noted at the end of its white paper that they were scouring the country for leads.

The final piece of the report was a CIA commentary on the possible motivations for the kidnapping in Colombia. They noted and dismissed political motives, financial motives, and normal cartel gangland-style reasons for the kidnapping.

The chairman's eyes were drawn to the fourth point on the list of probable causes. They surmised the general was being extorted for intelligence reasons. The death of his family was retaliation or intimidation, depending on if he'd been willing to share secrets or not.

The chairman wasn't buying any of their ideas. Why eliminate family members at the same time? You lose all the leverage they represent alive. It didn't make sense. That is, unless the FBI's viewpoint was correct.

It was an old-style, Colombian vendetta. A righting of wrongs to recover lost honor. The hostages weren't taken for ransom or to satisfy a shortfall in guerilla financing. These latest actions were personal and motivated by hate; they were deeply specific.

The chairman hit the intercom button. "Hey, Sam," he barked. "Yes, sir!" responded the aide.

"Could you come in here? I have a task for you." The chairman wanted to know more about the man indicated as the fourth probable cause in the FBI report. He wanted to have all his ducks in a row before speaking to the president. "Also make sure we are looking for any remaining members of General Alexander's family. We need to take them into protective custody as soon as possible."

The chairman's aide listened carefully before responding. He pressed the intercom button. "Understood. I'm on it, sir!"

The chairman leaned back in his chair. He hated this office. The walls were covered with memorabilia from his long career. Awards, plaques, gifts, and of course lots and lots of pictures of the chairman when he was a warrior. The man in those photos stared back at him, mocking him.

His office had the air of a fucking museum. It gave him the feeling that he'd died and someone had set up a place where others could visit and learn something about the man who had once been the Chairman of the Joint Chiefs of Staff. It was ceremonial, tradition; he got all that, hated it just the same.

If he had his way, right now he'd be in a desk smack dab right in the center of the operations and plans division of the Pentagon, where all the hubbub and activity occurred. Where brilliant young officers and enlisted men studied thick intelligence reports and embassy briefings trying to determine what the United States should do next. That's where he wanted to be, instead of being here, behind an ornate desk, waiting, always waiting.

The chairman put his hands behind his head and rocked gently back and forth. If the FBI's man was the culprit here, if this Chavez was responsible, then he needed confirmation and quickly. If it wasn't him, he needed to find who was murdering families, Americans on American soil.

Chapter Twenty-Six

Republic of Panama

The hangar was buzzing with activity. In the few short hours it required for Matt and his team to work the mission puzzle, more technicians and intelligence people had flowed into the large space. Matt pushed back from the table and stood up, stretching. He needed a break.

He heard the other two SEALs get up behind him. Oby and Boone followed him out of the confines of the secure cargo container and into the open hangar. As requested by Matt earlier, the mission support team had pulled the identified list of equipment from a second navy C-9 that landed and set it all up near the secure container.

The equipment was laid out on folding tables, two tables per man. One contained their weapons, their load-bearing vests, personal equipment such as hand-held radios, escape and evasion kits, flares, GPS navigation, night-vision goggles, camouflage face paint, water, and food.

The second table held each man's German LAR Five, closed-circuit scuba system. The LAR Five was a small, chest-mounted oxygen re-breather. It was capable of keeping a SEAL alive underwater for up to three hours, without emitting any telltale bubbles.

The second table also held a life jacket, fins with oversized pockets for their jungle boots, a face-mask, and aviator gloves with the fingers cut off. A weight belt completed the list.

A few feet away from the equipment staging area sat a sixteen-foot-long dugout canoe, a gift from Lane. After Boone's fruitless attempt to woo the attractive Army intelligence officer, he got to the point and asked about indigenous Colombian watercraft.

Two hours later, she knew the answer and had procured a local Panamanian version of the native canoes that they would find moving up and down the Ariari River in Colombia.

The long canoe was called a cayuca by the Panamanians. It was carved from the trunk of a single tree, a tree with special properties. When this type of wood was carved and shaped, it was dry and easy to form. Once it was placed in water, the wood swelled up, closing the millions of tiny holes in the material. It created a well-sealed, leak-proof boat.

The vessel was just long enough to handle the three men, all the equipment the SEALs would be carrying, and the thirty-five horsepower outboard engine they needed to propel themselves down the river.

The engine cover was dinged up and dirty. Purchased locally, it supported the visual and audio profile you'd expect to see and hear if a poor fisherman was navigating the Ariari. Rather than using a brand-new motor, Matt was banking on the idea that the locals on the river wouldn't pay attention to a sputtering old workhorse pushing a canoe downstream.

An American military-issued and maintained outboard engine would run flawlessly, humming, purring even as it effortlessly pushed the canoe down the waterway. This very signature likely would alert everybody on the river that a government boat was nearby, and they'd scramble to create some distance.

The locals also would pass the word along, using messengers and maybe even radios. Eventually, the FARC would be made aware of their presence. Matt was pretty sure they wouldn't run. The guerillas would come looking for the invaders and strike.

Matt watched as Oby took the time to check the outboard engine thoroughly, running it in a fifty-five-gallon drum filled with water. He knew a lot about engines, engines of all types. His dad had owned a couple of gas stations that catered to small repair, state inspections and the like.

He worked his way through high school fixing car engines, lawn mowers, just about anything that generated power. Oby stepped back and surveyed the machine sitting in the drum. Other than a little wear and tear and a dented prop, it was good to go.

While Oby finished up with the engine, Matt and Boone turned their attention to the Panamanian cayuca. It sat on top of a conventional boat trailer, trucked from the place of purchase all the way to the airport hangar. It was a solid piece of work, Matt observed.

He ran his hand along the side, marveling at the simplicity of the boat. Hand carved by a fisherman, these boats might perform their tasks for several generations if cared for properly. Boone started on one side, inspecting every square inch, Matt did the same starting on the opposite side. They met at the stern. He had a frown on his face

"What's the problem?" Matt inquired.

"The transom is cracked. We need to add a wood plank to make it sturdy. I assume that won't mess things up as far as the profile, correct?"

Matt looked at the transom. Boone was right; the place where the outboard attached to the canoe was worn out and cracked. It might be fine for another twenty trips or it might break in half during the mission.

"Good idea and no, it's not going to change the look of the boat in the dark. Let's get one of the logistics support guys over here to measure it and then go find what we need. Meanwhile, let's get back to the tables where the rest of the gear is staged. We need to conduct a complete inventory first, then function check everything, down to the sharpness of our knives."

"Roger that, chief!" Boone popped off, a big smirk showing he was joking.

Matt began to take the bait then stopped himself. "Okay, okay. You're right. I need to get out of the weeds and focus on something I can do well rather than do your job."

Boone didn't say anything. Instead, he walked to the corner of the hangar where the support guys had set up their little home away from home. Matt watched him for a moment, then ran through his mental checklist.

Time felt heavy, a crushing reality that was there waiting for him whenever he paused long enough to think. Senior Chief Auger must be feeling the same way, wherever he was.

Half an hour later, the three SEALs stood together by their tables. They first checked their personal loadout, then the assigned mission gear. Finally, they buddy checked each other's stuff until everything was locked down, mission-ready. Then they dive checked the re-breathers with Oby acting as the dive supervisor.

After thirty minutes, the rigs were good to go. This process was tradition and a lesson learned going all the way back to World War Two. It helped them find the little things that they might miss themselves, especially when the adrenalin was pumping and they were operating on little sleep.

If they discovered an issue, then the discrepancy was corrected on the spot. A little bit of tape there to cover up a shiny spot, some spray paint here, tighten up something that might rattle and cause noise.

Each little adjustment gave the three men the personal reassurance that their equipment and their buddies' equipment was ready to do the job. It was a proven pre-mission ritual.

Once the gear inspection was completed, Matt called them over to where a dry erase board was set up outside the secure container. There were four folding chairs staged in front of the board, where two of the men sat while each, in turn, stood at the board and ran down his part of the mission plan.

At any time, any of them could object to a procedure or argue with an intelligence assumption. They were a team of warrior equals, and each man knew the score.

Boone was responsible for navigation down the river and movement in and around the target area. He also was responsible for creating a coordination grid to use as an overlay on the target area.

The grid marked off a general area using an alphanumeric system. Letters down the left side, numbers across the top. Cardinal references such as south and north were difficult to determine at a glance and even more difficult to confirm while moving in the deep jungle or running around a target. Even a SEAL couldn't fight while holding a compass to his face.

By using the improvised grid, the three SEALs would be able to reference an object or an activity by calling out the grid reference just like the game, bingo. It was a very quick down and dirty way for people who were not in the same location to identify objects rapidly.

The coordinating data would be passed on to the assets supporting them, so that they also could pinpoint targets or the location of the recon team on the ground quickly and accurately. The air support was used to seeing this method on SEAL operations. They like the simplicity of the trick. It made directing air-to-ground supporting fire easy.

Oby was responsible for the reconnaissance and surveillance phase of the operation. He briefed Matt and Boone on how he wanted to conduct the initial recon when they found the target site.

Oby went over every detail of how he was going to set up the first surveillance hide. He explained how the observation shifts would rotate every two hours. One man would watch, one man would guard, and one man would sleep.

The last thing Oby covered was the surveillance logbook, something all qualified snipers were familiar with.

"Why the hell do we have to use the logbook?" growled Boone. "I don't care about sniper SOPs! Why can't we just write down what we see like we usually do?"

Matt could see that the lack of sleep and intense planning effort was wearing them all down. Time to step in. "We're using the sniper log because I told Oby to do so. It's the best format we have to capture everything and anything. We'll use it for the continuous reports we'll be sending back."

Matt's tone startled Boone. "Okay, sir, you don't have to get your panties in a bunch!" Boone waved at Oby. "Go on, brother SEAL, do continue!"

Oby smiled. "Happy to! Our surveillance logbook will be maintained, showing the time, place, activity, and impact of every event as it occurs in the target area. While we may not think all the information is important, during the post-mission debriefing intelligence professionals can pour over the logbook and match its data with that of other reports they have on the target. It has to be neat and accurate. That's all, boss!" Oby sat down.

Chapter Twenty-Seven

Matt was the last one to brief. He began by covering the command and control aspects of the mission. He emphasized the communications plan, starting with hand and arm signals while on patrol and finishing with the satellite radio they would use to communicate with the operations center. Matt was pretty sure this function would be performed by an aircraft orbiting somewhere near, but not too near the camp.

Matt also detailed the radio frequencies, call signs, code words, and the use of fire support if and when they needed it. Then he moved on to discuss how they were going to load the canoe into the helicopter.

"We have two primary and secondary extraction plans. One for us alone, if we don't link up with other friendlies; and the second plan is for when we leave with the rescue force."

Matt spent the next twenty minutes pouring over the details. In a way, having only three SEALs made it much easier to plan. They didn't have to explain a lot of things to each other and they didn't have to invent SOPs unique to the mission.

They'd worked together before and knew how each other thought and moved. There were no doubts about their individual skills as SEALs and no doubt of each man's courage under fire.

Matt looked at his watch; the planning effort was complete. "That was a great presentation. You two guys have really done a great job on this. We have about thirty minutes before we rehearse the canoe insertion. Grab something quick to eat and meet me out front."

"Okay, boss," Oby said, yawning.

"Moving!" Boone added. The two enlisted SEALs stood up and walked over to a table where overstuffed sandwiches had been prepared and left for them by the army cooks. Matt watched them eat and felt the heaviness again. Ten more hours until wheels up. Ten hours to go over the details in his mind a million more times. Ten hours to wonder whether or not Senior Chief Auger was still alive or if his small recon unit would survive the mission.

Ariari River, Colombia

Auger watched the young men practicing their warfighting skills off in the distance. The makeshift firing range was only a few yards back from the riverbank, and the far shore provided a simple but effective impact area for the rounds as they zipped across the flowing water.

The bullets made loud slapping sounds as they hit the mixture of clay and mud on the opposite bank. All things considered, Auger couldn't help but critique their efforts. What else did he have to do? The guerillas were firing a mixed bag of weapons: one or two bolt action rifles, a few automatic weapons from various countries, and one or two submachine guns (SMGs).

The small caliber SMGs were virtually useless here in the jungle. They looked cool in the movies, but rarely were the weapon of choice for professionals.

Most SMGs fired a nine-millimeter round, a bullet originally designed for use in pistols. The nine-millimeter bullet had very little penetration power, and while it could put out a lot of rounds, the bullets failed to blast through the dense jungle, where every living thing conspired to slow it down or deflect it harmlessly.

On the other hand, the rifles employed by the fighters utilized the deadly and highly effective 7.62 NATO round, excellent for punching through just about anything. One drawback with the weapons was the fact that most of these rifles used five-round magazines, not nearly enough bullets per magazine to lay down a heavy base of fire during a typical jungle firefight.

Jungle warfare tactics were considerably different than tactics employed in other terrain around the world, because you rarely saw the face of your enemy until you were right on top of him. Ambushes were set up on jungle trails within two or three yards of the intended victims.

The close proximity was critical; the ambushers needed to see their targets. Once an ambush was initiated and the lead started flying, the ambushers and their victims were locked toe-to-toe in deadly combat. In this situation, having weapons that pumped out a lot of jungle-penetrating firepower spelled the difference between victory and defeat.

The rifles the men practiced with were fine, but they were better suited for wide-open spaces. In desert and mountain environments, a man with a good rifle could kill you from half a mile away. Multi-round magazines were not as important.

He knew the best way to fight and win in this particular battle space was to use a belt-fed machine gun. It fired large-caliber rounds and penetrated everything, while delivering heat to an opponent in volume. Fire superiority could be gained in seconds, even if you were on the wrong side of a well-designed and initiated rifle ambush.

Auger understood why belt-fed weapons were so effective from listening to veteran SEALs discuss their experiences in Vietnam and from working in the Philippine Islands after the attack on the trade towers.

The pros operating in these brutal conditions preferred to arm themselves with as many belt-fed weapons as possible. It modern times, it wasn't unusual for an eight-man SEAL patrol to carry four M-249 squad automatic weapons, or SAWs, and two M-240 Bravo machine guns. The heavy firepower made SEALs the badasses of the jungle.

The mixed bag of weapons made perfect sense to Auger. The guerillas probably were picking up weapons wherever they could find, buy, or steal them. He watched intently as one skinny fellow in charge shouted, expressing his displeasure at how one lad was reloading his submachine gun.

The fact that they were even spending time on reloading drills impressed Auger. That implied that the man in charge had received some type of formal military training, maybe in the Colombian army or civil militia.

In Auger's experience, most of the time untrained irregular troops just fired the rounds they had in their weapon and then hightailed it out of harm's way. If anyone was coming to rescue them, these guys will be toast, he thought. Then, of course, there's American air power.

Auger sat back, leaning against the cage wall only eight inches behind him. He began his favorite pastime of late: daydreaming about the rescue. He'd created names for every pilot, aircrew member, and SEAL in the camp assault. In his fantasy, frogmen were coming to save him.

He knew what they carried, hell, he even knew the name of the drone operators located somewhere in the American southwest, directing the surveillance drones. In his mind, it all came together in perfect harmony and it always happened sooner rather than later. He never dwelled on the other possibility.

As the American sat deep in thought, a new group of men sauntered up to the makeshift range and took their positions on the line. The first group fired their last shots and greeted the newcomers with laughter and animated gestures, probably bragging to their fellow warriors about how well they'd done.

This second group was more organized. Their equipment also appeared to be more uniform. Auger stopped the movie in his head and took notes. He watched the range supervisor of the first group relinquish control of the range and walk away and saw another gentleman, who had the look of a professional warrior, take over.

"Can you see anything, senior chief?" The general lay in his cage in an awkward fetal position, twisted away from the river down below. His view was restricted to the jungle beyond the top of their high point, and there wasn't enough room for him to turn over and see the camp.

"Just a bunch of camp goons wasting ammo down on the range," the SEAL quipped. "They don't seem to be very proficient with weapons."

"Just how good do you have to be to shoot an American general locked in a bird cage?" he responded.

Auger grunted, acknowledging the wisdom of the older man's observation. These guys didn't have to be trained Special Forces to put a world of hurt on their two American captives. He watched as the dynamic leader of the second group of guerillas stepped forward and shouted a crisp command.

The shooters immediately complied, assuming proper assault posture, one leg forward, weight balanced over knees that were slightly bent. They opened up in unison, stitching the mud on the opposite side of the river in smooth three-round bursts. These guys were armed better, too. Russian style AK and AKM assault rifles and RPK belt-fed machine guns.

Every man was focused on attaining a tight impact zone, using the splattering mud to gauge their accuracy. They soon began practicing reload drills working in buddy pairs. They'd fire ten rounds, clear their empty magazine, and then reload, until all six of their thirty round magazines were emptied.

These guys were good, Auger thought. These guys were actually aiming their weapons and hitting what they wanted to hit. Their reloading was smooth as well.

After ten minutes or so, Auger realized the men on the riverbank weren't holding back on the ammo. Whoever they were, they were well-trained, well-equipped, and well-supplied.

They were the studs of the camp, and Auger hoped they were the only ones. Another twenty like them would cause a big problem for any special operations guys raiding the camp.

The supervisor, man in charge, or whoever he was, changed the drills and mentored those men having problems. This unit had operated together and trained together for quite some time, Auger believed.

They had a sense of purpose and a sense of unit pride. They also were older than the first group that used the range. Auger's mental image of the guerilla's capabilities altered a bit. He now classified the fighters in the camp into two distinct elements.

Chapter Twenty-Eight

The hard-core guerrillas who'd been out in the jungle for a long time were equipped much like their counterparts in the Colombian army. They had full combat vests with magazine pouches, canteens, knives, utility packs mounted either on their back or attached to the base of their vests, and medical supplies.

Most were armed with modern rifles, and they universally wore the same jungle pattern fatigues. Auger counted approximately twenty-five of these well-equipped, well-trained troops on the firing line.

The vast majority of the camp's inhabitants, however, were the second type of combatant. They were much younger, somewhere in the range of nineteen to twenty years old. They were draped in a hodge-podge of equipment and carried a strange mix of weapons.

From what the SEAL could observe, most of these men didn't use load-bearing equipment, and no special utility pouches or any other kind of survival equipment gear adorned their bodies. This indicated to Auger that this group likely didn't venture very far from camp.

Many of these inferior fighters were, of course, raw recruits. The guerrilla leaders, he surmised, probably brought in a new crop of trainees each season, worked them, and then selected the best of the group to either to replace the casualties in their primary guerrilla force or to infuse the primary guerrilla force with new blood.

"Well, I'm sure the Army Rangers or Green Berets will be here soon," said the general, interrupting Auger's mental critique.

Auger twisted to look at the senior officer. "What makes you think they'll send the army in here? We're next to a river, general. My guess is they'll send my buddies to save our asses!"

"Sailors? I seriously doubt it, son. They'll never send sailors to do an infantryman's job. These assholes would chew up your sailors." The general's words were delivered with a bit more contempt than Auger could ignore.

"With all due respect, sir, I've never met a Marine or army puke who was qualified to clean my rifle, let alone pull off a job like this one. I'll wager you a case of beer, American beer, that they do the smart thing and send team guys."

"I'll take that bet, senior chief!" General Alexander's voice was getting weaker. Tough guy or not, the steady diet of beatings had taken quite a toll on the older man.

Loud shouting from down below ended the debate between the two men. Auger twisted his body back around in the small cage until he was able to see the rest of the camp through a small space between his knees.

Down below his little perch, the guerrillas had gathered around two light-skinned Hispanic men. From their well-groomed haircuts and fancy clothing, Auger guessed they might be management types, probably from one of the big cities.

Kidnapping executives of multinational corporations working and operating in Colombia was a lucrative sideline for the guerrillas. They would hold these gentlemen for two to three weeks while they negotiated a ransom. Eventually, the hostages were freed, with the insurance companies paying the freight.

As Auger watched, the two men were ushered into a large one-room building that, compared to his accommodations, seemed like the Hilton. It must be the headquarters of this camp, he guessed.

Strangely enough, Auger was beginning to feel more comfortable as his reconnaissance of the guerrilla camp's interior opened up opportunities for a rescue force to exploit. He only hoped they sent in a surveillance team first. They would see the same things he saw and make sure the raiding force was dialed in before the shooting started.

There was a lot more to learn that could be important later on down the road, especially if he tried to escape. Auger knew the Colombians would be no match for Delta Force or SEALs rolling into the camp, guns blazing.

They'd pinpoint the scrambling guerrillas with laser aiming systems, taking people efficiently with double taps to the head. Aerial snipers sitting on a helicopter would compete with the ground force to see who eliminated all the competition first, the snipers or the assault team.

The silencers on their weapons would give them the vital first few seconds of surprise and make it hard for the fighters in camp to realize the assault had even started. It would be devastating and it would be quick. Hopefully, Auger thought, both he and the general would be alive to see the show.

SEAL Training Area–San Clemente Island, California

Jared knew instinctively they'd have to do it over again. His platoon was trained and well-versed in the art of hostage rescue, but these open field maneuvers, basic patrolling, and reconnaissance techniques were buried so deep in his men's memory banks that they were fumbling around like rookies.

That was one of the problems when a SEAL platoon focused on one specific mission area. You got extremely proficient at what you practiced, and the rest went to shit.

He turned to see a red-faced Chief Sampson wandering from platoon member to platoon member handing out his two cents worth on what he thought had gone right or wrong with the rehearsal. Very little had pleased his chief, from what the Jared could gather. Sampson was an expert at dressing down the boys without breaking their spirit. He watched and took mental notes.

The fact that the chief had spent a tour as a BUD/S instructor added a certain edge the men could appreciate. The men in this platoon trusted and respected the chief's judgment. His criticism stung only because the words rang true and they wanted his approval.

FOXTROT Platoon rehearsed the basic scenario of patrolling, approaching the objective, staging the rescue team on target, and attacking. It wasn't working, and the fact that the men were tired wasn't an excuse to stop and take a break. Fatigue was part of the job.

Four or five of his men had extensive experience doing cross-training exercises in Malaysia and in the Philippines. A few also had participated in the training activities in Thailand. These operators repeatedly voiced their opinions, reinforcing the need to execute the tactics well if they wanted to win a fight in the jungle.

The chief finished his walk about and released the platoon for a much-needed water break. He strolled back to where Jared stood, kicking up the dust with the tips of his boots. Jared noticed his chief also was dragging ass a little. He waited for the chief to come within speaking range and then asked the key question.

"Well, chief, how bad is it?"

Chief Sampson kept his head down for a moment before looking up. "LT, I think this whole deal stinks."

"What do you mean?" asked the puzzled officer.

"Well, sir, it goes like this. You and I are assuming this is a real tasker, and we are preparing for combat operations. The scenario has our SEAL brothers out there putting eyes on the target, maybe as we speak. When these guys are in place, they can easily help guide us, increasing our odds of success."

"So what is your point, chief?" The LT's voice was firm, indicating he wanted the other man to finish his monologue.

"Yeah, so I don't follow where you are going with this, chief." Jared was alarmed by the enlisted man's mood. Something was really bugging him.

"Well, LT," the chief continued. "We're a hostage rescue platoon. You know as well as I do that there is a downside to focusing on a specific mission area. Now, sir, we're great at moving through an urban environment, kicking down doors, and taking precision shots at terrorists and such, but we haven't practiced open field maneuvers and contact drills in over a year. Even then, it was a short review, not real proficiency training. Our guys are so rusty it's like we never even worked together!"

Chief Sampson looked his officer in the eye. "My point is this, boss. We shouldn't be doing this mission. As much as I like to participate in these shoot and loot gigs, this platoon shouldn't be going into the jungle. I've no doubt that we could get the job done once we're inside the target area, but there's a good chance we could get our ass handed to us patrolling through that mess."

He took a deep breath and let out, calming down a bit. "The locals know the terrain and they are acclimated to the heat; that means they'll have the upper hand. I just don't have any confidence that this platoon is going to react the way a SEAL platoon is supposed to react. We might lose guys for all the wrong reasons."

Jared put his hands on his hips and looked up into the blue sky. Whether he agreed with Chief Sampson or not, in a SEAL platoon, the prime mover was the chief petty officer. A smart naval officer didn't make a move without the chief's understanding and agreement.

The rest of the navy knew that, too. The wisdom of seeking the guidance of a chief petty officer was a tradition. Jared knew it was even more important in the teams.

Jared realized that if he continued to push this platoon, took them into combat, and got men killed, not only would he be liable professionally, but also morally. He'd be washed up in the teams if he was wrong.

He'd spend the rest of his life knowing he made a call that resulted in disaster and the death of his teammates. The SEAL community eventually would find out that he'd ignored his chief's advice and assume his decision to override that input was due to a need to seek glory and promotion.

The platoon commander stared back at his chief. "Chief, this is pretty serious stuff here. If you're asking me to pick up the phone and tell somebody we can't do this job, I need you to stand side by side with me, probably all the way up to the top."

The chief nodded, "I know it's damn serious, sir. But what's even more serious is our responsibility to these men. I'm sure there's a platoon at SEAL Team Four fully capable of executing these mission parameters. Their platoons are superbly trained and focused on jungle warfare. They have enough guys with rescue skills to put together a great assault group."

He paused, gathering his thoughts. "I mean, we are not talking about taking down a five-star hotel here. The target folder shows huts and lean-tos surrounded by a thousand miles of jungle. We are overqualified for the actions at the objective but we are not ready to get to that target on foot and in the jungle. Not the way we look right now."

The lieutenant understood what he had to do. "Well, let's go ahead and stand the men down for an hour. I'll make the call and wait for the shit to hit the fan. You and I should stand by to fly back to the coast or at least participate in a conference call. Do we have the secure line hooked up?"

The chief was relieved. "Yes, sir, the secure line is hooked up in the operations office and ready to use when we need to make the call."

"Good deal, chief." Jared said, beginning to regain some of his confidence. "I think the logic is sound, and we've had enough rehearsals to confirm what you are saying is true. I would put this platoon up against anybody when it came to breaking down doors and popping somebody in the forehead with two rounds, but this is different. I'll go ahead and make the call. You do what you have to do here, chief."

Sampson gave the officer a thumbs-up and marched away, with his face set in grim determination. He was under no illusion that his observation would be applauded by the higher-ups. The LT might be a good leader, but that meant nothing to the pukes who had left the real work of the teams two or three promotions ago.

Many of the officers in the staff in the senior command levels felt politics and saving face were more important than putting the right people in the target. His LT would be in trouble, no two ways about it.

Chapter Twenty-Nine

Jared walked to the building where the secure phone was located. He spotted a few of his men sitting around and casually getting hydrated. He tried to hide his concern about the mission, but the SEALs could see by the look on his face that something was wrong.

Most of the men probably believed the LT was frustrated by the botched rehearsal cycle. They would be very upset if they knew the truth, that their leader was about to request they abort the use of their platoon for a real-world combat operation. In other words, quit.

Jared sat on the dusty chair and dialed the number to the operations officer of Naval Special Warfare Group One. After three rings, the phone was answered. "Special Warfare Group One quarter deck, Petty Officer Hopewell speaking. May I help you?"

"Petty Officer Hopewell, this is the platoon commander of FOXTROT Platoon. I need to talk to the operations officer if he's in."

"Sir, the operations officer went home for the day. Can I take a message?"

"That's a negative," Stone said quickly. "Call his cell; tell him I ordered you to have him contact me. Make sure you convey that it's a very serious problem. If you can't get hold of him that way, send him an email on the secure intranet. He needs to call me on a secure line."

"Yes, sir!" the quarterdeck watch answered dutifully. "Will do!"

The lieutenant placed the handset back in its cradle and leaned back in the chair, sliding down a little bit further to get more comfortable. This is really going to stink up the place, Jared mused. The big boys are going to do everything from accusing us of being cowards to saying that we are trying to dodge a trip so we can stay home with our families.

The SEAL lieutenant knew for a fact that the senior staff types wouldn't see the crystal-clear logic of the chief's assessment. Somehow, Jared pondered, he had to come up with a strong enough argument to get his platoon off the hook for this mission.

Naval Special Warfare Group One–Coronado, California

Commander Jack Weasley was a former enlisted SEAL with ten years as a crazy frogman before attending officer candidate school and going over to what the enlisted SEALs referred to as the "dark side." He'd been having a quiet moment with his wife Ann in Balboa Park, just strolling and taking in the beauty of the place.

They'd gone there eighteen years ago on their first date, a safe public place for Ann, who'd never dated a military man before. He had his smart phone's ringer turned off, but he checked his emails and texts from time to time.

The email was cryptic, but provided sufficient information that he had to reluctantly put his wife in a taxi. He drove the twenty minutes over the Coronado Bay bridge through Coronado Island and onto the seaward side of the naval amphibious base to his headquarters.

Jack walked into his spacious office, unintentionally slamming the door behind him. The duty officer had greeted him at the door to the secure headquarters, a collection of officers and enlisted men responsible for managing and supporting all the SEAL teams on the West Coast.

As the operations officer, he'd been read into the SPECAT traffic and knew more than FOXTROT Platoon did about their end objective and location. He assumed the lieutenant was getting antsy and wanted more information, details they could work with. He didn't blame them if this was the reason for the call.

He walked down the hall to the crew's lounge, poured himself a cup of over-warmed coffee and then moved purposefully to the secure communications room. He was still angry at the disruption and knew he had to make it up to Ann somehow.

She'd been a trooper throughout their entire marriage. Long deployments, three tours of combat in Afghanistan, and much more. He punched the code into the cipher lock and opened the door. Jared Stone was on his shit list.

San Clemente Island – California

Jared sat next to the secure phone, falling in and out of a lazy cat nap. Each time he heard a sound, his head snapped up and he felt an electric shock course through his body. He was overtired, BUD/S student kind of tired.

This call might be a symptom of his fatigue and not his good judgment. SEALs hated quitters, and he was about to tell the chain of command that he and his platoon were dropping out. The ring of the phone startled him, and he fumbled with the handset.

"Jared Stone."

"This had better be good, lieutenant!" The commander's voice conveyed anger, and the message was received loud and clear by the leader of FOXTROT Platoon.

"Sir, this is about Operation Dagger."

"No shit! Now get to the reason for this call!"

Jared swallowed hard. They'd been out at the island working so hard he'd lost track of the days. He just realized it was three in the afternoon on a Sunday. "Sir, we are CASREP'd for this mission."

Commander Weasley wasn't sure he's heard right. A CASREP is a navy casualty report, usually reserved for reporting mechanical failures on a ship. SEAL platoons didn't fail in this manner. "What the fuck are you talking about? Are you shitfaced?"

Jared covered the phone and took a deep breath. He just needed to get it all out, no wind up. "Sir, FOXTROT Platoon is not proficient enough to execute at a C1 combat-ready status in the jungle. We are, and have been, an urban and underway hostage rescue unit for over eighteen months. I said CASREP because that's the closet readiness concept that makes sense. You need to tell WARCOM you need another platoon that's ready to fight and win in that environment."

Naval Special Warfare Command – Coronado, California

Admiral Fitzpatrick arrived wearing golf attire. He sat down behind his large walnut desk and punched the speed dial button on his telephone. The automated system dutifully dialed up the desk phone of the Naval Special Warfare Group One Commodore, located a half a mile away on the San Diego Bay side of the Coronado Strand. The Commodore, Robert Morris, picked up immediately.

"Admiral, I'm ready to go secure on my end." Bob Morris's voice was calm. He'd been in a lot of tough scrapes in his twenty-five-year career. Getting yelled at by Admiral Fitzpatrick wasn't even close to the worst he'd lived through.

The admiral found the right button on his phone. "Roger, I'll initiate."

Commodore Morris had received a call an hour before from his operations officer, Commander Weasley. His staff officer had conveyed the need for his presence at headquarters without breaching communications security, and then filled him in on the situation when they were face-to-face in the commodore's office.

The commodore heard the tone signifying they were on a secure communications line. "What the hell's going on, Bob?" the admiral said through clenched teeth. "I've only been told Foxtrot Platoon wants to abort. How the hell can they abort before they even begin the fucking mission?"

"Well, admiral, the commodore began, "The platoon commander of FOXTROT Platoon has requested that we relieve his platoon of their assignment." The commodore took a deep breath.

"What?" Admiral Fitzpatrick jumped to his feet. "You dragged me in here because some lieutenant is getting cold feet? What the hell's going on here? Where did we get this guy?"

The commodore took a deep breath, then began to explain the platoon commander's logic. "Admiral, I happen to believe he's right. Lieutenant Stone's concern and that of his platoon chief is based in fact. Their specialized hostage rescue platoon is ill-suited for an engagement in the jungle, especially on such short notice. They are highly-trained and combat ready for the job they've trained to, primarily in urban environments and ship boarding operations."

The admiral's voice rose from a steady tone until he was shouting. "Maybe I'm delirious, Bob, but if I recollect correctly, THIS IS A FUCKING HOSTAGE RESCUE MISSION!"

Commodore Morris was used to dealing with the admiral. He'd worked under the officer in a coalition special operations task force in Jalalabad, Afghanistan, in 2010. He always had been an emotional man, a screamer. Bob knew he had to wait out the storm before he'd be able to get his point across. They were wasting time.

"Admiral, they're having great difficulty making up the deficit in jungle training in the time allotted them. They're also training on San Clemente Island. That's damn near desert terrain, a far cry from the jungles of Colombia."

The admiral was having a hard time controlling his temper. "Bob, they're SEALs, damn it! I was against this specialization bullshit from the very start! Now all my troops are drill bits. They only fit a precise requirement. What good is it expanding the force if you're still running short on C1 ready combat units?"

The admiral was right. Overspecialization had created teams and platoons designed for a specific task and environment. It looked great on paper; Bob Morris had been one of the advocates for the change. But it hadn't stood the test of time. Now the community's leaders were arguing that it was time to get back to its roots. The core value of special operations is flexibility and adaptability. Assess, plan, and execute. He grudgingly had to agree.

The admiral's voice became calm. "What am I supposed to do now? Send an East Coast platoon from SEAL Team Four?"

The commodore knew the real problem here was East Coast–West Coast politics. The old man was supposed to be in command of both, but it was clear he was trying to throw a bone to the West Coast because his roots were in Coronado.

Bob wasn't a stickler for boundaries. Maybe it would've made sense if they'd tapped a seasoned West Coast platoon for this job. There were several working in the Philippines that were ready and available to support Dagger, but these units were still engaged against Abu Sayyaf and committed to Pacific Special Operations Command or PACSOC for several more months of counterterrorist operations.

"Admiral, these men haven't touched an M-240B machine gun or conducted open-field fire and movement in almost two years, and they don't have much time left. They could receive the green light to launch the rescue at any moment. Sir, the bottom line is simple. If they don't feel they're ready, my recommendation is we reassign the mission to the East . . ."

The admiral cut his commodore off in mid-sentence. "Bob, I don't care what you think, and I don't care what that lieutenant thinks. This is a West Coast show. Nobody, and I mean nobody, is going to tell me who goes on a mission and who doesn't. I don't buy this crap about SEALs not knowing how to patrol and not knowing how to do fire and movement; and if I remember right, this specialization shit was your idea!"

Chapter Thirty

The commodore knew the admiral had him pinned to the mat. He'd been an advocate for creating super platoons capable of transcending all previous high-water marks in every mission category.

The old standard of SEAL platoons being "jacks of all trades and masters of none" was inhibiting the pursuit of operational excellence; and the better SEALs performed around the world, the more Washington demanded of them. In the new special operations era, the national command authority wanted elegant precision. Cadillacs not Chevys.

The commodore tried one more time to convince the admiral to change his mind. "Admiral, this is a request from the platoon chief and platoon commander. If we force them to do this mission against their recommendations, we run the risk of a disaster. One we could've prevented. It's my opinion that a SEAL Team Four jungle warfare platoon would be better suited for this operation."

He paused for effect. "Consider for a moment that the target is not a sophisticated hostage scenario in a built-up urban area. It's nothing more than a bunch of huts, lean-tos, and makeshift buildings. There's no need for a precision hostage rescue team." The commodore stopped talking.

The admiral barely waited for the commodore to finish. "Bob, you will order that lieutenant to continue preparations for mission execution. You will tell them it's his responsibility to get those men ready for combat. You tell him that and when you are done telling him I want you to schedule a meeting. Next Tuesday, just you and I. We have some serious issues to discuss regarding the readiness of your SEAL teams. Do you understand me?"

The commodore realized he had lost. "Yes, admiral, I'll pass on your answer and your orders."

"That right, Bob, my orders. Not suggestions!" With that, the admiral slammed the phone down.

Staging hangar – Panama

Matt fiddled around with his equipment for what seemed like the fourth or fifth time in the last hour. He knew all his gear was finally good to go, but it helped ease his mind. Nearby Oby and Boone were putting the finishing touches on their gear.

In the few minutes left to them before mission launch, they'd mulled over every detail of the operation. They worked the phases, running down individual mental checklists to detect anything that might be amiss. It was overkill and they knew it, but the only thing that would stop the process was mission launch.

Lately, Matt spent a lot of time thinking about his father. It felt like a million years since he'd been burdened with the emotional baggage of his old man. His father's hero status as a holder of the Medal of Honor had cast a shadow over Matt for all of his childhood and into his mid-twenties. It rarely came up in the teams, but that didn't matter; it was still in Matt's head.

He realized he'd thought about his dad and the big blue less and less after the operation in Egypt. His combat experience removed his low self-esteem regarding his dad; and in a strange way, being a leader brought him closer to his dead father. Matt still felt the man's presence during times of stress and that was probably why he was thinking about him right now.

For the past two years, Matt had sat on his ass at the training center in San Diego, fooling himself into thinking he might have a chance for a normal life. His mental focus had shifted off the warrior mind-set expected of a SEAL, and instead he'd focused all his energy on trying to establish a lasting relationship with Tina.

Team guys never spoke about getting out, unlike all the cliché war movies; members of elite units operated like professional athletes. Honing their skills, expanding their knowledge, and getting ready for the next event. Matt wasn't sure if he was going to stay in the teams for the long haul or quit and give civilian life a shot.

The other thing that nagged him when he was getting all introspective was Tina. She was gorgeous, smart, and when not complaining about his work schedule, funny. Yet in his gut, he knew she wasn't the one. She wasn't Sherry.

The more time passed, the more he realized he'd been in love with the Virginia Beach beauty. Sherry was scared away by the combat risks and the severity of Matt's wounds.

After the fight in Alexandria, Egypt, she had ended the relationship. Maybe he was ready for her level of commitment, that is if she wasn't already married with three kids back in Virginia Beach. Almost five years had passed. Maybe . . .

"Hey, boss, you okay? You're standing there staring off into space like you're in a trance or something." Boone's voice held a slight tinge of real concern.

Matt took a breath. "Yeah, I'm fine. Just running through the op in my head. I can't find any issues. You?"

Boone shook his head. "I just asked Oby and he's solid, too. I think we need to get out of this metal box and into the field. It'll all shake out once we're locked and loaded."

Oby walked over and waved his hand. "Come on, ladies, chow is ready, and we don't want to go into harm's way on an empty stomach, do we?"

Matt and Boone laughed. Oby loved two things in this world: guns and food. "You join Oby, Boone. I have one or two more things to check here, then I'll join you. Make sure Oby doesn't eat my share."

"Roger that, boss!" Boone jogged to catch up with his swim buddy.

Matt wondered if Oby or Boone ever thought of leaving the teams. Most enlisted guys expected Templar-like devotion to the brotherhood and would see a crack in a man's commitment as a serious sign of weakness and potentially a liability. In the teams, you were all in or you were not in at all.

Most enlisted men tended to stay in the teams a full twenty years or more if physically able to operate at a high level. Officers, on the other hand, would eventually rise up the ranks, leaving danger behind and fighting new battles in the staff environment. A good percentage left the teams and the navy, jealous of their enlisted brothers.

Matt feared the day when he would have to tell operating SEALs what to do while not sharing the risks they were taking. Maybe that was the time to depart the life; he wouldn't be the first officer who got out of the teams for that same reason.

Matt stepped back and took a last look. He was mission ready. He needed to clear his mind of all this bullshit and switch to operator mode. He'd never promised Tina anything as far as the future was concerned.

It was an unspoken understanding between the two of them. But Matt was aware that she was ready to make the next step. He might have been sucked down that rabbit hole but for the oddly-timed call to arms.

The last thing Matt expected was to be assigned to a SPECAT combat mission while on shore duty. It was crazy, but he was glad it happened. It'd stirred up his sense of purpose again.

As he stood there, being honest with himself, he knew he wasn't ready to settle down, and he also knew he needed to tell Tina about this decision when he returned to Coronado. It was time for her to move on with her life.

His mind was clear. His job was to take Boone and Oby into Colombia and save Senior Chief Auger. Boone and Oby had the same determined look etched on their faces and felt the same desire to pull their friend out of the mess he was in.

The intelligence types had continued to express their pessimism, telling Matt there was a little chance the two American hostages would survive their ordeal. At a minimum, they believed the enlisted hostage was already dead, since he wasn't valuable enough to ransom.

Matt didn't buy into that bullshit. Auger was alive, and they were going to find his ass, rescue him, and give him shit about getting caught over beers back in Coronado. He suddenly felt really hungry. Matt walked over to the table covered with food. He pushed all thoughts of the future and Tina aside; it was time to lock it down.

The sound of an approaching helicopter grew steadily until the hangar doors rattled. Their ride to Colombia had arrived. As Matt joined his teammates for their last hot meal for the next few days, he pondered the object of their reconnaissance, Senior Chief Auger.

His intuition told him that his friend and mentor was still alive. He was a tough son of a bitch, that was for sure; so if anyone could survive this ordeal, he would.

Matt took another bite of his sandwich and looked back over his shoulder, peering through the open hangar doors. He watched as the MH-53 helicopter crew loaded the versatile aircraft. The dugout canoe was sitting nearby, mounted on a standard boat trailer. Would that thing fit?

Matt observed the army aircrew take the commercial boat trailer and roll it straight up into the cargo bay. The canoe was too long to fit and allow the rear cargo doors to close, so the tail ramp would have to stay down for the flight. The ass end of the dugout poked out of the helicopter a good three feet or so. It looked goofy, but he was sure the air force boys knew what they were doing.

Chapter Thirty-One

The overall load of boat, trailer, and SEALs was no problem for the heavy lift MH-53. Once the boat and trailer were cinched down, one of the crewmen walked toward the mouth of the hangar and caught Boone watching him.

The two professionals gave each other a thumbs-up. Both had a job to make this all come together and a shared desire to see this particular mission go well. America didn't leave her fighting men behind.

Boone looked at Matt. "All right boss, the crew chief signaled they are ready; it's time to saddle up!"

"Okay, Boone." Matt saw that Oby was grinning at him. The waiting was finally over.

The three SEALs gulped down the rest of their meal, jogged back to the equipment staging tables to gather up their gear, and then walked together toward the helicopter. The engines were beginning to crank up, whining loudly as if in protest.

The reconnaissance team climbed up the tail ramp, tossing their backpacks and weapons into the boat. The re-breathers and dive bags had been secured in the canoe earlier. All the mission equipment needed to be secured in a way that prevented loss if the boat capsized during insertion.

There were no connections inside the dugout to attach equipment, so Oby had drilled holes along the top edge of the canoe and placed small eye bolts in each. This created a system of anchoring points to snap or bungee in their backpacks.

Oby finished the job by running a piece of parachute cord through each eye bolt, around the entire circumference of the canoe. This gave the three SEALs even more flexibility to stow things where they made the most sense once they were in the river.

Oby checked the outboard motor lying in the bottom of the boat. It was secured to several of his attachment hooks, but he double-checked to make sure it wasn't going to shift around during the flight. Meanwhile, Boone checked the rest of the mission loadout, making sure their packs and weapons were tied into the canoe.

The rotors were up to full speed now, making it impossible to be heard. Matt stood at the tail ramp reading over the flight path to the DEA refueling spot located in the northern region of Colombia.

The DEA controlled access to their forward base for a distance of ten miles. As a result, Matt and the senior planners believed the short refueling stop would not compromise the reconnaissance mission by giving the FARC advance warning of their operation.

The crew chief grabbed Matt by the arm and directed him to join Oby and Boone on the passenger seats, made of interwoven red nylon webbing. He looked at his teammates and gave a questioning thumbs-up.

They both responded with a solid thumbs-up, indicating they were satisfied with the mission loadout and personally ready to go. Matt nodded, then sat down and snapped his seat belt in place.

The helicopter crew chief gave them all an okay sign to check that the SEALs were ready for takeoff. The team responded in kind and the crew chief dropped his hand. Thirty seconds later the big MH-53 rose into the hot Panamanian air, spun right on its axis, dipped its nose, and accelerated as it gained height. They were on their way. Operation Green Dagger was underway.

Once at cruising altitude, the crew chief handed Matt an aircraft headset, allowing him to check in with the pilots. From this point forward and until landing in Colombia, the pilot in command was leading the mission.

He would keep Matt updated on their progress and on any changes passed to him regarding the operation, such as weather or intelligence updates. He also would pass the word if the mission was scrubbed before they landed at the refueling site.

DEA Camp Twenty-Six - Colombia

After more than two hours of flight time, the MH-53 began reducing power, easing down incrementally in the thick jungle air. The DEA forward operating base or FOB was constructed of earth and light materials. The mix of simple buildings and tents gave the impression that the site was a mining operation instead of a secret counter-narcotics base.

The United States had a vested interest in interdicting the flow of coca leaves or coca paste from Colombia to processing centers in Mexico. This was accomplished, in partnership with the Colombian Army, by using American surveillance technology to detect coca fields and their associated harvest camps.

Once the coca leaves were mashed, they were transported along thousands of tiny jungle trails, traffic nearly impossible to distinguish from the normal movement of legitimate farmers.

Once the coca-growing areas were discovered, the Colombian Army took over. They used a wide range of methods to totally destroy the crops and timed it so there was little to no time left in the growing season to reconstitute the lost crop. Ground forces descended into the camps and continued the process of destroying the product that had been harvested but not transported.

Matt and his team were landing at camp twenty-six for only a few minutes. As much as he would love to get out of the helicopter and explore the FOB, talk to the DEA agents, and learn about their operations, the crew chief had told the three SEALs in mid-flight that they would not be exiting the aircraft during the ten-minute refueling event.

The MH-53 stopped its forward twenty feet above the metal plates marking the landing pad. The pilots descended slowly, losing altitude a few feet at a time until it finally settled on the metal landing pad and stopped moving.

The rotors continued to spin at a low rate of rotation as Matt watched a four-man team pull a long black fuel hose from the large flexible fuel storage container nearby.

The field storage devices being used to refuel the aircraft were called fuel blivets. The flexible storage containers could be delivered by boat, truck, or were transportable by air, sling-loaded under a helicopter. Their thick rubber walls were strong enough to hold the liquid and not leak or burst when handled roughly or dropped from less than forty feet in the air.

Matt checked the digital map on his tablet. They were close, only a short flight away from their primary river insertion point, designated by the code word SPLASH. He estimated that adding together the time left in the refueling exercise and the transit time to SPLASH, he and his team had thirty minutes left until feet wet.

As always, Matt ran through the mission from front to back, checking off each critical element to ensure for the last time that nothing was overlooked. Once finished, he relaxed. Maybe he could catch a cat nap before SPLASH.

He saw that his two partners were having no problem relaxing. Boone and Oby were passed out; enlisted SEALs could fall asleep anywhere, another skill learned at BUD/S. Get some shut eye whenever and wherever you can.

The helicopter finished fueling. The crew and pilots went through their pre-flight checks and, when satisfied, confirmed again that their cargo and passengers were secure before lifting gently into the air. The MH-53 hovered for a moment, slowly twisting to the right.

Once aligned with their navigation heading, the helicopter tilted forward, accelerating rapidly as it climbed. Matt felt the sensation in the pit of his stomach. Now he could finally enjoy a little naptime. The crew chief would wake the team with plenty of time to prepare before insertion.

The area on either side of the river was mountainous. The helicopter pilots believed it should be possible to slide in under the Colombian civil and military RADAR by following the river basin and staying below the ridgelines on either side of their course. The Americans needed to conduct the insertion without tipping off the highly unreliable Colombian military.

The MH-53 was equipped with technology that muffled and muted the sound of its engines. The pilots also were flying with night-vision goggles. There were no safety lights or navigation lights of any kind operating on the aircraft during this mission flight.

Intelligence experts supporting the mission planning had determined that if the helicopter dropped down low enough in the river valley, the terrain would provide additional dampening of the noise made by the big titanium blades.

The MH-53 dropped down every ten minutes in increments of five hundred to a thousand feet. Once they were ten miles upriver of the drop point, they descended one last time to settle into a low, terrain-contouring flight path only fifty feet above the dark jungle below. The pilot pushed the throttle forward and followed the dark green ribbon of water visible through his night-vision goggles.

Matt felt the jump in speed and woke up. Oby also was awake. At this speed, they should be at the drop point in less than ten minutes. He trusted the crew to keep him in the loop, but he was wide awake now and planned to monitor their flight progress actively from here on out, even as he suited up and prepared to leave the helicopter.

Matt woke Boone by jabbing an elbow into the point man's ribs. Boone had fallen into a deep sleep, so he woke up disoriented and groggy. Oby, Boone, and Matt checked the critical equipment connections one more time to ensure that everything was in its proper place. The crew chief stood by his station near the nose of the canoe, ready to pull the quick release on the green light.

Boone stood up and went back to the canoe to retrieve his vest and weapon. Oby and Matt waited in the cramped environment, then took turns accessing the mission gear in the boat. It only required five minutes before all three SEALs were dressed and ready. The crew chief walked over to the recon team and flashed four fingers, four minutes until arrival at the drop point.

The SEALs took turns going to the tail ramp and charging their M-4 rifles by placing a live round in the chamber. Next they made comms checks with each other on the tactical network. The waterproof, VHF radios were encrypted and connected to a light headset. The headset had an earpiece for one ear and a waterproof, adjustable boom microphone.

Matt checked the UHF radio, his link to tactical air support, and received a solid copy from the pilot up front. The SATCOM radios were checked before takeoff back in Panama. Matt would use them to pass the execution checklist code words, so the operations folks could track their status against the mission timeline and key milestones. The SPLASH call would be passed by the helicopter pilot as soon as the SEALs inserted.

The time remaining burned off quickly, and before Matt knew it, the crew chief was giving him the one-minute warning. Boone and Oby removed the extra cargo straps holding down the canoe and stashed them to the side. Each man inspected the sides of the boat to ensure nothing would block or inhibit its movement off the trailer when the time came.

Matt positioned himself at the tongue of the trailer and placed his hand on the release mechanism. Once at the drop point, the helicopter would hover four feet over the river and allow itself to move forward slowly, while at the same time lifting the nose up at an thirty degree angle. This would allow the canoe to slide off the trailer's roller system using gravity, that is once Matt pulled the release mechanism.

The big bird stopped in mid-air and pivoted around until it was facing back the way they'd flown in. The pilot eased the speed up a few knots to assume the drop parameters for the boat launch. He smoothly brought the helicopter down to ten feet above the river.

The crew chief signaled to the SEALs that they had thirty seconds to go. Matt took off his headset and gave the crew chief a thumbs-up. He gestured for Boone and Oby to get behind him. Once the boat began to roll out of the helicopter the three SEALs would follow in single file down the right side of the boat trailer.

A few seconds later, the crew chief moved back out of the way, and Matt turned his attention to the red and green stoplight positioned near the ramp entrance. He took a deep breath and let it out. The green light flashed on and Matt pulled the release mechanism. They were committed.

Chapter Thirty-Two

Bogota, Colombia

Chavez arrived in Bogota, traveling by armed motorcade from a small military airfield outside the city to his personal residence downtown. The final phase of his plan was about to unfold. Now the stage was set for the final moment of vengeance. This last act had to be completed face-to-face, his family honor demanded no less.

Chavez made arrangements to be escorted on foot through the jungle to the base camp on the Ariari River where General Alexander was being held. Flying by helicopter was far too dangerous.

The Americans or Colombian Special Forces would track the flight and pounce. The jungle patrol would take longer, but it was a safe way to get to the camp undetected. Once in the camp, he'd have the pleasure of executing the man who'd ordered the death of his only son.

Chavez had many informants within the US intelligence agencies. They were telling him the Americans were convinced the general was being held somewhere inside the city of Bogotá. That was a good thing. Their technology and rescue forces would be focused on the wrong place.

They also passed on that the Americans believed the soldier taken hostage with the general after the ambush was dead. Chavez didn't care about the soldier, but his men had made it clear to the uneducated morons living in the jungle that General Alexander was not to be harmed.

Nobody in the Colombian military was trying too hard to find the Americans. A little money in the right places, a few threats here and there, and the Colombian military was firmly in Chavez's back pocket. Most of the military leaders who would have opposed him hesitated to do so when they remembered how swiftly he'd dealt with the Colombian pilots who participated in killing his son.

The Colombian military wanted to end the violence in their country, but they were afraid to face the terror of Chavez's organization. So, they played their part well, showing the Americans a feigned interest in searching for the hostages while at the same time improving their personal wealth, capitalism at its best. Chavez was told the bogus government search effort was reported daily to the US ambassador in Bogotá. He was sure the Americans found comfort in this level of local commitment.

The hotel phone rang. Chavez picked it up and listened for a moment before slowly placing the receiver back on its cradle. His escort was in position and everything was in order. He went to his luggage and pulled a set of well-worn camouflage fatigues that he knew would help him blend in with his escort.

It'd been many years since he'd patrolled through the jungles of his homeland. It might be tough on him, the jungle was an unforgiving place; but he was determined to show the men of his escort that once a warrior, always a warrior.

Tocumen Airport – Republic of Panama

The C-141 transporting FOXTROT Platoon to Central America touched down and taxied for ten minutes toward the commercial side of the airport facility. Cargo trucks waited near a cluster of large hangars, apparently waiting for the air force cargo plane to stop moving in front of them.

An air force sergeant in civilian clothes waved the aircraft into its final position, giving the pilot arm gestures that signaled him to stop and shut down once they'd arrived on the mark. Jared looked out through the small window trying to ascertain their location related to the tower and the main terminal.

As briefed, the commercial hangars were well away from the tourists and business flyers. A twenty-foot concrete barrier stood between the three hangars in front of the C-141 and the rest of the airport. Once on the ground, his platoon would be difficult, if not impossible, to observe.

The tail ramp lowered and the sides of the tail split open, peeling back to create a large opening at the back of the plane. A bright yellow forklift promptly rolled up and was so quick it startled the crew chief, who jumped off the tail ramp and signaled frantically for the forklift to stop.

Jared was informed by the crew chief that his team had at least ten minutes of post-flight checks and cargo preparation before they'd be ready to begin the offload process. Jared laughed. The air force was so precise and focused on their rules. Then again, that approach probably paid off when you were trying to keep a plane in the air.

Six minutes later, the crew chief walked over to Chief Sampson. The chief nodded and then turned to the SEALs of FOXTROT Platoon and gave the men the signal to unbuckle and grab their personal packs. He looked over at Jared. "You going to join us, lieutenant?"

Jared was going over the phone call with the Group One Operations officer for the tenth time since leaving San Clemente Island. The request to be removed from the rescue mission was the right thing to do, yet he felt it had only served to put a black mark against himself, the chief, and the platoon.

Jared snapped out of his funk and unbuckled his seat belt. He stood up, snatching his pack off the seat next to him as he did so. "You seem to be in quite a hurry, chief."

Sampson shrugged. "We got more sleep in this machine than we've had in the last two days. These guys are still loopy. I want them fed and in the rack, as soon as that can happen."

Jared walked up to the chief and waited as he watched the enlisted leader direct the platoon to exit using the forward side door instead of the tail ramp. "There's enough crazy going on back there, gents! No need to add another sixteen swinging dicks to the problem."

Jared and his chief watched until everyone was gone, then looked around one last time to make sure nothing was left behind in the cargo area. "I think we're good to go, chief."

Sampson nodded, then, having satisfied himself that all was in order, he led the way through the side exit and into the thick Panamanian air. Jared followed his chief down the steps to the concrete taxiway below. The rest of FOXTROT Platoon stood twenty yards off to the side. One of the men waved Chief Sampson over.

"What's up?"

"Chief, that lady over there, the hot looking one to the left of the forklift, she told us to get our ass into the hangar; but I wasn't doing anything until you directed us to move."

Jared spotted the attractive woman and noted she wasn't wearing a uniform. "Spook?" he guessed.

"Fuck if I know, sir. Could be the agency, but whoever she is she'll make this place just a little bit easier to endure." The chief winked at Jared.

Jared waved the chief forward. "It's okay. Let's get everybody out of the sun."

FOXTROT Platoon moved with a purpose toward the big doors. As he got closer, Jared could make out multiple cargo containers and a beehive of activity inside. This was the real deal. He stopped at the entrance and waited until all his men were inside, and that's when he met Captain Singer.

"Welcome to the mission isolation area, lieutenant!" The army captain was built low to the ground, probably a college wrestler, Jared thought to himself. He took the offered hand and shook it.

"My men are tired, but eager to get briefed. We were in iso status in California and assumed our target area was the Philippines; clearly that is wrong."

The captain nodded. "Your confusion makes sense, lieutenant. Major Lane Sanchez is the lead on mission background, weather, and enemy order of battle. She's air force. You probably saw her outside when you arrived."

Jared raised his eyebrows. The hot Latina lady wasn't a spook after all. If all air force women looked like her, he might have to consider a cross-service transfer. He followed the captain to a container and was told to drop his gear next to the pile of SEAL backpacks already piled up in front of the metal box.

"Your team is over there, by the large refrigeration units. We have your mission bio-planning down to the calorie, and we have your sleep cycle programmed for peak efficiency. First, you eat, then the general briefing, then a nap. We'll get into the details of the operation this evening."

The captain shook Jared's hand and left him alone. Jared watched him walk away and then looked around for the attractive major. If she was the intel resource, maybe she'd share a preview of the job right now.

Jared saw the major speaking with an enlisted airman near the back corner of the hangar. He strolled over, casually soaking in the environment's sounds and smells. The smells were pretty strong.

Lane spotted him walking in her direction, and Jared noted her attempt to focus her attention on what was in front of her. Ten feet away, Jared stopped and politely waited his turn. She was worth waiting for.

Chapter Thirty-Three

River infiltration point, Ariari River, Colombia

As rehearsed, the weight of the canoe forced it to roll cleanly off the boat trailer. Matt, Oby, and Boone moved, trying to keep pace with the speed of the canoe's departure.

They didn't want to fall too far behind and become separated from their boat in the dark. All three of them remembered to crouch down as they were exiting the aircraft to avoid smacking their head on the upper portion of the exit door.

Matt wasn't ready for the warm water hitting his body. It felt like a comfortable bath, he thought, struggling back to the surface. He spotted the bobbing heads of his two partners and moved with several powerful strokes toward the silhouette of the canoe. Thankfully the canoe had landed right side up.

Matt, Oby, and Boone reached the canoe at the same time. Matt and Boone grabbed the boat and stabilized one side to allow Oby to crawl inside. He quickly checked the equipment and gave Matt a thumbs-up. They were in luck; nothing had fallen out during the insertion.

Matt realized he couldn't hear the helicopter at all anymore. That was a positive sign. The aircraft was loud, but once it was around the bend in the river the trees muffled the noise surprisingly well. I guess that part worked the way it was supposed to, he thought. Boone climbed into the canoe, then Boone and Oby helped Matt scramble into his position in the middle of the boat.

Boone and Oby spent the next two or three minutes untying the outboard engine and getting it into position at the aft end of the boat. The dugout was flat, providing a transom for the outboard motor.

The motor was lowered onto this section of the boat and screwed into place. The lower part of the engine was then placed into the river. Oby messed around with the engine cover for a minute or so while Matt checked his watch.

They were right on schedule. Boone and Matt both had donned their night-vision goggles or NODs, and their weapons were in their hands. Each SEAL took a bank of the river and scanned both sides of the shoreline, pointing their M-4 rifles at the darkness. Although the engine wasn't running yet, the canoe was staying midstream, pushed rapidly toward their objective by the current.

The rough coughing sound of the outboard engine coming to life startled Matt. For the ruse to be effective, the three SEALs must look and sound like locals moving down the river on their way downstream. Matt lowered his rifle so it couldn't be seen from the riverbank and placed it across his lap, but he kept the barrel pointed outward. Boone saw his leader and followed suit.

Matt was concerned. Had they done too good a job making the engine sound like an old piece of crap? The outboard didn't sound like it was going to make it much further than the next bend. Boone reached inside the equipment pack stowed near his legs in the bow of the boat and pulled out a small transmitter.

The communications device was just like the beacons carried by US pilots for search and rescue response. He pushed a rubber-coated button, and the beacon began emitting a pre-designated signal, specially coded to indicate the SEALs were safely in the canoe and en route to the target. The execution checklist code word was PADDLEWHEEL.

Somewhere out there someone was noting the beacon and crossing the code word off the list after noting the time it occurred. The beacon had the added benefit of marking their exact location; satellites, drones, even strike aircraft could see where they were and track their progress to the camp.

The beacon was a great way to communicate the situation on the ground without spending too much time exchanging verbal signals. Matt didn't need confirmation that the signal had been heard. It was only sent to make the boys back at headquarters feel warm and fuzzy about the progress of the reconnaissance mission.

He knew there was a fifty-fifty chance their mission had been compromised by the loud insertion event. If it was, the easiest way to take the SEALs out was to hit them with a river ambush. The guerillas would radio ahead and set up where the canoe had to slow down as it curved around a tight bend.

Matt caught himself; there wasn't necessarily an ambush up ahead and the bad guys here were not JSOC superheroes. These guys were farmers converted to poor riflemen by people who didn't understand tactics or how to fight an elite American unit.

Too often SEALs allowed the opposing force to grow in size and capability in their minds. The normal result was overplanning and overloading men with too many bullets that resulted in slowing down their mobility, a key requirement in a fast-moving firefight. They weren't compromised, and they had darkness and the element of surprise on their side.

The recon team traveled down the Ariari River at a fairly quick clip with the steady current helping them. That was a good thing. Matt didn't want to arouse suspicion by pushing the outboard hard enough to draw attention. The average Joe out there wouldn't push their precious engine just to go home or to go fishing. In this part of the world, things moved slowly anyway.

The three navy men rode in silence for the next thirty minutes. Matt's GPS indicated that they were making a solid five knots in speed. He had to be careful not to get too close to the camp or overshoot the position. He was about to tell Oby to slow down when Boone poked Matt, jabbing him in the shoulder to gain his attention.

Boone pointed to the bottom of the boat. "Aqua!" he said, with a poor Spanish accent. "Mucho aqua!" he continued, sounding alarmed.

Matt looked but wasn't able to see anything in the inky darkness. He reached down with his hand and felt around. His fingers found six inches of river water lying in the bottom of the canoe. The scooped-out interior of the canoe was shallow.

The design allowed enough room for a few people, sitting one behind the other, the walls of the cayuca were only twenty-four inches above the bottom of the boat. Any leakage could be a big problem.

Matt didn't understand how water possibly could have seeped or slopped into the boat. He leaned forward and whispered to Boone, "You think this is from the drop?"

Boone considered it for a moment then shook his head. "No way, boss. When I was scrambling around looking for the radio, it was bone dry down there. The water's been rising steadily for the last thirty minutes."

Matt reached outside the edge of the canoe to feel how much freeboard there was between the top of the canoe and the river's surface. The canoe was noticeably lower. There was no accurate way for him to determine how fast the water was coming in or whether it was still coming in.

Oby couldn't hear what the other two were whispering about, so he reached out and kicked Matt in the leg. Matt scooted backward to get closer to the sniper.

"What the hell's going on?"

"The canoe has water in it," Matt said. "Hey, look out!" Oby had inadvertently steered to the right when Matt started speaking, causing Matt to duck a low-hanging tree branch.

"Make sure you keep this thing in the middle of the river."

Oby shoved the tiller hard over to the right, moving the canoe away from the dark line of jungle foliage at the edge of the river. He moved back into the river and resumed course. Then he leaned forward.

"Okay, so there's water. It's probably from the insertion."

"It is not from the drop," Matt said. "Boone said it was bone dry when he went for the radio half an hour ago, and it's getting worse."

In the time it took to discuss the leak, the water had risen another inch. If the wet stuff kept coming in at this rate, they'd be sitting in a bathtub within ten minutes.

"Boys, I think we're sinking." Boone expressed his alarm louder than a whisper, but it went unnoticed by the others.

Oby was first to pose a plausible theory. "You know, these boats are supposed to be waterproof. They're carved from one tree trunk, then put in the water so the wood can swell up. I mean they are virtually unsinkable."

Matt countered, "Yeah, yeah, yeah. I know all that, but we still have water coming in."

Oby continued, "Boss, we had this canoe out of the water for a good two or three days. It's possible this thing just dried out. I mean, consider how many cuts and cracks this boat has. It's likely the water seeped right through since the wood shrank in the heat. You know, I didn't think to check the bottom of the boat once it was staged on the trailer."

Matt moaned, "Shit, Oby, I see what you mean!" Meanwhile, Boone was getting tired of trying to decipher the quiet debate going on in the back of the boat.

"What the hell are you guys talking about?" said Boone. Matt leaned forward to bring his frustrated point man up to speed.

"Oby thinks we left the boat out on the trailer too long and it dried out. The holes and dings in the bottom of the boat would have gotten bigger once the wood shrank in the sun."

Boone nodded in the dark. "Makes sense. So we are a bunch of dumb shits! Now what? Do you think this thing's going to swell back up in time?"

Matt checked the depth of the water in the boat again; it was now ten inches high. "I don't think so," Matt said to Boone. "It looks like we're going to be swimming and sooner rather than later."

"Sir, why don't we try to increase the speed of the boat and get as much distance as we can before it sinks completely?" Oby asked from the back of the boat.

Matt smiled; that was a great idea. They were still a good five miles out from the target. Every mile forward on the river closed the distance to the camp and reduced the possibility they'd have to abort the mission.

"That sounds like a plan, Oby. Go ahead and accelerate; but if that outboard starts making a racket, slow down. We need to eat up the distance, but we also don't want to wake up the neighbors."

Oby throttled up and the canoe reacted. Although the three men traveled in silence, Matt had a million problems flying through his mind. Using the LAR Five scuba was out of the question now.

There wasn't any guarantee they'd be able to find them later so they'd have to destroy their capability to operate and sink them with the boat. Could they swim with all their equipment to the objective, still using the river's current to help them or should they go on land and hump through the jungle?

Chapter Thirty-Four

In BUD/S training, every SEAL candidate had to swim five nautical miles. Five nautical miles was the equivalent of about seven land miles. If they could get another mile or so out of the boat, they'd be within reasonable swimming distance with the current in their favor. It would be the same as BUD/S, except they had three times as much crap strapped onto their bodies and at BUD/S nobody was shooting at you.

Boone must have been thinking along the same lines. He moved closer to Matt and whispered in his ear, "Well, boss, at least we don't have to worry about navigation, just point our nose downstream and start stroking!"

Matt agreed, "Yeah, and the river current will make the trip much shorter timewise. What do you think, do we need every piece of gear or should we strip down the loadout a little?"

Boone studied the question for a moment before answering. "Sir, I think we should keep everything with us except the dive rigs, of course. It's all waterproof and neutrally buoyant. All we should have to do is tow it along behind us or lay on top of it and float. We may need all that stuff before this job's over."

Matt made the decision. "Okay, Boone, we'll take all the equipment." By now, the water had risen up to their waists. Luckily it was warm; SEALs hated cold water. "Take your fence cutter and start disabling the LAR Fives. When you're done, start handing out our gear so we can rig up while we're still afloat."

Boone complied with Matt's order, disabling the scuba rigs so they would have to be rebuilt by an expert before they were functional again. Next, he untied the mission bags, and in turn handed them to Matt and Oby. Matt received his and snapped it into his combat vest.

Isolation Hangar – Panama

A JSOC officer Jared hadn't seen around the hangar approached Jared as he was walking away from the dining area, his belly happily full. The navy commander carried a large package under his left arm. Jared stopped and waited until the commander smiled and extended his hand. Jared shook it, but his eyes never left the package.

"Here you go, lieutenant," the commander said, handing Jared the large yellow envelope. "You now have all the frequencies and communications information you'll need to conduct your operation. As you know, the reconnaissance mission has been launched already, and we received the insertion and underway codewords right on schedule."

"When will the recon be in a position to begin reporting what they see on the ground?" Jared asked.

"Good question. We expect to begin receiving a real-time feed of target data in four to five hours. For now, you're to focus on planning your infiltration. The helicopter crews are at your disposal. Ask for any other information that you need from us to complete your analysis or to support your mission planning. Use any information the reconnaissance team provides you to modify how you might strike the target. You don't have a lot of time, lieutenant. I suggest that your men get as much rest as they can when they can."

Jared nodded, quietly taking the package, "Yes, sir, thank you." Chief Sampson walked up as the staff officer departed.

"Problems, sir?" he asked.

Jared watched the staff officer leave the hangar. "What's that, chief?"

"Never mind, lieutenant. So what's the good news?"

"I have the comms package." Jared patted the envelope. "When all the guys are done eating, have them muster over there, the corner of that storage container. I'll go and find that air force major. It's time we were briefed on this gig."

Twenty minutes later, Jared and the rest of FOXTROT Platoon were snuggled into the long metal cargo container that was designated the secure planning and briefing room.

Major Sanchez stood at the front of the room, very aware of the sixteen pairs of eyes scanning every inch of her body. Matt knew she was a distraction, but all he cared about at this moment was her information.

Lane took a deep breath and began to walk through the weather indications for the next ninety-six hours. Weather in the Colombian jungle was based on the seasons more than pressure fronts and offshore storms. It was the end of the rainy season, so their helicopter flight should be workable for the duration of the mission window.

Then she segued to the background profiles of the key people involved. The first face to flash up on the smart TV's screen was an older man in an army uniform, an officer, a general.

"The FBI and CIA both believe General Alexander was targeted as part of a vendetta. The justification appears to be personal and not business. The general was involved in ordering an attack on FARC and Colombian assets associated with the drug kingpin known as Hernando Chavez."

The name meant little to Jared. He'd spent the last few years going through the SEAL training pipeline, BUD/S, SQT, then a platoon deployment to the SEAL detachment in Guam. The Central America game was all SEAL Team Four's responsibility.

Lane flashed a new picture. The man was in his early thirties, handsome and athletic. He was wearing polo gear.

"Hernando Chavez made his way up the Pablo Escobar organization as a mule, then as a hit man. He learned fast and made a name for himself.

As reward Escobar gave Chavez the Bogotá market. By age twenty-eight he was on top. Escobar was captured by US special operations and extradited to America. Chavez fought for two years to defeat the competition and ended up on top."

"He looks like a rich guy. Polo, really?" One of Jared's men pointed out the obvious and the disconnect. If Chavez was a street hood who killed his way to the head of the Colombian cartel, why the façade?

The major nodded. "This picture is dated. We do not have an image of what he looks like now. Once Chavez was in control, he got married, had a child and attempted to become accepted in upper-class society. This is a picture of him in Venezuela, where he was a fairly good player from what we can gather."

Chief Sampson was getting irritated. The pace of the brief was glacier slow, and so far, none of the information aided them in their mission planning. "With all due respect, major, who gives a shit about his pony riding skills. When are you going to get to the mission?"

Jared felt the same way, but he winced at the tone used by his platoon chief. "What he's trying to say, major, is we've been fed shit and kept in the dark about this op from the moment we were recalled and stuck on San Clemente Island. Can you answer the chief's question? Is this information relevant?"

Lane kept her cool and looked down for a moment. When she looked up, she looked straight at the chief. "Chavez ordered the ambush that killed several Special Forces soldiers. He ordered and directed the kidnapping of the general and your teammate, Senior Chief Auger.

"Over the last two days, his hit teams have brutally executed the general's daughter and son and their children. It is

206

the CIA's opinion from their profile of this asshole that he will go to the FARC camp and execute General Alexander himself. Is that relevant enough for all of you?"

Chief Sampson kept a straight face, but he knew he had just been subtly called an idiot. "My apologies, major. Please continue. There will be no further interruptions."

Lane smiled. SEALs were straight shooters in more ways than one. "Not to worry, chief. My wind up may have been a bit slow. Now for the last key profile, Senior Chief Auger."

Jared listened to the list of Auger's deployments and decorations. He was impressed. This guy had been around the block and then some. No wonder he'd taken the personal protection assignment; he probably needed a break. Some break.

When Lane finished, Jared raised his hand. "What can you tell me about the recon team?"

The Ariari River – Colombia

The SEALs were following their standard operating procedure of keeping their combat vests open at the waist and chest. Frogmen learned long ago that it's impossible to get all the stuff off of you if you start to sink under the weight. The crisscrossed straps added to the mess, making staying above water a difficult proposition.

They had checked their equipment and added foam blocks or thin foam pads here and there to offset the weight, making the loadout neutrally buoyant. If they did their rehearsal preparation correctly, then the three of them wouldn't end up on the bottom of the river.

Once their personal gear was ready and the mission equipment was snapped into their vests, Matt indicated to Oby by pointing. It was time to drive the boat over to the right side of the river and disembark.

Oby reduced the thrust of the outboard and glided to the right until he was bumping up against the low-hanging tree branches. Once up against the riverbank, all three of them started getting smacked by the trees and vines they couldn't see, even wearing NODs.

Matt signaled it was time to get out by simply rolling himself over the side. The boat didn't require stabilizing; it was almost underwater as it was. Getting out of the boat was a trick. Muddy bottom, swirling current, and trying to stop the boat long enough to jump out.

Oby unscrewed the outboard motor from the transom, disconnected it from the fuel bladder, and dumped it over the back into the river. It sank immediately. Then he grabbed the fuel can, took off the cap, and dropped it into the river, too.

Boone took a piece of five-fifty nylon para-cord and tied off the boat to a low hanging branch, picking a spot further back on the branch under the leaves to hide the line. The river was supposed to be no more than fifteen feet in the dry season and twenty-five feet during the rainy season.

He allowed for twenty feet of parachute cord. That way the boat would sink but not go anywhere. There was always a chance someone would come back for the LAR Fives.

Oby slid into the water and joined Boone and Matt hanging on to the para-cord. When Matt saw Oby enter the water, he gave his instructions. "All right, guys, we stay in physical contact. We don't have buddy lines connecting us to each other, so grab the man next to you with one hand and hold on. If we get separated out here in the dark, we'll never get back together again."

"That's for damn sure," Boone muttered under his breath.

Matt kept talking. "We're going to float down the river hugging the right-hand side. We still have the fins in our equipment bags, so let's take turns putting them on right now."

Oby unsnapped the fins from the side of his equipment pack and put them on one at a time while Boone held on to his equipment harness. Once his fins were donned, Oby smacked Boone on the shoulder, holding him while Boone went through the drill.

Matt was the last to put his fins on while Boone made sure he didn't float away from the group. The canoe was almost completely underwater now and painfully banged up against their knees.

Once all of them were ready, Matt checked his watch. "Okay, don't stroke hard, let the current do most of the work. Boone, Oby, let's go."

Base Camp–The Ariari River

Auger's head snapped up. He was having a great dream about his high school girlfriend when the commotion in camp woke him. Down the hill and to his left there was a flurry of activity that after a moment he realized weren't sounds associated with a rescue force hitting the guerillas.

Oddly enough, he didn't feel threatened in the camp. He'd been in his cage for several days, and for the most part his captors had kept their distance. He twisted his head to look down through the vertical slats of his prison and he saw that two gentlemen that he didn't recognize had entered the camp.

The strangers were talking excitedly to the other guerrillas around them and more men were gravitating toward the group to listen. One man yelled a name that brought even more men to the huddle.

The senior chief couldn't hear the words being spoken down below; and even if he could, his Spanish was restricted to Chipotle dishes. But he didn't need a degree in the language to understand the word yelled by the men in the camp, the name Chavez.

Senior Chief Auger wasn't an intel-type, but he wasn't an idiot either. He knew who Chavez was by deed and reputation. Anybody working in the southern command area of operations knew about the notorious Colombian drug lord. Auger guessed there were only two plausible reasons for the excitement below. Either Chavez was dead or he was coming to the camp.

A contingent of ten guerrillas was pulled aside by a man Auger hadn't seen before. Within minutes, the ten men linked up with the apparent leader. He watched them separate from the others and make their way down to the riverbank. Once there, they began filling their canteens with water.

A few minutes later several women approached them carrying armloads of food. The guerillas stuffed the food into their pockets. These guys were preparing to leave camp for a while.

Was this the welcoming committee? He leaned back and rubbed his neck. Anything that reduced the enemy strength in camp was a good thing, he mused. Fewer assholes to kill when the cavalry arrived, a higher probability of a short fight, and that was a plus for the good guys.

The senior chief could hear the general's strained breathing nearby as he slept. The old guy hadn't said much today. Auger wondered if it was fatigue, depression, or a combination of both that kept the older man so quiet.

General Alexander wasn't a whiner, but it worried Auger that the guy was sleeping so much. Sleeping too much was also a sign of concussion. Lord knows the general had suffered a lot of vicious blows to his head during the long trek in the jungle.

On the other hand, he was thankful he didn't have to hand hold the officer through his ordeal. That would have been irritating as hell. Auger smiled, remembering how the navy pilots gravitated to the SEALs in SERE school, looking for leadership and tips on how to cope.

SEALs were selected for traits inconsistent with flying a technologically-advanced fighter aircraft, but they were perfectly suited to endure a game of fuck, fuck. During the POW course, Auger and the other prisoners were allowed to execute a mass breakout. Men ran in every direction, being expected to practice the survival and evasion skills taught in the classroom prior to the camp phase of the course.

While most of the pilots were solid and handled themselves well, a few always decided to follow a SEAL into the woods. Auger unfortunately had picked up three pilots as ducklings, impossible to shake and noisy as hell. They were detected by roving patrols and wrapped up within forty minutes of leaving the camp. He appreciated the general's mettle more than the old man could know.

Auger turned his attention once more to the patrol down by the river as it prepared to leave. Fifteen minutes later, the guy giving orders earlier joined them. He gave a short speech and turned on his heel.

The rest of the men fell in behind and walked out of the camp. According to his rough beer math, their departure reduced the number of effective shooters in the camp to about thirty. Auger didn't count the fifteen or so trainees or the camp serfs. That population wouldn't be an issue if an American force hit the camp.

If the boys were going to attempt a rescue, this would be a good time. Even worse, if they waited too long, the camp's firepower would be increased by whoever was coming with Chavez. If his theory was correct and they were meeting the drug lord to escort him back to camp, he'd have his own firepower and his force would reinforce the fighters in camp.

Auger believed in his heart that somewhere out there, there were snake eaters planning a rescue mission and there was no way he could get this information to them.

Chapter Thirty-Five

Auger looked around the edge of the jungle and then across the river to the other side. He'd spent a lot of his time evaluating the camp as a special ops target set. "That's where I would be right now if I was watching this camp," he said under his breath. "You can see the whole horseshoe shape of the encampment from right there."

Auger had planned the rescue assault in great detail many times while sitting in his cage. A sniper positioned across the river with the observation team could reach out and touch five, maybe ten targets in less than three minutes. That would be the signal to the assault force to attack, sweeping from left to right across the open space, engaging all the targets the sniper didn't eliminate.

In his mind, it was always a one-sided fight and always over quickly. It'd be a piece of cake, he thought. Come in, hose everybody down who isn't an American, and let God sort them out. That is unless the general was correct and they sent in Rangers. Then the rescue would become a fifty-fifty toss-up. A real Wild West show.

No precision shooting required, just maximum firepower and lots of shit blowing up and burning. Either way. Auger wasn't picky. He didn't care if a troop of heavily armed Boy Scouts took the camp down; he just wanted out.

A black cloud interrupted Auger's thoughts, a feeling that he was wrong. The little voice in his mind had been growing in power and volume for several days. Its message was always the same. Nobody knew where he was and nobody was ever going to come to save him. In a nutshell, he was truly fucked.

Five miles from camp – Ariari River

They each grabbed the other with one hand and let go of the boat. Within seconds the cayuca was gone, behind them somewhere in the dark. Matt and the two SEALs laid on their bellies in the dark water, floating like a human raft, scanning both riverbanks with their NODs.

The water was so warm it actually felt good to Matt. Warm was a lot better than the alternative. SEALs were known for their prowess over, on, and under the water. What wasn't so well-known was SEALs hated being cold, and the ocean was invariably always cold. If it wasn't the temperature, then it was the time in the water that sapped the heat from the body and turned a pleasant mission swim into a BUD/S torture session.

Matt's attention shifted to another irritant. His butt was numb from sitting on the hardwood of the cayuca. At least that was over; now he needed to concentrate on the time distance factor. If they swam hard, they'd be at the observation point ahead of schedule but way before first light.

If they just relaxed, saved their energy, and drifted with the current, they might meet the planned timetable and show up none the worse for wear. But if by drifting they fell behind schedule . . .

His best guess was they had between five and six miles of river to navigate before arriving at the guerrilla base camp. He decided to track their speed using the current for thirty minutes and then use his GPS to calculate their speed. That would give him the missing piece of the puzzle.

He could then plot the speed into the GPS, apply it to the target location, and query the GPS for a time on station estimate. If they were moving too slow to meet his planned arrival time, he'd have the three of them kick it out and turn on the afterburners.

The three men continued to float in silence, kicking their fins once in a while to stay close to the riverbank. They tried laying on their equipment bags, then trailing them behind, and eventually ended up the way they'd begun. This posture also allowed the men to keep their weapons at the ready in front of them. It was decided by trial and error.

Matt and his teammates were wide awake and fully attuned to the reality that there were bad guys out there in the dark who would love to end their little midnight swim with a blast of gunfire. The next thirty minutes passed slowly. Matt checked the GPS, and after plugging in the time factor, the display showed they were making five knots.

That was really good, Matt thought. Then he applied five knots against the current position and time to target. The GPS display showed he was going to arrive at the feet dry point with forty minutes to spare. There was no need to swim; the current was doing their work for them.

Matt was the first one to recognize they were getting dehydrated when his calf cramped up so bad that he couldn't move his right leg. He whispered to Oby and Boone to start drinking water. He quickly followed his own advice, reaching down for his plastic canteen. Dumb mistake, Matt thought.

All SEALs knew that once you got inside the water, cold or warm, your body heat began to escape rapidly. Your body compensated by trying to change its fluid distribution to either cool down the body or warm it up. For the last hour or so, the three SEALs had been dumping body heat into the river, much of it through sweat.

Matt didn't feel chilled yet, but the river no longer felt like bathwater to him. Matt checked his watch; it was fifteen minutes after two in the morning. He'd wanted to be scouting the target observation point by four in the morning. At five knots they'd be exiting the river around three twenty.

After a long pull on his canteen, Matt returned to the task of scanning the riverbank and checking his watch. Everything looked the same in the jungle, even more so in the dark. He kept thinking they might miss the exit point and shoot right across and past the FARC. The strain of looking through the NODs and seeing little or no detail in the trees was causing a headache.

He felt the cramp in his left leg starting to relax and took that as a cue to drink more water. A few minutes later, the cramp went away completely. Their initial intent to avoid people along the shoreline by detecting campfires with the night vision equipment was working.

There was nothing out here generating a heat or light signature. Even if someone was sitting on the riverbank and awake, he doubted they'd see, let alone identify the dark blob that floated by. They maintained strict silence, whispering only when absolutely necessary. Matt glanced at his watch yet again; another thirty minutes and they would pull into the shore, just thirty more minutes.

Isolation hangar – Republic of Panama

The air force major's breakdown of the recon team was thorough and impressive. The three SEALs were hardcore combat vets, solid operators, and more importantly, they'd worked together as a team before. This Matthew Barrett was impressive in his own right.

A senior lieutenant probably up for lieutenant commander very soon, Jared guessed. A planner, a thinker, and a proven war leader. Jared waited for the brief to end, but he'd made his mind up; FOXTROT Platoon was dealing with professionals they could rely on. Now came the waiting.

After the intelligence presentation, Jared walked outside the container and became immersed in his own thoughts. Chief Sampson exited the container and walked up to the lieutenant, waiting patiently for Jared to acknowledge him. Jared snapped out of his fog and smiled at his chief.

"Get a load of this heat! I think we should go touch base with the aircrew. Let the guys chill out for a while longer."

"Sounds good to me, LT. I'll have the rest of the platoon spread out in the hangar and stage their mission gear for a quick departure, then stand them down for a few hours. When do you want to visit the pilots?"

"As soon as you finish with the platoon. I'll wait here for you."

The chief spun around and made his way to the gang of young men nervously standing by the pile of equipment. Jared made a mental note to set aside enough time for one last personnel inspection of the group in full mission gear.

Jared wiped his brow with the back of his sleeve. Some of the men already were starting to look a little pink, he observed. The heat here was different than the desert. It was wet and sticky and seemed to suck the energy right of you.

Jared watched as Chief Sampson passed the word for everybody to drink as much water as they could hold. He knew from painful experience that dehydration snuck up on you when your body was preparing for battle. Anxious warriors forgot the basics. It was his job to remind them.

The heat just made it worse, of course. The chief directed everyone to add an extra canteen to their loadout. Jared knew they were already carrying about twenty-five pounds of water each. That might cause a little grumbling; but one thing was true about water, once you drank the precious liquid, you didn't have to carry it around anymore.

The SEAL officer walked over to a situation map pinned to a large bulletin board on the side of the container wall. The situation map showed the Ariari river area and the suspected location of the base camp where the two hostages were presumably being held.

The op plan was straightforward: let the recon team find and fix the FARC target and report. Passing the confirmation code phrase CHEESE WHIZ meant the American captives were located and that phase one was complete. That was FOXTROT's signal to board the two Blackhawks.

It would be a straight flight to the target from Panama, taking just over two hours. Once inserted near the target, the Blackhawk helicopters would climb up to a higher altitude, conduct an air refueling event, then drop down into a low orbit one mile from the camp.

The SEAL platoon would assault the target and rescue the two Americans. Once they were safe, phase two was complete. The phase three role of the Blackhawks was to provide fire support if needed and extract the team and the hostages when alerted to do so by the SEALs on the ground.

On a table nearby lay a metallic clipboard with the words Top Secret printed in large red letters. Jared flipped the top metal flap back to reveal three inches of intelligence message traffic relating to the operation.

He read the material with interest. The briefings had been excellent, but the underlying story unfolding in the United States and in Colombia hadn't been discussed fully. The messages made for tedious reading, but the details were there and worth the effort.

Ten minutes later Jared found a series of short messages covering the assassination of General Alexander's family. He read with sadness at first; but as the gory facts piled up, he became angry. He hoped Chavez was really coming to the camp to kill the general. That put him on a collision course with the United States and, more specifically, FOXTROT Platoon.

Chapter Thirty-Six

Jungle trail–Colombia

Even with the flashlights illuminating the ground, it was difficult to see where he was going. Chavez tripped for what seemed like the hundredth time on an unseen root reaching out across the path. He was getting too old for this shit.

For the young men who were escorting him, this was their way of life. To be comfortable in the jungle required time, and Chavez was out of practice, even growing soft in the last couple of years, flying wherever he wanted to go, a limousine taking him here and there.

His workout routine was strict; but he never pushed himself that hard, not this hard. They'd been moving on the jungle trail for three or four hours, taking only one fifteen-minute break. Chavez ran out of his water quickly, but the men around him weren't going to let "el jefe" suffer.

All he had to do was look thirsty, and he was offered a canteen. The escort patrol consisted of twenty-five fighters, warriors he'd paid for and nurtured at a distance. He knew they were aware of his patronage and felt proud to be chosen as a member of his escort.

Their plan was to continue moving through the night until somewhere near the camp they would link up with a group coming out from the base camp. The rendezvous point was near a large loop in the river, where the trail meandered to within fifty yards of the fast-moving water.

The loop was easily visible from the air and easy to identify when you were walking on the trail. Except for that terrain feature, the trail tended to follow a straight line moving north by northeast. Chavez peeked at his digital watch.

He still had a ways to go before the linkup. He knew he had to suck it up and put a good face on it. He must show these men that he was tough, tough like them. Chavez straightened his back and tried to walk with a sense of purpose.

Nobody seemed to pay attention. They were too absorbed in patrolling and professionally scanning the jungle for threats. A few more hours, he thought, a few more hours. The thought of putting a bullet in the brain of General Alexander suddenly gave him a second wind.

The Ariari River–Colombia

It was time. Matt reached across to squeeze Boone's shoulder. Boone nodded acknowledgment and repeated the gesture, giving Oby the signal to swing in toward the riverbank. They only had ten yards or so to swim before their feet touched the shallow muddy bottom.

The SEALs formed a triangle, with Oby focused on the potential threat from the jungle immediately above them. They spent five minutes at the water's edge, looking and listening. Trying to absorb the natural sounds and condition of the jungle after the numbing ride down the river.

Oby eased forward and leaned on the bank, extending his M-4 rifle. That was Boone's cue to exit the river and crawl ashore. He established a defensive position four feet to the left of Oby and squatted down. Oby next exited the water and stepped a few feet to the right before kneeling down.

Matt watched the quiet exercise in combat discipline until it was his turn. He exited the Ariari and took up a position between and just forward of the other warriors, created a new triangle. It was time to look and listen again.

The SEALs were known as violent commandos, sliding down fast ropes, zooming in on attack boats, and kicking down doors. The myth was far from reality. SEALs were thinking warriors, men who used anything and everything to gain an advantage.

Stealth was a key component in SEAL tactics. As the old-timers from Nam used to say, better to kill the bad guys in their beds than get into a pissing contest.

Matt took a quick look at his GPS display; as he did so, Oby moved forward a few feet to relieve Matt at point security. There wasn't a need to plan every move or give endless commands. His men knew what needed to be done. Endless hours of training had resulted in a feel for each other and the job that was instinctive.

They were shivering. They'd been in the water for a long time, and the light wind blowing down the river wasn't helping. To make matters worse, the three men had consumed nearly all their water. The muscle cramping was becoming a real problem, a problem they hadn't anticipated. Matt studied the digital readout and checked it one more time.

According to the GPS, the bearing from their position to the target was parallel with the river, but the distance was two hundred yards. He was surprised. He checked his figures one more time. It was hard to believe they could already be so close to the FARC base camp.

Maybe the intelligence guys plotted the camp's location incorrectly on the terrain map, or Matt's beer math on their speed of movement was way off. In either case, they were dangerously close to the enemy.

Matt gestured until Oby noticed and slid sideways to hear what Matt had to say. On the other side, Boone saw the movement and copied it, easing next to the lieutenant.

"The GPS has us two hundred yards upriver from the camp. I've checked it twice and there's no mistake."

"Next move, sir?" Oby whispered back.

Matt checked his watch. It was three forty-five in the morning. If they tactically moved through the jungle, it would take approximately an hour to move the two hundred yards. Once there, they would move into an observation position on the edge of camp and take a look.

A concern he had was visibility. They might have to go right up to the edge of the camp's jungle perimeter before seeing anything of value. The rising dawn was going to make it worse.

Matt wanted Boone's advice. Boone was a great point man, and he'd have an opinion on their ability to move through the dense cover and make the timeline. "Boone, can we make it through this mess in the time we have left?"

Boone thought for a second. "No, I doubt it. But I've got an idea, boss. Why don't we go back into the river and move down about another hundred yards or so? That should only take about ten minutes. Then we'd only have to patrol the remaining hundred yards through the jungle. By that time our NODs should pick up campfires and any other lights in the base camp. Then we'll move up to the edge of the jungle and establish an observation position. Of course, it's your call, LT."

Of course it was his call. Matt understood. It was always his call, his decision to make. What were the odds this camp was holding the American hostages? What were the odds Auger hadn't already been dumped off someplace on a jungle trail, an expendable piece of baggage? Matt struggled to erase the negative thoughts from his mind. He had to make a decision. The shivering wasn't helping.

"All right, guys, let's get back into the water. We'll swim until we can determine the position of the camp, then we'll go back onshore." Matt had a sudden inspiration. "What kind of range can we expect to get from the NODs?"

Oby answered for Boone, "You'll only be able to see campfires when we get sixty yards out."

Boone disagreed, "Forty yards is more like it, boss, especially with no moon through this dense growth."

Matt smiled in the dark. "Good, then that is what we will do. We won't move a hundred yards down river and get out. Instead, we'll keep moving down the river until we hear or see something; then we'll exit the water. That will give us more time to sneak into the observation position."

Matt heard whispered responses; they were onboard with the plan. "Boone, you take point. Oby and I will move behind you. We'll float and swim in single file. Maintain physical contact. Boone's responsible for looking forward and spotting the camp, I have left flank security, and Oby has the right side. All good?"

"You got it, boss!" Oby whispered.

"Roger that, sir." Boone was good to go.

The three SEALs eased back and into the river. The water seemed ten times colder now, Matt thought, sucking in his breath. They immediately took hold of each other's cammie pants with one hand and started down the river, swimming and bobbing and drifting their way closer to the enemy camp.

They stayed closer to the riverbank, and as a consequence, they were making contact with the muddy bottom and getting tangled in the loose vines dangling from trees that leaned out over the river. Matt suddenly had a thought: what kind of creatures were moving around in this muddy soup?

His imagination conjured up images of deadly schools of piranha staring at his legs and licking their little lips in anticipation. He didn't even know if there were any piranha in Colombia. He shut down the movie playing in his mind and focused on the right bank. He had a job to do.

Matt felt Oby's body shivering under his cammie shirt. They'd been in the water for a long time, no thermal protection and nothing warm to consume that might raise their core temperature.

He wasn't sure how early the dawn expressed itself here in the jungle. He glanced across the river from time to time to see if the treetops were visible from the growing backlight of the rising sun. Once that happened, daybreak would come fast.

At best they would have thirty to forty minutes to stalk through the underbrush and get into the recon observation point. The GPS map indicated that they would be on an elevated ridge to one side of the camp, allowing them to look down and see most of the activity there. He realized if they didn't get set up soon, he'd be flirting with the mission's expressed abort criteria.

Well, he was committed to trying, he thought. They owed it to Auger to make it work. While Matt was daydreaming, Boone had stopped. Matt bumped into his point man. Oby ran into Matt next. The three SEALs dropped their feet into the muck and crouched together, shivering, their weapons held at the ready.

Matt and Oby waited patiently for Boone's verdict. Instead of saying anything, Boone raised his right hand touching two fingers to his eyes. The hand and arm signal communicated that he was looking at the enemy.

Boone extended his index finger, pointing at the shoreline. He changed his hand position, spreading his fingers wide and slowly bringing them together until there was a very short distance between his fingertips and his thumb. That indicated the bad guys were very close, too close.

The shivering stopped immediately as the three SEALs forced their bodies, through force of will, to face the threat. Matt and Oby moved up alongside Boone. They both realized from the last hand signal that they must be so close that someone could hear or spot them at any time.

Once Matt was up next to Boone, he was able to see what Boone was seeing. Through the NODs, he watched three or four spots of light dancing and flickering through the trees. The spots of light he knew to be campfires from the way the light moved back and forth. He heard a sound that sounded like pots or pans being hit together. Then Matt saw the two men sitting on the edge of the river.

Chapter Thirty-Seven

Matt couldn't take his attention away from the two guerillas. They appeared to be sleeping, slumped against the trunk of a large tree. He reached to his left and squeezed Boone's shoulder. Boone watched as Matt placed his free hand against his neck and made a cutting motion.

Boone understood the command. He slid his hand across his chest and placed it on the rubberized grip of a pistol hanging under his left arm. Boone pulled the weapon out of its specially designed holster. The holster was extended to allow for the four-inch silencer.

Oby observed his friend's body language and eased his weapon up. He wouldn't open fire unless Boone failed to take out the two men on the riverbank. Boone raised the pistol an inch at a time until he was finally sighting down the short black barrel.

Normally, he'd double tap a target, placing two shots into each man. But he needed to finish these men in a total of just two rapidly aimed shots.

Boone squeezed the trigger, focusing on the front sight of the weapon. The pistol jumped in his hand as the first round was fired into the forehead of man on the left. Boone didn't wait to see the result of his marksmanship. He smoothly shifted his point of aim to the second man, taking up the trigger slack as he moved the weapon.

The pistol spit out the second shot, hitting the target squarely between the eyes. The quiet zipping of the bullets was as loud as the smacking sound their impact made. The jungle would absorb the louder sound of the automatic pistol's slide going back and forth as it fired, ejected a spent casing, chambered a second round, and fired. Both guerillas were dead and the SEALs were falling behind schedule.

Matt swept the shoreline one more time before turning off the night-vision scope. He didn't need to congratulate Boone. The point man knew this was only the beginning. Matt leaned toward Oby and cupped his hand around his ear.

He brought the sniper up to speed on what had transpired since the two guerillas weren't in his direct field of view. He then explained their next move. Matt then repeated the instructions to Boone.

Boone was to move down the shoreline closer to the camp. All three of the men knew they were in great jeopardy. Eventually, someone would come looking for the two dead men.

Once the alarm was sounded, the chance of rescue for General Alexander and Auger would be lost. The recon team's survival was also at risk; the three SEALs didn't have the firepower to fight a protracted battle if tracked down by searchers from the camp.

Matt had instructed Boone and Oby that, if detected before going onto land, the three of them should go under water and allow the river current to take them away from the camp.

That was the same plan for getting hit or spotted on land. Head back to the river and go under. It was a lame way to end a rescue operation, but Matt's responsibility was to preserve the lives of his two teammates as much as it was to recover the two American hostages. There were never any easy choices in combat.

They crawled up on the bank, repeating the security drill exercises earlier. Once the triangle was established, Matt gave Oby a little push. Oby stood up and began to patrol toward the flickering lights. Matt took one more look over his shoulder. The high trees on the opposite bank of the Ariari river were clearly silhouetted against a light pink sky. They weren't going to make the timeline.

Oby eased forward, step by painstaking step. Listening, scanning, and then moving. Matt had no exact idea of how far the perimeter of the camp might be, so he trusted in Oby's skills and watched his flank. For now, he was a rifleman.

After fifteen minutes, the dawn was bright enough it interfered with the NODs. Oby stopped and placed the headset in his side pouch. He waited for Matt and Oby to do the same. When they were ready, Matt squeezed Oby's arm.

Oby moved again, crouching more now that he didn't have the fires and lights of the camp to guide him. A few minutes later Oby froze. He raised his left hand up and made a fist signaling a reason to halt. Then he turned his hand over as if he was palming a basketball. It was the hand signal for a building; the recon team had arrived.

DEA Camp Twenty-Six - Colombia

FOXTROT Platoon was directed to exit the two aircraft and move to the far right of the landing pad. Jared watched the refueling operation, but from time to time he looked skyward. The little birds were late.

The Boeing MH-6 helicopters were a versatile aviation platform designed to carry a maximum of four men. They could be configured in ground-attack mode with rocket pods and machine guns added, but they were too light to carry a lot of ordnance.

Their preferred use was as a scout for route reconnaissance or as an airborne sniper platform. Two of Jared's long gunners stood off to the side of the platoon a little, waiting for their ride to the target.

A minute or so later, Jared saw rather than heard the small helicopters. They did look like little birds from this distance, he mused. The refueling hoses were being pulled back from the Blackhawks. The SEALs would wait until the little birds were on deck and loaded with the two snipers. Then Jared and the rest of the platoon would board the larger aircraft.

He checked the time, a quarter to five in the morning. Here on the raised plateau, it was easy to see the spreading light of the dawn across the far skyline.

It took another ten minutes for the little birds to top off their tanks, load, and be ready to lift off. The departure was dramatic: four black war birds powering up and surging into the Colombian sky. Jared watched the DEA camp get smaller and then disappear; that's when the warm, moist air of the jungle hit him.

He knew they weren't acclimated for this mission; he'd petitioned for FOXTROT to stand down to be replaced by another team more used to the environment, the tactics, and the climate. His request was shot down, and here he was, leading men into combat for the first time and knowing they weren't ready, not at their peak performance level.

The two MH-60 Black Hawk helicopters cruised side-by-side with the little birds trailing behind by fifty yards. The SEAL platoon and the insertion platforms had been advanced methodically by the mission coordinators in Tampa, Florida; but as they left the DEA camp, control was handed to a mobile special operations unit onboard the USS San Diego.

The USS San Diego was an amphibious transport dock designed from the keel up for advanced amphibious warfare support. Normally the San Diego carried a complement of Marines and their support capabilities, such as landing craft and helicopters; but it also served as the command vessel during amphibious landing operations.

The ship and its crew were now home to a JSOC command and control team and twenty Army Special Forces soldiers, staged onboard as a quick reaction force or QRF. If the

SEALs found themselves in deep shit, the green berets were the reinforcement force riding to their rescue.

Jared had the entire picture in his mind. The hand off the ship, the QRF, it all had been briefed to the SEALs in their isolation area back in Panama. It seemed too complicated to Jared; too many things could go wrong.

Chief Sampson was a student of war, and he frequently stated that too much help added too much complexity. Historically, complex plans fell apart upon contact with reality. Better to plan simple and adapt on the way. Jared saw his chief's point even more clearly now. This operation could turn into a royal clusterfuck.

In keeping with their preference for simplicity, Jared and Chief Sampson had worked out a plan that didn't rely on split-second timing or perfect coordination on the ground and in the air. Rather than vertically assaulting the camp by fast roping into its interior, they'd figured it was best to infiltrate by sliding down fast ropes onto a jungle path two hundred yards away from the guerilla base camp.

Jared's intelligence petty officer had detected a path on the satellite photos that ran parallel along the river and straight into the encampment. If it was visible to a satellite, then the helicopter pilots should be able to locate the insert point quickly from the air. The little birds would release and start their orbit around the perimeter of the camp, the two SEAL snipers engaging targets on the ground.

An air force door gunner with a machine gun sat on the side opposite the snipers. The little birds could fly in figure eight patterns that brought either side to bear against the enemy below.

Precision sniper fire or devastating machine-gun fire, it all worked when it worked. Jared's hope was that this part of the plan provided his ground team the distraction they needed to cover the two hundred yards to the camp.

Jared also was hoping for an assist from the reconnaissance team in position on the edge of the camp. All they needed to do was to eliminate critical threats to the assault force, such as killing anybody who manned or shouldered an anti-aircraft weapon.

They also should be mindful of the hostages. If the guerillas became desperate or vengeful, they might kill the Americans or even use them as human shields to aid in their escape.

He knew this guy Barrett was a pro from reading the man's record of combat service. He would do the right thing. It was time for Jared to clear his mind of the bigger picture; the time for planning was over, it was time to lead.

Lieutenant Jared Stone checked his watch; it was five twenty-five in the morning. From the helicopter's point of view, they could see the sun peeking over the far horizon.

A voice crackled to life in his headset. "Lieutenant Stone, we have received the execution checklist code phrase CHEESE WHIZ, I say again CHEESE WHIZ. Your team is cleared hot for insertion. Good luck!"

Jared's palms began to sweat. For some reason, he'd half expected the mission to be aborted. Things usually didn't go this smoothly on SEAL missions. Jared twisted around to give a thumbs-up to the seven other men on his bird. The same code phrase had been passed to his chief in the second Blackhawk. Jared thanked the pilots and then removed the headset.

The helicopters were already dropping rapidly. The closer to the jungle canopy they got, the faster they flew. By Jared's best calculations, he put them next to the camp in five minutes. He signaled his men by passing an okay hand signal.

Each man, in turn, flashed the same signal back at Jared. They had a 120-foot-long fast rope just in case; but as Jared glanced at the aircraft's altimeter, it hinted that the treetops were only twenty- to thirty-feet high in this area. A shorter drop and less time exposed to enemy fire. So far so good.

The rapidly approaching dawn was a concern he couldn't shake. Maybe the guerrillas would be groggy from sleeping in. They surely weren't expecting an air-to-ground special operations assault on their camp. Satellite coverage showed little to no activity that might indicate a heightened state of readiness.

Jared checked his watch one last time before moving to the door. They were the world's most deadly killers. FOXTROT Platoon would execute; they would lay waste anyone who tried to stop them. Jared was supremely confident in himself and in the long process that had brought him to this moment of truth.

The right side door gunner patted Jared on the shoulder then held up one finger. Jared repeated the one-minute warning for the rest of the SEALs. It was showtime.

Chapter Thirty-Eight

Oby held up his fist and then slowly sank down until he was in the prone position. Matt and Boone mimicked the body language of their point man and once on the ground began to crawl up until they could also see the camp.

There were two feet of leaves and branches shielding their position from observation by anyone in the camp. Matt saw that they were on the high ground, a perfect place to work from. A sound to their left alerted the three men, and they flattened their bodies, pressing down into the soft earth.

Matt watched as three men walked up the steep hill, making a beeline for a large wooden box. When they stopped at the box, one of the men bent down and fumbled with something before standing up and backing away.

"Come, come now!"

Matt was surprised to hear English. He was even more surprised when after a few seconds' delay, he watched a large man crawl out of the box, moving with great difficulty. There wasn't enough light to positively identify him, but he looked too big to be Senior Chief Auger.

Another of the armed men stepped up and delivered a severe kick to the ribs of the man on the ground. This didn't speed things up; the man moaned and collapsed, holding his side.

The man who originally called for the prisoner to come out shoved the overly aggressive guerilla with his rifle at high port. He said a few terse words and then ordered the two men to help the prisoner to his feet.

The man was at least six feet tall, clearly not a Colombian. He was so dirty it was hard to confirm he was Caucasian. The man in charge moved around the prisoner and poked him in the back with his barrel. "Move, general."

Alexander! Matt was looking at one of their two objectives. He stared at the second box. Was Auger in the other container? The three SEALs stayed quiet as the general and his escort moved down the hill and into the camp. The hostages were separated. This wasn't good.

Matt had an idea. If he could confirm exactly where they'd taken the general, then he, Boone, and Oby could snatch Auger and pass the results to the assault force. Right now they were only twenty yards away from the two wooden boxes. If they moved around to the right some more, they could cut the distance in half.

Matt turned to his partners and presented the plan. Boone's only amendment was to communicate the plan to the assault force now before they moved. Matt agreed. He pulled out the UHF handheld radio dedicated to aviation communications. The assault team was flying by Blackhawk, and the call signs were given to Matt before they'd left Panama.

"CYCLOPS FOUR TWO - CYCLOPS FOUR TWO - this is DAGGER ONE - SITREP - OVER."

The response was immediate and strong; they were close. "This is CYCLOPS ONE - GO."

"CYCLOPS ONE - this is DAGGER ONE. Sitrep to follow. Time five one four, position northwest perimeter of the camp. Little activity in camp. Hostage One moved from containment to the main camp. We are twenty yards from Hostage Two. Will extract Hostage Two at time five two five. Pass to DAGGER TWO. DAGGER ONE out."

"Copy all DAGGER ONE - good luck - CYCLOPS FOUR TWO - out."

Matt smiled. That was all the other two SEALs needed to see. Oby eased back four feet and turned right. Matt and Boone followed close behind. The tree line curved in close to the back of the second wooden box, and the height of the hill made it impossible for anyone in camp to see them as they crawled out of the jungle and toward their friend.

Auger was weak from lack of food and barely heard the guards take the general away. He'd been fading in and out of consciousness for a day now. The sleep never was deep enough to refresh him. He was aware he was no longer able to contemplate an escape. He would either be rescued or die here in this box.

His mind had been playing tricks on him: hallucinations, weird lights, and sounds. So when he heard his name whispered he didn't react. The second time the voice was louder and more emphatic.

"Auger, you piece of fucking shit, are you in this fucking box or not?"

Auger twisted around to look at the back of his wooden prison. The back wall was solid wood; only the front had slats to allow air into the small space. Auger's memory was triggered by the voice, it was familiar.

"Damn it, Auger, if you're in there rap on the box with your fist. It's Boone."

Auger's eyes opened wide. That voice, it was familiar because he knew that voice. He freed an arm and knocked on the wall three times. "I'm in here, I'm here!"

Oby and Matt had been studying the back of the box. They didn't know if there was a lock on the opening, but they didn't have a way to remove the lock anyway. Shooting it off would wake up a hornet's nest of shit in the camp below.

Boone pulled out his Leatherman tool and began to separate the one-piece wood backing by wedging the tool in between the seam and rocking it back and forth.

Matt took his knife and did the same thing on the other corner while Oby maintained security. It was five twenty-eight.

Three minutes past the time they told the assault team they'd be done, and the sun was filling the jungle with light all around them.

The creaking of the wooden panel seemed like a siren going off, but they were committed now. The back came off in two pieces, and suddenly they were looking at Auger's shredded shoes.

"Fuck you, too," Auger said hoarsely. "Now get me the fuck out of here."

Matt and Boone pulled the senior chief out a few inches at a time, while in the background Matt heard the camp waking up. Men's voices, metal clanging. When was the assault going to hit the camp?

Once Auger was out of the box, they continued to drag him to the tree line and another four to five feet beyond that. Matt set him upright in a sitting position. Auger's eyes opened in shock.

"You? What the fuck. It's you?"

"Hi, senior chief." Matt gave the man a hug. "We can catch up later. Right now I need to get you as far away from this place as possible. All hell is about to break loose."

Auger's response was interrupted by the sound of a SAW machine gun stitching a line of death across the center of camp. The attack had begun. "Move!" Matt pulled Auger to his feet and followed Oby as the point man punched through the dense foliage heading northeast.

If the assault went sideways, the guerillas would be swarming the jungle looking for their precious hostages. Matt's improvised plan was to move fast, putting distance between them and the camp. Once in a safe location, they could always make comms and call in an emergency extract. For now, it was time to haul ass.

The escort from the camp had been waiting at the rendezvous point for his special visitor for hours. Their leader was excited. He'd never met Chavez, and it was certainly a great honor to meet him personally and escort him into their camp.

The rumor going around was that Chavez was coming in to kill the hostages himself. He was smart enough to know Chavez would be angry if anything happened to the two Americans, but especially the older man.

Once in camp, the guerillas had quickly matched General Alexander's photo to the taller American. They assumed the second American was either an assistant or a survivor of the personal protection detail ambushed a week earlier.

He'd ordered the general moved today into the interior of the camp, closer to the entrance. He'd be standing there when he brought Chavez in from the jungle.

He'd already received a radio signal from the patrol escorting Chavez telling him they'd be at the rendezvous location in fifteen minutes. He tried to relax by getting his mind off the impending visit. He liked his life; it was simple, but again everybody in Colombia led a simple life.

His position in the guerilla army gave him dignity and a sense of purpose. He was a good leader, trusted and respected by his men. If he handled himself well today, he might even get a chance to work for Chavez. They all knew Chavez looked for talent; and if chosen, a man could advance as a member of the drug lord's inner circle.

At the very least he should receive a promotion. A promotion meant being put in charge of more men, possibly a sector of his very own to control. It wasn't about money or rank. It was about power. He was ready, and maybe, just maybe, Chavez would think so, too.

A sound reached his ears, something different, a sound coming from the direction he expected Chavez. His eyes widened as the sound grew louder; he knew this sound. The Americans! Just then a long, ripping sound of machine-gun fire filled the morning air behind him.

The two MH-60s flew in low, skimming twenty feet over the water, one helicopter at point and the second close behind. The lead helicopter used its advanced navigation system to determine the exact location of the insertion point.

The light from the blossoming dawn helped the army pilot to identify key terrain features in the jungle and the surrounding hills. According to the map, the large bend in the river corresponded with the bend in the trail.

The insertion plan was going to lean heavily on established procedures. Nothing fancy. Pop up off the water to an altitude of a hundred feet when they were three hundred yards short of the loop in the trail. The Black Hawk shifted upward in small increments until it reached the right altitude. His co-pilot pointed ahead. The bend was easily distinguishable.

In clipped professional tones, the lead helicopter pilot explained to the trailing aircraft where he was and what he was about to do. At the same time, the little birds were attacking the camp, providing the confusion the SEALs needed to insert nearby.

The lead Blackhawk banked hard right at the bend in the river. He slowed down and eased his nose up slightly. The crew chief reported the bend in the trail, ten seconds to go. The pilot gained a visual and began the maneuver to slide the helicopter sideways until it was directly over the terrain feature below.

The crew chief yelled, "GO!"

Jared was the last man down the fast rope. A few yards away, the second helicopter was unloading the chief and the rest of FOXTROT Platoon. Jared's troop held security until the two

Blackhawks rose up into the air and flew away. He knew they wouldn't go far.

An orbit had been established one mile away. The Blackhawks would now shift to the role of emergency casualty evacuation and air gunnery support, should Jared need more than the two little birds to get the job done.

The young guerrilla leader sat watching in awe as the Americans appeared directly over his ten-man escort. He was even more surprised when he saw bodies sliding down ropes into the jungle only yards away from his position on the trail. They were after Chavez!

The Americans obviously found out about the linkup with Chavez and were here to kill or capture him. The patrol bringing Chavez couldn't be far away. It was his duty to eliminate the threat and protect Chavez.

One hundred yards away, a nine-man protection team stared up at the helicopters in amazement; not one had his weapon at the ready. The young leader turned and whispered his battle instructions to the Colombians, directing them to protect Chavez. He directed six of his men to follow him up the path and quickly deploy around the curve of the trail.

Not far away, Chavez and his patrol stopped abruptly as the helicopters passed overhead. The drug lord glanced up and instantly recognized the aircraft for what they were: American special operations helicopters, MH-60 Blackhawks.

Were they after him, he wondered with alarm, or were they after the hostages? He suddenly realized that his sweet revenge could be thwarted by the arrival of the Americans. He was too close to let this happen.

Chavez owed it to his dead son to finish the job, to have final vengeance. He ordered the three men guarding him to follow him up the trail and toward the camp. One protested that it wasn't safe, but Chavez wasn't listening. In a minute he'd caught up with the leader of his detail, and he quickly gave him orders to advance and kill any Americans they found on the way to the camp.

The patrol leader nodded. He had some reservations about fighting the Americans. He gave the command for his men to follow quickly. Chavez and the ten guerrillas jogged down the trail with their weapons at the ready. They were only thirty yards from the bend in the trail.

Chapter Thirty-Nine

FARC Base Camp–Ariari River

Matt halted the four SEALs after they'd covered forty yards. He turned around and watched the two little birds spinning in orbit around the camp. One was hosing down everything that moved with a Squad Automatic Weapon or SAW light machine gun and the other was directly opposite in the orbit, selectively shooting key targets. It was textbook, and he second-guessed his decision to get far away from the camp.

He considered the odds JSOC would half-ass the assault and decided that wasn't possible. His best bet was to stay close to the target area. That's where all the surveillance and communications attention would be focused.

He looked at his GPS and found a landmark that was easy to find on the ground and in the air: a sharp bend in the jungle trail that paralleled the river. It was only sixty yards away, and they'd still be putting more distance between them and the camp.

Jungle insertion point - Colombia

When the hot blast of ripping lead screeched across the trail, the tail end of the FOXTROT's Platoon formation had spun backward, immediately going to ground and returning fire. Chief Sampson's troop was fully engaged and Jared had to make a decision. Fight here or pull back toward the target objective.

He decided to reinforce his second troop and gave the command. His troop jumped to their feet and ran to the right side of the firing line established by the second troop. Jared ran in behind them and made the call to the Blackhawks.

"CYCLOPS FOUR TWO - troops in contact - I say again TANGO INDIA CHARLIE - OVER."

The pilot in command of the lead Blackhawk checked hi swatch. The SEALs were in trouble, and the two little birds would run out of ammo and fuel if the assault didn't happen pretty damn quick.

"DAGGER TWO - give me your status. Do you need emergency evac? OVER."

Jared didn't have time for all the radio protocol. "We were hit in our six o'clock immediately after your departure. We have not advanced to the target. Standby."

Jared paid attention to the fight. The attackers were backing off; they'd had enough for now. Chief Sampson called a ceasefire and the jungle went quiet, all except for the constant sound of gunfire back in the camp. Jared wasn't going to waste any more time.

"Let's go! We need to get to the camp, now!"

Chief Sampson grabbed two M-240B heavy machine gunners and pushed them into the point position. Jared approved. Everybody knew they were there now. Better to come in with their heavy guns forward. The men of FOXTROT Platoon started running down the trail.

Chavez screamed at the patrol leader. He was a coward, an idiot. But Chavez knew the call was the right one. A few more minutes and his entire protective team would have been wiped out. Chavez grabbed the unit leader by the lapel and growled new orders.

The man saluted, a gesture lost on the drug lord, and barked out instructions to the six men left who were capable of fighting. He formed them up into a file formation and began a wide fishhook movement back to the camp to avoid the Americans.

Chavez still had a chance. The Americans were on the trail and not in the camp. It was a race to see who would get to Alexander first. With the sunlight pouring through the trees it was easy to jog through the trees and bushes, eating up the two hundred or so yards to the perimeter of the camp. His fatigue had vanished; he was full of energy and determination. Time was still on his side.

The guerilla leader halted at the sound of the engagement ahead. He directed his men to melt into the jungle on the right side of the trail. They were only fifty yards from the bend in the trail, and a thousand crazy thoughts ran through his mind. Did the Americans ambush the patrol? Was Chavez alive or lying dead on the ground? He had to make a decision, but what was the best move to make?

The sound of men running made the decision for him. A patrol wouldn't be running and certainly not with Chavez in tow. So far, his instincts have served him well. By pressing back into the jungle, he was in a perfect position to ambush the approaching men. He whispered instructions not to fire if they were friendly, but hit them hard if they weren't.

The two machine gunners burst from the bend in the trail and kept running. Behind them were many American soldiers. The patrol leader said a prayer and raised his rifle. The burst of automatic fire caught the SEALs by surprise.

The two machine gunners from FOXTROT Platoon had been located on the far left of the kill zone when the ambush was sprung and didn't get a scratch. They immediately hit the ground, firing into the trees.

Jared felt a hammer hit him in the left side, knocking him to his knees. He struggled to get flat on the ground while the rest of the platoon deployed in a skirmish line on the opposite side of the trail from the attackers and let loose a withering fire. Chief

Sampson grabbed two riflemen and pushed out to the left of the ambushers, moving three to four feet into the jungle.

He trusted that the rest of the platoon saw his maneuver and were ready for what came next. Jared saw the chief swing out and started to remind his men to shift fire once the chief and his two riflemen opened up on the Colombian's right flank. As he opened his mouth to give the order, he was struck in the neck.

One of the M-240B gunners also was hit and lying on his side. He took his belt of ammo and shoved it toward the other machine gunner, then he rolled over and kept firing until he lost consciousness.

The Colombians were located behind a four-foot-high ridge paralleling the trail. It was a great defensive position, elevated slightly above the path. However, once the Americans went to ground, most of the ambusher's bullets flew high and over their heads. This little problem required the Colombians to stand up in order to aim down at the road where the platoon lay.

A few of the SEALs figured this out right away and began lobbing fragmentation grenades into the trees, aiming for the backside of the ridgeline. Several others picked off the Colombians whenever they stood up to take a shot.

The SEALs also were at a disadvantage. From the trail, they were unable to apply heavy, direct firepower on the ambushers, at least not without standing up themselves.

The platoon's 18 Delta corpsman crawled to the wounded M-240B gunner, who was close at hand. The wound wasn't life-threatening, and with a minim of prompting, the SEAL regained consciousness. He pushed the corpsman away and opened fire. The two belt-fed weapons were critical in a firefight, and this firefight wasn't going their way, at least not yet.

On the flank, Chief Sampson took a deep breath and opened fire. The entire ambush was only sixty seconds old; but to him, it felt like an hour had gone by. The three SEALs advanced at a walk, their bullets finding the prone bodies of the guerillas as they cowered behind the dirt ridge. No one even tried to fire back.

The rest of the platoon heard the chief open up and they shifted their fire to the right. The two SEALs closest to the chief crawled on their bellies up to the dirt ridge and tossed frag grenades on the other side.

A few seconds later, the guerillas broke, running back toward the camp through the jungle. The chief continued his sweep through the ambusher's position and yelled for the rest of his platoon to cease fire.

The pop, pop sound of the chief finishing off the few guerillas still moving echoed through the now still jungle. The chief held up his hand and the two riflemen stopped firing. It was over. Chief Sampson walked straight out to the road announcing his intention.

"COMING OUT!"

"COME OUT!" several men replied, completing the standard communications drill.

When the chief stepped out onto the trail, he took a quick inventory. The machine gunner on his left had passed out again. The other machine gunner was oriented down the trail looking toward the camp and holding security. The chief became irritated that no one was working on the wounded machine gunner. He turned his gaze to the right and spotted the reason.

Jared was on his back. The corpsman had removed his combat vest and body armor to get access to the wound in the lieutenant's side. Another SEAL was trying to apply pressure on the neck wound, but there was so much blood it didn't seem to be working.

The chief snapped out of his momentary fog and looked around the trail. His men were deployed appropriately. He had three hundred and sixty-degree coverage, but he knew they couldn't stay there.

Sampson walked up to Jared and kneeled down. The lieutenant's eyes were wide open and afraid. The chief looked at the corpsman, who had just finished examining the wound in Jared's side.

"Chief, if we don't get him to surgery, he'll die. We need a casualty evac bird in here now!"

Chief Sampson nodded. He looked at Jared again. The officer grabbed his chief with his left hand and pulled him closer. Then he raised his right hand and pointed in the direction of the guerilla camp. His eyes said it all. Continue the mission, save the hostages.

Chief Sampson removed Jared's hand and stood up. "Roger that, sir! You get better, you hear me? I'll have no quitters in this platoon."

Jared began to smile, but the smile faded before it was fully formed. Jared Stone, United States Navy, was dead.

Matt hit the ground when the crazy firefight erupted sixty or so yards in front of them. Bullets ripped through the trees all around them. The shooting went on forever, and all Matt and his patrol could do was hug the jungle floor and hope nobody started lobbing heavy stuff their way.

After two minutes, the engagement petered out. A few pops here and there indicated someone was cleaning up the opposing unit.

"That's five five six ammo, LT," Boone whispered. "The goons use seven six two in their AKs."

"The guys in camp were carrying all kinds of different weapons; there's no way to know for sure if the survivors of that fight were friendlies or not," Oby countered.

245

Matt pulled the UHF radio from his vest. "CYCLOPS FOUR TWO - this is DAGGER ONE - interrogative - do we have blue forces on the ground? OVER."

"DAGGER ONE - this is CYCLOPS FOUR ONE - that is affirmative. They just called in the two little birds for an emergency CASEVAC. One KIA and one WIA - OVER."

Chapter Forty

Matt considered the ramifications of what he heard. Were the engaged Americans the rescue force? If so, were they still an effective fighting unit? Were they at least capable of continuing the mission?

"Guys, I'm going to try and link up with the American unit that was just engaged. They have one KIA and one WIA. The little birds are breaking off their attack and heading to the place where the fight happened. Once I get a communications relay between us and their officer in charge, we'll be moving to link up with that unit. Any questions?"

Nobody had any questions, so Matt called the airborne command post again and worked with them to coordinate a linkup. The last thing he wanted was to surprise a unit that just lost men and start a blue on blue engagement in the jungle. It was hard enough to tell friend from foe as it was.

A minute later a new voice erupted on the UHF radio. "DAGGER ONE - this is DAGGER TWO. What is your current position? OVER."

"We are fifty to sixty yards from the attack site. We'll be coming in on a bearing of two four seven degrees. Three frogs and one rescued frog hostage - OVER."

"Roger that. I'll brief you on the situation when you get here. No need to patrol; just beat feet here and we'll link up. It'll be a regular frogman reunion."

Matt realized the casualties were team guys, maybe even people he knew. It was great that SEALs were the rescue force, but one was dead and one wounded. He passed the linkup information to Oby, Boone, and Auger, then directed Oby to move out on the bearing he'd given the rescue force leader.

Oby pushed hard, and before long the four SEALs were close enough to hear people talking. Matt signaled for Oby to stop and he went down to one knee.

"DAGGER TWO - this is DAGGER ONE - we are twenty yards from your position. Sending my point man forward - he'll be whistling - OVER."

Chief Sampson had just finished briefing the little birds for the emergency CASEVAC. The Blackhawks were racing in from their off-target orbit to pick up the aerial gunnery support role ceased by the smaller helicopters. He almost forgot to switch back to the linkup frequency. As he did, he heard enough of DAGGER ONE's callout to understand.

"DAGGER ONE - this is DAGGER TWO. Understood - go ahead and send your point man forward."

Chief Sampson heard the roaring sound of the Blackhawks as they arrived on station over the camp. His men were in a defensive circle with the casualties in the center. He walked around the circle briefing each man on the CASEVAC plan and on the linkup. When he was finished with that, he positioned himself on the edge of the jungle and waited.

He saw Oby before he heard the whistling. The chief waited patiently until he clearly saw four men, three heavily armed and one who was not, exiting the trees.

The Colombian watched the Americans step out onto the trail and embrace the man waiting for them. He immediately recognized the prisoner. Where was the tall American?

He'd held his men back during the firefight to make sure he knew what was going on. They'd snuck forward a few yards at a time until they were able to barely see the Americans as they finished off the survivors of what he assumed was the escort patrol. Was Chavez dead?

He wasn't afraid of dying, but he didn't know if fighting here was the best choice. His welcoming committee crouched behind him, some with concern etched across their faces and others showing grim determination. That was the problem; his group was a mixed lot, good fighters with experience and others who had never faced fear in combat.

The sound of a helicopter came closer and closer until he spotted the small aircraft hovering over the trail. He wasn't sure what the Americans were up to, but he'd made a decision.

The camp commander needed to know what happened here. He also needed to be aware that Chavez might be dead. The patrol leader moved back and his men followed suit. They would fight these intruders, but not now and not here.

Matt surveyed the perimeter and took a knee next to the SEAL chief. "I'm Matt Barrett. This is Oby, Boone, and Senior Chief Auger. We were able to snatch him after the guerillas moved the general into the center of camp."

The little bird arriving drowned out the chief's response. He held up a finger to pause the conversation, then moved over to the center of the defensive circle. As briefed, the SEALs stretched the circle out to twice the diameter to allow for the little bird to land. There wasn't really enough room, but the slow descent allowed the titanium blades to cut a path down to the trail.

FOXTROT's sniper jumped out of one side and the army SAW gunner exited the other side of the helicopter. Sampson directed his men to place Jared's body and that of the wounded machine gunner into the aircraft. They strapped them down and gave the pilot a thumbs-up. The bird rose into the air, pivoted, and darted away.

The second helicopter appeared, acting like a hummingbird as it flitted around looking for a good place to land.

Sampson waved and pointed to where the first one had landed, and the pilot pushed the stick to center his aircraft over the spot. It repeated the crude landscaping exercise as it landed. Cutting more of the tree branches and leaves on either side of the trail.

The second FOXTROT sniper and door gunner exited the little bird and joined the SEALs on the ground. Sampson gave the okay signal, and the pilot rose up into the air. It spun around one hundred and eighty degrees then took off to join its partner, already en route to the DEA refueling camp.

Matt took a head count. FOXTROT was down two shooters, but they'd gained two armies SAW gunners. Adding Matt's recon team brought their strength up to nineteen men and Senior Chief Auger, who wasn't armed and didn't have body armor.

The Blackhawk door gunners had picked up the tempo of the air assault over the camp. He needed a sitrep. Chief Sampson had pointed to a body in the center of the perimeter when Matt initially asked where the officer in charge was.

He'd never met Jared Stone, but grieving for a fallen brother would have to wait. General Alexander was the mission, and with nineteen SEALs and air support, there was still a good chance they could succeed.

Matt spoke up, "Chief, I know this is an awkward moment, but I'm taking command of FOXTROT Platoon. We had more than enough strength to make a rescue attempt and we owe it the general. We don't leave our warriors behind."

The chief was relieved. He wanted payback almost as much as he wanted to complete the mission. "Okay, sir. What's the plan?"

Chapter Forty-One

Chavez halted the escort patrol leader for the tenth time. They were lost. He closed his eyes and tried to remember the map of the camp area. Without navigation aids, their big hook movement had become a wandering noodle. They should have found the camp by now; but when the helicopters stopped shooting, he'd lost his reference point.

Chavez opened his eyes and grabbed the patrol leader. They would turn hard left and walk until they found the river. Then once at the river, they would turn left and that way they'd find the camp.

He gave the order and the patrol began moving again. A minute or so later, the American aircraft began shooting again. He needed to keep that sound to his left and that would guide them to the Ariari.

The patrol leader brought his welcoming committee into the camp at a run. The bunkers were crude, deep holes in the earth lined with logs, but they were positioned away from the center of camp and therefore difficult to see and strike from the air. He asked where the camp commander was, and a terrified teenager wearing a camouflage shirt pointed to the next bunker.

The patrol leader sprinted to the next bunker and found his commander. He poured out the story of his patrol's attempt to meet Chavez and his escort only to witness a vicious gun battle. He told him he wasn't sure if Chavez or any of the escort patrol survived.

The camp commander waited a moment before responding. When he did, the patrol leader felt a huge weight fall off his shoulders. He was ordered back to the other bunker; he was no longer responsible for anyone but himself.

Oby led the long line of determined SEALs back through the jungle heading for their earlier observation point above camp. He was being cautious, but moved fast. Matt watched his point man's back, but his brain was working overtime. His plan was simple, but nothing in combat was simple and Murphy's Law was always in play.

He intended to place Oby and the two FOXTROT snipers on the hill overlooking the camp. Their job was to find the general and, when Matt started the assault, to kill any guerilla within thirty yards of the hostage.

Matt had briefed the Blackhawk pilots and they were onboard. Matt would take sixteen SEALs down to the river and turn right until they assembled on the edge of the camp. On his signal, the SEALs would run out and stretch across the open area where the camp met the riverbank before pivoting right. As one long skirmish line, they would sweep the camp from the water to the main gate.

The Blackhawks' task was to keep the Colombians pinned down long enough for Matt's new command to cover the fifty yards, killing everything in their way. If all went according to plan, the snipers would preserve the general's life and the SEALs seeping up would find the hostage and rescue him. Matt didn't need to secure the camp or defeat everyone there. His mission focus was the general.

Matt watched Oby and the two other SEAL snipers detach from the patrol and head up to their firing point on the hill. He waited a minute or so to give them time to cover the thirty yards to the top of the hill, then moved forward. Boone assumed the point man position, and the SEALs patrolled in silence for another two minutes.

Above their heads, the Blackhawks continued their race track orbit above the camp. There were few targets now; the guerillas were staying under cover and many had run away. Boone froze and sunk down low to the ground. Matt and the long

252

string of warriors behind him copied the point man's body language.

A few seconds later, he turned slightly to wave Matt up to the front. Matt crouched low and slid up next to Oby. "There you go, boss. The camp stretches that way, across the gap, for about seventy yards. If the guys space themselves out in five-yard chunks, they'll be able to cover all of the exposed riverbank."

Matt studied the camp and agreed with his point man's assessment. He turned and whispered his final instructions to the man behind him in patrol order. The man standing behind him was Senior Chief Auger, and he was carrying a SAW.

Matt realized it must have belonged to the wounded machine gunner in FOXTROT. Well, better to have the senior chief along for the ride as a fighter rather than a liability.

Auger turned and passed the word down the line. Matt waited another sixty seconds before standing up. Boone stepped off to the right side, and Matt motioned for Auger to join them on the side of the trail. He called Chief Sampson up and placed his hand on his shoulder.

"Good luck!"

Sampson grunted, took a deep breath, then let it out. Matt thought the senior enlisted SEAL was having second thoughts; but in the blink of an eye, he was gone, sprinting as fast as he could run to the opposite end of the camp.

The rest of the SEALs chased after Sampson. The Blackhawks saw the move and opened fire on the camp's perimeter bunkers, forcing the guerillas to eat dirt and hopefully giving the SEALs a chance to get into position before they had to fight.

Oby had his spotter scope set up and would act as spotter and shooter for the three-man sniper element. He scanned the camp from the water to the camp entrance. As he was doing so he missed Chief Sampson's sprint along the riverbank. He focused on the area around the only substantial building in the camp, which he presumed was the headquarters structure. It had windows and, fortunately, they were open toward his point of view. Inside, on a chair, sat General Alexander.

Oby told his two partners and they confirmed they could see the general through their scopes. There was no one else in the building; the guerillas were all hiding in the dirt bunkers outside. He briefed them on the drill and that is when he spotted the long skirmish line stretching from one end of the river opening to the other.

The Blackhawks had accomplished their objective. The SEALs were able to deploy without being engaged. Oby watched Matt, Boone, and Senior Chief Auger trot into the center position of the line, and as they did so the SEALs began to move.

Oby didn't need the spotter scope anymore. The three snipers adjusted their bodies into a firing posture and snugged their rifles onto their shoulders. Oby took a breath and let it out slowly.

He felt his pulse and watched the end of his barrel move slightly in rhythm with the blood coursing through his veins. If anyone even took so much as a step in the direction of the building, they'd be dead before their body hit the ground.

Matt jogged along keeping pace with the formation. It reminded him of the first phase of BUD/S when he'd learned how to do a beach survey. All the students were dropped from a speed boat. The twenty or so swimmers were to swim away from each other and get online, twenty-five-yard intervals between each man.

The student in charge would move them forward in twenty-five-yard chunks until they reached the beach. Once there, the entire formation shifted right and headed out to sea. The students collected depth soundings all the way in and all the way out. The drill was always a total mess.

Some swimmers swam too fast and others too slow. Matt was watching closely for this same problem to manifest as the skirmish line advanced deeper into the camp.

Chief Sampson was doing his part to keep the left part of the line in order, and Matt had to wave the right side back twice to keep the line straight. They were thirty yards into the camp when someone finally spotted the SEALs and the shit hit the fan.

Matt opened up and it was as if a timed explosion had been set off. The SEALs of FOXTROT Platoon were out for blood. Every man was advancing, riflemen picking point targets and SAW gunners sweeping the guerilla positions.

The Blackhawks broke off their attack, fearful they might hit the advancing special operators. One took station to act as a blocking force further up the trail in the jungle while the second aircraft orbited the riverfront.

The pilot in the second helicopter saw two bodies left behind by the SEALs, two men wounded or KIA. He radioed the DEA camp to expect more casualties.

Oby spotted a guerilla running to the headquarters building. Apparently, someone realized their ace in the hole was tied up inside. He took up the slack in his trigger, but the gun next to him cracked and jumped before he could shoot. Oby saw the runner drop and remain still.

"Nice shot!" Oby observed.

"Anytime you want some instruction, old timer, just let me know." The younger SEAL cracked a smile.

"Fuck you, man child," Oby responded. It was game on. All he needed was a few targets to teach the punk a lesson.

The FARC camp commander directed the men in his bunker to focus on the center of the approaching line. He had spotted the man with blond hair giving commands, and he knew that removing the Americans' leader might break up the attack.

Matt suddenly felt the pressure of rounds zipping all around him, tearing up the ground but only around him. It took a second for him to determine their origin. They knew he was in command and they were trying to decapitate the attacking force.

He gave the command for the left side to leapfrog forward. As they moved the right side of the long line provided covering fire. Once the lead group reached their objective, they went to ground and opened fire, allowing Matt and the right side to stand up and advance.

On the hill, Oby saw a man in the bunker to the far left of the camp entrance waving his hands around. The other men in the dirt pit were deferring to him and reacting to his commands. Oby aimed one mil dot to the left of the man's head and fired.

Oby watched the camp commander flip sideways in mid-sentence. Two of his men had acted on his last command and were already out of the bunker, sprinting for the headquarters building.

The FARC camp commander's eyes were staring blindly up into the overhanging jungle canopy. Oby looked through his spotting scope. No one else was picking up the reins of leadership.

The SEAL sniper farthest from Oby marked his target. "I've got the squirter on the right."

The other FOXTROT sniper responded, "ROGER - I've got the one on the left."

Both long guns fired at the same time. Seventy yards away and down the hill, both guerillas took rounds in the center of their chests. After sixty seconds of direct assault, the hostage was still safe. So far so good.

Matt got up for the last time and ran forward. His side of the line was now at the cluster of buildings; so when he went down, he refrained from firing and took stock of their situation. He saw three bodies lying in front of the headquarters building, testimony to his plan to protect the general using his snipers.

The left side of his new command was up and running directly at the closest bunker. The SEALs threw grenades as they closed the distance, and once on the lip of the dirt hole they fired into it for a second before shifting fire to the next bunker. There were five such defensive positions, and each was assaulted in much the same way.

Matt pointed to the entrance to the camp where the trail ended at the camp perimeter. He had Senior Chief Auger and two others secure access to the camp and then took three men into the headquarters building. The firing behind him ended abruptly. The camp belonged to the SEALs.

Chief Sampson called in the Blackhawk to evacuate two of his men who were hit during the assault. The wounds were not life-threatening, but both men were hit in the leg so they couldn't move on their own. He left a small perimeter around the wounded SEALs and jogged over to the headquarters building.

Matt went into the building and directed his teammates to untie the general. The older man was unconscious and beat up pretty badly. Bruises and cuts covered the general's body. He was pale and Matt yelled for a corpsman. They lay the general on the floor as one of the FOXTROT Platoon corpsmen entered the building. He immediately checked the man's vital signs.

"Weak pulse and possible concussion. He's lost a lot of blood, but my biggest concern is sepsis. He's been in the jungle for two weeks, and this is a bad environment be exposed to in his condition."

Chief Sampson entered the building and appraised the scene in front of him before reporting to Matt. "I have a

Blackhawk coming in to evacuate two of my--I mean our--men. We need to get the general out there, too. I'd like to send half my guys, say five, out with the bird. The other Blackhawk is staying on station to provide whatever services we request."

Matt nodded. "That sounds like a good plan, chief. Can I ask a favor?"

"Shoot, LT."

"Take Senior Chief Auger, too. He's manning a SAW at the main camp entrance. He's operating on pure adrenalin, but he's bound to crash soon if he hasn't already."

"Sure thing, sir. I'll take care of it."

Chapter Forty-Two

Chavez fell hard. His plan had worked; they'd found the river. The downside was the effort it was taking to bash and crash his way through the much denser vegetation close to the water. He was exhausted but not demoralized.

The six men traveling with him were not saying much. They'd all heard the massive escalation in gunfire at the camp, and after three minutes, the eerie quiet that followed. He wiped his brow and redoubled his efforts to reach the camp.

As the pilot turned for what must have been his twentieth orbit over the river, the right side door gunner reported armed Colombians on the riverbank. The enemy combatants were only fifteen yards from the camp perimeter and definitely moving toward and not away from the camp.

"We are still weapons-free, gentlemen. Let's do a gun run. Standard figure eight flight pattern. The right side is up first then left side. How copy?"

The two door gunners rogered up and braced themselves. The figure eight maneuver was a dynamic roller coaster ride that allows first one side then the other to fire at the ground. The pilot shot out of the orbit and flew away from the camp and downriver before pitching over and racing back toward the enemy patrol.

On the hill overlooking the camp, Oby was collecting his gear, getting ready to link up with the rest of the SEALs down below. He watched the Blackhawk turn up the river and then come roaring back down river.

He heard rather than saw the M-240B firing from the right side of the helicopter. Then watched as the aircraft turned its nose up into the air and fell back to earth ending up with its nose pointed upriver. The left side door gunner was ripping the riverbank to shreds. Oby half wondered if they were just having fun.

A constant stream of machine-gun bullets were ripping apart the jungle all around Chavez. The ground at his feet came alive as it jumped and popped with the impact of the hundreds of rounds. His men tried to return fire, but half were wiped out with the first blast from the American helicopter.

After the second gun run, most of his guerrilla escort lay tossed about the jungle floor like rags dolls. A few were moving here and there, but most were dead. Chavez was furious. More bullets shredded the ground at Chavez's feet, showering him with debris. He drove to the right and rolled, screaming a command.

"Open fire!"

There was nobody left alive to obey his command.

The Blackhawk helicopter landed in the center of the camp and waited as the SEALs loaded the two wounded men into the aircraft, followed by General Alexander. The rest of the men designated to leave climbed in and buckled up. Matt grabbed Senior Chief Auger by the arm and held him back.

"We need to spend some quality time over a beer when this is all over. It's been way too long."

Auger nodded. His face was etched with fatigue and he was unstable on his feet. The adrenalin had worn off, and the sum total of his ordeal challenged his ability to remain conscious.

"LT, we will definitely need to do that. But let's make it a case of beer; we have a lot of things to catch up on!"

"Will do!" Matt responded with a grin.

"Hey boss, do me a favor."

"Sure what do you need?"

"Get a message to the general. Tell him – Hardywood Bourbon Barrel Porter."

Matt was confused. "What's that?"

It's my favorite beer, he'll understand."

Matt shook the senior chief's hand and helped him into the helicopter. A few seconds later the Blackhawk rose up into the air, turned north, and then roared away, disappearing beyond the treetops. He looked at the river. Why was the second Blackhawk still attacking?

The second Blackhawk pilot asked the door gunners if there was any movement on the ground. The left side door gunner responded. "Sir, I think we should do one more run and then break contact. It's time to get the SEALs off this target."

The pilot acknowledged and then pushed the nose to the right in a tight turn. The Blackhawk screamed down the river dropping a little lower to get a better visual of the kill zone on the riverbank.

The right side door gunner had just finished reloading a belt of ammo into the gun and was waiting until the bodies came into view before firing. As he watched, a man staggered out of the trees lining the river and began moving toward the camp.

The M-240B burped a stream of fifty rounds into the lone target on the riverbank then put another thirty rounds into the area where the bodies were lying. The young staff sergeant didn't realize it, but he'd just killed one of the worst drug lords in the world.

Boone put down the binoculars. He'd watched the last helicopter gun run and saw the guerilla at the edge of camp ripped apart in seconds.

"Sir, nothing like a little overkill. I mean it was only one dude. I could've popped him easy if he'd reached the camp."

The second Blackhawk floated down into the camp. Matt knew that Operation Green Dagger was over. "Boys, let's go home!"

Exhaustion suddenly washed over Matt as he sat down in the helicopter and felt it rise. All the stress of command, the fear of failing his friend, and worry over failing the mission all evaporated, leaving an empty shell.

Matt had expended all the energy he had left in that last assault. He was proud of all the guys and especially happy to know Senior Chief Auger would live to fight another day.

Matt couldn't avoid the obvious; he loved this shit. The fear, the challenges, the whole damn thing. He'd been thinking a lot about his future lately and had been confused about who he was and who he wanted to be.

The path was crystal clear to him as he stared out of the helicopter side door at the light blue sky. Tina and her plans for a life together would have to be put on hold. Matt was a warrior, a navy SEAL. It was his destiny, and he was going to live that destiny.

THE END

Made in the USA
Columbia, SC
02 October 2021

46566054R00159